UNBEARABLY

Yours

ELODIE COLLIARD

This novel is entirely a work of fiction. The names, characters and incidents portrayed in it are the work of the author's imagination. Any resemblance to actual persons, living or dead, events or localities is entirely coincidental.

First edition

Editing by Caroline Acebo and Beth Lawton.
Book cover and design by Leni Kauffman

ISBN 9781778137921

BY THIS AUTHOR

PLAYLIST

You can listen to the playlist on Spotify by searching "Unbearably Yours"

1. Wouldn't Come Back – Trousdale
2. Northern Attitude – Noah Kahan
3. The Bolter – Taylor Swift
4. Deep End (Paul's in pieces) – The National
5. I Hate It Here – Taylor Swift
6. The Sweet Sound of You – The Paper Kites
7. stranger - Olivia Rodrigo
8. Love of mine – Benson Boone
9. Regret Me – Daisy Jones & The Six
10. Can't Stop Loving You (Live from the Treehouse) – Half Moon Run
11. closure – Taylor Swift
12. When We Drive – Death Cab for Cutie
13. Motion Sickness – Phoebe Bridgers
14. The Alcott (feat. Taylor Swift) – The National
15. I know it won't work – Gracie Abrams
16. Colour Me In – Damien Rice
17. cardigan – the long pond studio sessions – Taylor Swift
18. Fire and the Flood – Vance Joy
19. this is me trying – Taylor Swift
20. All My Love – Noah Kahan
21. Pancakes for Dinner – Lizzy McAlpine

22. Forever and a Day – Benson Boone
23. Falling in Love – Cigarettes After Sex
24. Missing You (with Ashe) – Stephen Sanchez and Ashe
25. Moon – Renée Rapp
26. Would That I – Hozier
27. Comfortable – H.E.R.
28. Evermore – Hollow Coves
29. Sweet – Cigarettes After Sex
30. Big Time – Angel Olsen
31. Bloom – The Paper Kites
32. Everywhere, Everything – Noah Kahan

TRIGGER WARNINGS

Alcohol use on page, deaths of loved ones off page
(breast cancer and smoke inhalation)

AUTHOR'S NOTE

Writing this book was a very personal experience that not only made me grow as a writer, but also challenged me to look inside myself and explore things I'd never had the courage to do before. It's been quite healing.

There's a little bit of me in Charlee and a lot of me in Oliver. His hypersensitivity is mine, and although I haven't gone through all the steps to get an official diagnosis, my therapist has strongly encouraged me to get tested for giftedness.

There are many stigmas around hypersensitivity and the personality traits that come with it. I've been called "hypocrite," "fake," and accused of having ulterior motives every time I've been "more" and did "too much" than what's socially acceptable. It hurt for a long time and often made me question my actions.

But writing this book was the balm to my heart I didn't know I needed, and it made me realize that as long as I know what's really in my heart, I'll be okay.

I hope you go into this book with gentleness, not only for Charlee and Oliver but also for yourself. And for my hypersensitive tribe, I hope this book makes you realize that there's nothing wrong with feeling everything harder.

Far from it. You are the best there is on this earth.

To David,

For loving me so sweet and tender, in all your quiet, intentional ways.

And for proving to me at every turn that a love like ours isn't only confined to the pages of romance novels.

Toronto, August 18, 2017

Well, this is weird. Never thought that I'd be writing a handwritten letter to a complete stranger in 2017.

I don't believe I've bought a stamp (do we still use those, or are they just collectibles now?) or set foot in my post office in the last five years. But I suppose that's what you get when you decide to earn some extra credit for your resume and sign up for a program that hasn't evolved since it was created in 1879.

Full disclosure: I wouldn't be doing this if I didn't think it would help me land a decent job in journalism, but I've heard through alumni that this program is the gold standard for newspapers looking to hire and I need to hone my skills. So let's see how well I do writing these articles . . . It's nice that we get to choose our topics, though. I might dare a little in my article themes, see how far I can push my research and journalistic writing as if it were actual facts.

My teacher gave me your info last week when he told me I was being paired with a fellow senior attending college in British Columbia. And that's all I know about you, with your last name and the first letter of your name. It's the only thing I like so far, the anonymity of it. How mysterious . . .

Hope you have a better excuse than me to do this. If you're here of your own free will, forget what I just said. I was just kidding, obviously.

I guess I'll hear from you soon! Hope you'll enjoy this first article. Starting off strong (it's a true story).

C.

<u>Attached article</u>
Dating in 2017: When swiping right gets you killed

CHAPTER ONE

Wouldn't Come Back

Charlee

"**W**hat do you mean you *lost* it?!" I can't help my voice rising three octaves as I turn around and find the hulk of a man I picked up in the bar tonight staring in horror at his half-wet, half-hard dick.

"I-I don't know," the guy stutters in a thick Scottish accent. He's still holding his penis like he's afraid it might fall off if he lets it go. "One second I was in ye, and n-next thing I know, it's—it's . . . *gone*."

I take a deep, controlled breath. *This is what happens when you make horny decisions, Charlee.* "How does someone lose a condom, though? Wouldn't you, I don't know, *feel it come off*?" Not that I don't appreciate having access to efficient healthcare while in Europe, but the hospital isn't where I want to end up tonight.

"You were just feeling so *good*," he says, finally dropping his now flaccid dick from his hands and locking his eyes between my opened thighs, his brows knitted together.

If only I could say the same, but alas . . . Although "gifted" could be used to refer to what is hanging between his legs, I would certainly not apply that word to his techniques.

I groan, my head slumping against the mattress. How long do I have until something gets infected? I reach down and push my fingers inside, feeling, probing, searching.

"I think I'm gonna need some help," I mutter, pressing the heel of my other hand against my eye. "I can't find it."

"Aye . . . hmm. Let's see. Maybe . . . maybe you can get up and jump a bit? Maybe that'll get it out?"

I prop myself up on my elbows. "Are you fucking serious?"

"I dinnae ken! Gravity and all, no?"

"What I meant," I enunciate slowly, "is that I need *you* to help me *find it*. Come on, big boy. It's fishing time."

Scottish Guy turns red at my words, and I would *almost* feel sorry for asking him to get up close and personal with my vagina on a one-night stand if it weren't for the fact that *he lost his condom inside me.*

"Aye, of course." He kneels down, his mane of strawberry-blond hair the only thing I can see. He licks one finger, and as gently as he can, slides it in.

I wince.

God. Of all the dating stories I've accumulated over the years, this one might take the cake. Forget the man who meowed to his cat when the feline jumped on the bed as we were halfway through it. Or the one who kept asking me if I had come yet, like I was some on-demand orgasm machine. Oh! How about the woman who rubbed my clit like she was scrubbing some tough stain she couldn't get rid of? Nope, still not as bad as right now.

"You need to relax a wee bit if you want me to stand a chance at getting it."

Need to r—

"I'm sorry, yes, I'll do just that," I say flatly. "Relax while a guy I met two hours ago is playing lost and found in my vagina."

A guttural sound leaves his throat. "Look, I'm doing my best with the situation. This isn't very pleasant for me either."

He's right. I'm sure this isn't how he imagined his booty call would go. Lucky for me, tonight is my last night in Stirling before I travel to the Highlands.

"I think I'm feeling something . . . Aye, wait, hang on, don't move . . . I got it, I got it!" He holds the soggy condom in the air as if it were an Olympic gold medal.

"Thank god." I sit up, gathering the sheets over my body as I look around, desperately trying to locate my clothes. But the sound of Scottish Guy fumbling in his nightstand drawer catches my attention. "What are you doing?"

"Are we picking up where we left off?" he asks, as he pulls a brand-new condom out of the box. He sounds genuinely confused by my question, which makes me wonder if the past ten minutes all just happened in my head.

"No, we're not. I honestly don't feel like having anything else inside me right now." I offer him an apologetic smile as I get up. "Plus, I have an early start tomorrow, and it's getting late."

"Of course. No, I get it." He yawns and stretches for emphasis. "I'm tired too anyway."

I hurry to slide on my jeans and black T-shirt. "Thanks for the evening," I say when I reach the door. "I'm sorry you had to . . ."

Scottish Guy waves me off. "Don't worry about it. Made my week a wee bit more interesting than usual. I had fun. Minus the condom part."

I give him a tight smile and walk out the door into the crisp air of Stirling. The walk to my quaint hotel is a fifteen-minute stroll down cobblestone streets and across vast cow pastures. Not a soul in sight. Exactly how I love it—peace, quiet, and nothing for miles and miles. Just the sound of my boots squishing the wet grass beneath them, the wind rustling through the leaves.

And the high-pitched ringing of my phone.

I groan. Apparently, not even Stirling can escape cell service.

"Hello?"

"Charlee! It's Ben."

"Hey, boss. Sorry, didn't recognize that number. Everything okay in Toronto?"

"Yeah, I left my phone at the office. Am I waking you up?"

I wish. "Nope, just taking a little stroll around town."

Ben chuckles. "Sounds just like you to be out at this hour. Listen, there's been a slight change in the schedule. I need you to board the next plane to Toronto and come back to the office."

I frown. "But I haven't even gone to the Highlands yet. I'm meeting with a local guide tomorrow who's supposed to show me around the Caledonian Forest so I can start my piece on deforestation."

"Forget the assignment," he cuts. "We have something bigger coming up. I can't tell you more on the phone because of some NDA shit, so get back here ASAP, please."

"You got it," I say, then hang up.

Well, that's a first. In all my years working as a journalist covering climate change for *Wild Planet*, I have never gotten a call from Ben asking me to ditch a feature story in the middle of it. Sending journalists all over the world to cover the environmental downfall of our planet isn't cheap. I can almost hear him repeat the words he's said to everybody a thousand times: "Money doesn't grow on trees, and with the massive deforestation going on, it wouldn't even be viable if it did."

So for him to bring me back before I get to the nitty-gritty of this assignment, it must be something major.

I don't know if I should be scared or intrigued.

I'm kidding.

I never get scared. Especially when I can sniff an adventure from miles away.

I'm fucking excited.

Hey, C.

Nice to meet you.

Agree, the program is a little outdated, but it's such a fast and practical way to learn the job. Plus, I like writing letters. Something personal about it, you know? Like I purposefully spend time crafting a message meant for that one person.

Sorry, I'm getting sappy (already, god . . .).

You already have more information on me than I do on you, as the only address I got for my letters was the one for your dorm. I'm lucky enough to live at home while I finish college. Though fair warning: my mailman and I are playing a game called "catch me if you can, asshole." The rules are pretty simple: if I miss him, he never delivers my mail. So if you don't hear from me within two weeks, write to me again. Emile probably burned the letter or shredded it in his office. It's a long story . . .

You chose an interesting topic for your first article! Hope you didn't know someone or haven't lived through something similar yourself. Dating apps are the worst. I don't do well online. I prefer organic ways to meet, which is a short way of saying that I've been single forever. Maybe I should rethink not using the apps. It's clearly not working well for me.

Anyway, I won't take any more of your time.

Till next time!

O.

<u>Attached article</u>
What makes a town live: Jerry's famous grilled salmon becomes a must-see tourist destination

CHAPTER TWO

Northern Attitude

Oliver

The For Sale sign across the street hangs on the door of what used to be my grandparents' beloved restaurant. It's taunting me, mocking me for failing to honor my legacy and keep the restaurant in the family.

Almost failing.

It's not over yet. Although I don't see how I'll be able to gather the kind of money I'd need to buy it back from the town before Oscar sweeps in and closes the deal.

It'll only be a matter of months now, I guess.

I look down at the empty notebook page on my lap, the weeping willow shading me from the unusually hard-beating sun as I wait for Matt to arrive with the setup for the festival. It's September, for crying out loud, yet here I am in shorts and a T-shirt, sweat coating my temples.

I miss fall. Real fall. The kind of fall when the best place to be is under the covers on the couch, with the rain splattering gently outside and playing that oh-so-melodious sound on the orange leaves that have slipped to the ground. The kind where draping a cardigan over your shoulders, and with a hot cup of coffee in hand, is the only way to go outside. The kind where, when hiking, there's no escaping the brilliant palette of colors bursting to life, nor the smells of earth and maple leaves that fill the senses, that perfect blend of musky and sweet that's so distinctive of this time of year.

I miss the fall of my childhood.

And none of these thoughts are helping me with the ones I need to put on paper.

I sigh, brushing my fingers through the waves of hair falling into my eyes. I've been writing these letters for years now, and I've always found the words to express what weighed heavily on my heart. And although they no longer make their way to her, they've always been healing for my soul.

But today, nothing's happening.

Maybe it's a sign that I need to stop. Let go of my past and forget about her. Maybe I don't have anything to say anymore, or maybe she feels so distant to me now that my brain doesn't understand that she was more than just a memory.

From the corner of my eye, I spot my friend's red pickup parking in front of the town's park.

"Hey, Oli! Can you give me a hand?" Matt calls from his truck.

"Coming!" I set my pen and notebook on the grass beside the old wooden bench.

Matt makes his way toward me, a folding table in one hand and a gorgeous flower arrangement in the other.

"Who are these for?" I ask, taking the flowers. "Is this an order, or did you just make it for today?"

Matt grunts as he sets the table down and opens it. "For today. I had time last night and was inspired. I'm manifesting fall."

"I see that." I chuckle before nodding to his red-and-black-checkered shirt. "Might be a tad overkill?"

I set down the bouquet on the table, admiring the tasteful arrangement of yellow sunflowers, orange daisies, chrysanthemums, and burgundy berries wrapped in golden oak leaves.

"What?" He laughs, looking down at his clothes. "You don't like my plaid shirt?"

I shake my head. "I think you're gonna be drenched by the end of the day." I point to his boots. "Although I'm sure the tourists will eat this up."

Matt laughs again. "What can I say? I need to be on-brand for the Autumn Festival kickoff. I even trimmed my beard, see?"

I snort. "Trimmed" is a pretty strong word for the half inch he cut from the dark-blond beard gracing his face. Matthew looks like the mountain man stereotype: long hair, long beard, gruff around the edges, but with a heart of gold. There's still something funny to me about a guy like him handling delicate flowers daily, but I couldn't picture him doing anything else.

"You have a lot of stock this year," I say as we walk back to his truck to pick up some pumpkins. We pass by curious onlookers who are already starting to gather at the entrance to the park, looking at the artisans setting up their stalls and putting up their signs. It's still early, and the Pine Falls Autumn Festival doesn't open for another hour, but that's the way it's always been. People are excited to get the two-day celebration started.

Our little town of six hundred twenty inhabitants nestled in the heart of British Columbia has already tripled in population since last week, the hotels are full, the streets vibrate with activity, and the local stores are readying themselves for the most important event of the year. Even my normally peaceful hiking trails have been busier than usual.

I get it. Nothing comes close to the show fall puts on in this town. I've never seen anything like it. Between the colors, the river, and the mountains, it's nothing short of postcard worthy. And my own paradise.

"It's been my busiest season this year, man," Matt says. "Business is going so well I don't know if I'll be able to take time off before next year."

"You've been putting your heart and soul into this. I'm not surprised people can't get enough." I set the pumpkin down before clapping his back. "We'll celebrate your success at the festival with the whole gang next Friday."

"Why don't you rent a stand this year?" he asks, plopping down on the folding chair he brought from his truck. "You've been making amazing wood pieces. It could help, you know. With the money and all."

"I don't want to sell them," I tell him, adjusting the pumpkins and haystacks until both sides of the booth look perfectly symmetrical.

"I'm just saying. You're very talented, and people would grab them like hot croissants." He squints his eyes. "What are you doing?"

I pick up one of the arrangements and reposition it so that the flowers face the festival goers. "You might be good at making those bouquets, but your placement is all off. Look." I point at the cornucopia centerpiece. Half of it is hidden by the dried pampas grass standing tall in front of it. "How can you expect people to buy your beautiful creations when they can't even see them?"

I move things around and give the table a little more breathing space. "And voilà! That's your eye-catching piece now."

He whistles. "Thanks, Oli." His gaze falls on the notebook, and his eyebrow arches. "Still going at it, uh?"

"Yeah, well . . ." I sigh. "I think I might hang up the pen and focus on what's ahead."

"Good." He nods. "About time."

My phone vibrates in my back pocket before I can offer any further explanations. My boss's contact information flashes on the screen.

"Oliver, thank god," Donna says when I answer. "I'm sorry to bother you on a Saturday, but I have something urgent we need to discuss. I can't say on the phone. Can you meet me in the office today?"

"Today?"

I live about three hours north of Vancouver, but my work doesn't require me to come into the office except for an emergency. I'm closer to nature here, and that's where I need to be for the type of stories I cover as a journalist for *Wild Planet*, a global monthly publication dedicated to shining a light on issues facing our planet.

"Yes, today," Donna replies. "I'm sorry. I wouldn't ask you to drive all the way down if it weren't important."

I check my watch. "Sure, yeah. I'll be on the road in a few." I hang up, then slide the phone back into my pocket.

Matt's head whips in my direction. "You're leaving?"

Guilt is already digging its claws into me. "I'm needed at the office. Something urgent. I'm sorry, man. I know I said I'd be here all day to help you with the stall."

He looks around, and I see that the thought of handling this all by himself is overwhelming, especially with how busy he's already been this year. I told him that he could count on me, and here I am, already bolting.

Where are your priorities, Oliver?

But despite the panic settling on his face, he says, "Don't worry about it. Work's important."

"And so are you," I counter.

Matt chuckles. "Yes, but I think I'll handle it just fine. Worst case, I'll call Lola. She said she could lend a hand this afternoon if we needed one."

I smile at the thought of our best friend being forced to make small talk with strangers all day. *Yeah, she'll hate that.*

"I'll make it fast, okay? Maybe I can be back before tonight and help you close."

I hope whatever news Donna needs to break to me won't wreck the rest of my day.

Toronto, September 1, 2017

Hey, O.

I understand the dating-in-real-life struggle. I'm off the apps too. They're such a time suck anyway. Maybe you haven't met the right person yet.

You think you can just leave me hanging after what you said about your mailman? I'm not sure I fully grasp what's going on, but it sounds like a very interesting story, and I want to hear it. What did you do to the poor guy?

Thank you for the article you wrote. It was very moving. I take that you've been to Jerry's before? Is it a restaurant in your hometown? I feel like it means a lot to you. I'll keep the recommendation in mind if I ever visit BC.

Hopefully, this article won't scare you as much as the first one, although it's a true story (I secretly love that little terror, and I like to think he loves me back).

Oh, by the way, are you left-handed? I'm only asking because the left side of your letter was a little smudged, which made me wonder. Anyway, a very random question, ha!

Talk soon!

C.

Attached article
There's a new sheriff in town: How a cat is terrorizing this Toronto neighborhood

CHAPTER THREE

The Bolter

Charlee

"**Y**ou better have a darn good excuse for pulling me out of Scotland, Ben, because there's no way in hell I left that little slice of paradise, working my ass off on this deforestation article, for this shithole," I say when I storm into our office on Monday, two little days after my plane touched down in Toronto.

Our *empty* office. Huh. Where *is* everybody?

"Ben?"

"In the conference room, Charlee!" he shouts from the end of the hallway.

I roll my eyes.

Welcome back, Charlee. Thank you for coming this fast. Aren't you jet-lagged? Here's a coffee. Maybe it'll help.

Nope, it's just *Get your ass in here.*

Classic Ben.

I walk into the small conference room to find him buried in paperwork, his glasses perched on top of his balding head, his brows knitted so tightly that he looks like a shar-pei. Or a sphynx if you're a cat person. No shame in that, though; cats are the best.

"What's up, Ben?" I throw my bag on the table and plop into a chair across from him.

At the thump of my bag, Ben looks up, startled. Dark circles color the skin under his eyes. "Hey, Charlee. Nice to see you." He gathers the paperwork into a neat pile. "Sorry for the mess. They're drowning me in legal stuff. I haven't slept in three days."

"Who's 'they'?"

He slides his glasses onto his nose. "Yes, yes. That's why you're here. But first, I need you to sign this NDA."

He skids a document across the table.

I pick it up and read. "'Except as otherwise provided in the Agreement, *Wild Planet* must not disclose the Confidential Information included in this document by Movie Night Live, with the exception of the identified members of their team.' Ben, what the fuck is going on?"

"Keep reading and sign the damn thing, Charlee, and I'll explain the whole caboodle."

I skim a few pages, landing on the list of what the agreement considers "confidential information."

"My location, the parties present, any material used, any information discussed during meetings, any *filming*-related matters?" I slam the document down. Not this shit again. "Ben."

"Sign. It."

Last year, Ben was in touch with some execs from a multibillion-dollar streaming service. The deal fell through before we even got a chance to celebrate because one of my stupid-ass colleagues had run his mouth off to anyone willing to listen. When the streaming platform heard about it, they ended our contract, no explanation necessary. We'd fucked up big time.

I know that Ben has been trying to diversify the company's income streams because revenue has been shrinking over the years, but this is starting to look a little obsessive.

"Why do you keep booking me for TV gigs?" I whine. "I'm a print journalist! Ask someone else. Claudia loves that shit."

"They don't want someone else, Charlee. They specifically requested you after they saw the videos you made on the fires in Australia."

"And who showed them those, huh?" I mumble. "It was material for my articles, not an audition tape."

I have a feeling I'm going to regret it, but I sign the document with a sigh. I need to know what he got himself into. Actually, what he got *us* into.

"There."

"Thank you," he says, like he was holding his breath the whole time. "We finally have a way out of the financial mess we're in, Charlee. And I made damn sure to keep my mouth shut this time so only the people involved are in the know.

And as you can see," he nods toward the NDA, "I'm not even taking chances with those who *are*."

"Indeed, Ben. Indeed."

"So, here's the deal. We're sending you to British Columbia this Friday. You'll be there for two weeks with a filming crew from Movie Night Live to make a docuseries on the Great Bear Rainforest and the impact climate change is having on it. Don't worry," he adds when he sees my arched eyebrow. "They put their most experienced team on this project. People who are used to venturing into wild places like that. It won't be like the coyotes' news report you did two years ago with that awfully inexperienced local station."

The Great Bear Rainforest.

The words linger in my mind. I used to know someone who loved that place with all his heart. Someone who was supposed to show me the beauty of British Columbia.

"Am I gonna have any training before I leave?" I ask, shifting my attention back to Ben and what matters. "And there are a lot of Indigenous communities living in the area. Do we have the okay to cross their lands?"

Ben shifts in his seat. "I'm working on it. Everything will be in order by the time you get there. As for training, you will be paired with a BC-based *Wild Planet* reporter who holds a wilderness & remote first aid certification and will provide the necessary gear and preparation for you and the rest of the team." At my look, he adds. "We need to spare every expense we can, Charlee. If the guy can lead the team through the forest, we'll use it to our advantage."

I sit back, just enough to relax my tense shoulders. "So let me get this straight. You're sending me to the other side of the country with a film crew that cornered me into signing an NDA prohibiting me from disclosing my location. There's not enough time to prepare properly. And I'm being forced to rely on and trust some local journalist turned rescuer who found their certification in a cereal box, instead of having a real guide accompany us like we always do. Am I missing anything?"

I can't keep my question from dripping with sarcasm, but he should know better.

We usually receive a week's worth of briefings on our next assignment's locations, and those are planned months in advance. Then we go through multiple safety protocols, which are long and boring. Only then do we get to hop on a plane.

Don't get me wrong, if I could skip half of it, I'd jump at the chance. There's nothing I love more than the thrill of being faced with the unknown. But when I'm working, I'm not only putting myself in danger. There's a whole crew behind me—coordinators, photographers, equipment handlers. Not to mention the local help we usually enroll to guide us and provide useful information on the environment. A lot of people count on me to keep them out of harm's way, and as much as I don't mind being careless with my own safety, I'm not about to compromise theirs. And now I'm suddenly supposed to accept that we're throwing our protocols out the window just because a film crew decided to dictate the rules?

Hell no.

Ben puts his hands up. "Listen, Charlee. Truth is, we need the money. You and I both know that the future of print media isn't looking good. We have to appeal to younger audiences and look at partnerships that can keep us afloat."

I frown. "Keep us afloat?"

His silence is louder than whatever words he could have used. After what feels like an eternity, Ben clears his throat and stares right at me, almost pleading. "*Wild Planet* is implementing company-wide budget cuts. If you refuse to do this, they'll close the Toronto branch. You're our last hope, Charlee. I know it's . . ."

Whatever comes out of his mouth is muffled by the ringing in my ears. It grows louder and louder as the seconds tick slowly on the clock hanging next to the door.

I can't lose my job. I can't. My mind cannot even fathom it. This is all I have.

For the last five years, I have given everything to this job. Days and nights running around the world. Missed birthdays and Christmases. My sister's wedding! But I would have done the same thing a hundred times over, because it's what I was made for. I don't know who I am without my hiking boots and my duffel bag.

If this job ceases to exist, *I* cease to exist, simple as that.

"Charlee?" Ben's voice cuts through the noise and snaps me back into the room.

"Okay," I breathe, pushing my fingers against my scalp. "So all I have to do is film this thing for two weeks, and that's it? We stay open?"

He nods. "Just two little weeks, Char. And then back to your assignment in Scotland or wherever you want to go."

"Fine." I get up. "But this is the last time you're putting me through this shit, you hear me? I'm the best journalist you have, but next time, just fucking ask first. Instead of forcing my hand."

"You're right. I'm sorry."

I grab my bag and sling it on my back. "I know I am. See you in two weeks, boss."

And just like that, the fate of two dozen people, my career, my passion, and my *raison d'être* all rest on my tiny shoulders.

No big deal.

Hey, C.

Yep, you got me. I'm left-handed. I'm a little bit embarrassed about it, if we're being honest. I haven't written on paper in a long time and kind of forgot I have to hold my palm up if I don't want the ink to smear. Or maybe I should just change pens and use a ballpoint instead. I'm very sorry if it made it harder for you to read. I'll be more careful with the next letters.

I'm impressed that you were able to understand me so well with so little. I guess I'm an open book to you, huh? My nan used to say that a lot when I was younger. Apparently, I have the worst poker face, which isn't a bad thing, I'd say. Don't you think? Fewer chances to deceive people like that, at least.

Anyway, yes, I do hold a very special place in my heart for this restaurant. Jerry is actually my great-grandpa's name. He opened the restaurant with all the money he had, and since then, it's been a town staple. My grandpa, who's also named Jerry, took over when his dad died, and I was basically raised among busy waiters and hot stoves. I don't think there is anywhere else I would call home more than this place.

And my grandpa is still going at it! Still flipping the burgers and doing his famous grilled salmon that tourists go nuts for. It's quite the place, like you said. Add it to your list of locations to visit if you ever come to BC. I'll tell him to give you a discount.

Also, what do you mean what did *I* do to the "poor guy"? Trust me, don't spend a second feeling sorry for him. That stubborn rascal is a seventy-year-old French jerk who refuses to retire. Don't be fooled by his sweet charms. He's been the town's mailman for decades. One day, he came into my grandparents' restaurant for lunch, and three days later, he barged in screaming that he got food poisoning from what he ate there. But that's impossible, because I know my grandparents and the quality of the ingredients they use. The one and only goal of his miserable existence since that day has been to make our lives a living hell. If I'm not out at 8 a.m. ON THE DOT when he comes by, you can bet your ass that my mail won't be delivered. And if I'm there and manage to grab it, Emile spends five minutes throwing French curses at me (I've picked up a few by now). He's a stubborn and resentful mule.

Anyway. I wouldn't say the article you sent me this time scared me, but I'm definitely intrigued now. That's an . . . unusual cat, let's put it that way. Are you a cat lover?

O.

Attached article
Here are the ten weirdest animals you'll find in BC (yes, they all exist)

CHAPTER FOUR

Deep End (Paul's in Pieces)

Oliver

The sound of my miter saw drowns out all outside noises and internal thoughts swirling in my head. There's nothing but the strident melody of the blade cutting through the wood as splinters fly all around before the dust settles on the ground.

I haven't set foot in my woodshop in months, but the news my boss bombed me with last week got me hopeful for the first time in god knows how long. Hope is a frivolous and dangerous concept. One that I've been purposely avoiding for years.

Yet last week, hope felt more like a tangible possibility than it ever had.

And today, as soon as work was done, it was hope that made me open the doors of my woodshop next to my cabin and pick up a project I left behind years ago, resurrecting the dream I thought was long buried.

I run my hand along the piece of wood lying on the table, feeling the imperfection of the oak under my fingers. Every single piece of lumber in this workshop has been meticulously handpicked by me. Some I even cut down with my grandpa.

I walk to the woodpile next to the furniture I've made over the years and kneel down with nostalgia. My grandfather taught me everything I know about wood. He always told me to take a good look at the grain. "It'll reveal a lot about its history," he used to say. "Look at it carefully, each detail, and the rest will come to you easily." How to choose the right timber for the right project, how to bend and dry it to the exact shape you need, and how to sand and stain it to best reflect its natural color. We used to start early in the morning and stay buried in the shed until night set in and Grandma yelled at us to get our asses to the dinner table.

We built my cabin, right in this room, piece by piece.

For a long time, I couldn't set foot in this place. It was too painful, too fresh. A constant reminder of my loss and the gaping hole he left.

But today, as I'm picking up a piece of cedar we chose together, I feel closer to him than I ever did during those last years. It's as if he's standing right here next to me, pressing the miter saw into the wood, his cologne and clean-soap scent wrapping me up in the comforting cocoon of my childhood.

"Ols!"

I turn around and spot Lola, eyes wide, standing in the doorway. I stop the saw, then take off my safety goggles.

"Hey, what are you doing here?" I throw my gloves on the table, walk toward her, and pull her into a tight hug, noticing how dark it is outside. How did I miss the sun setting? I've been buried in here for hours.

"What are *you* doing? What's happening? I haven't seen you here in ages." She moves around me, inspecting the wood on the table. She looks up at me. "Are you . . .?"

I nod. "Maybe."

"Why? How? Since when?"

I laugh, wrap an arm around her shoulders, and drag her outside, toward my cabin. "Let me brew you a cup of coffee, and I'll tell you all about it. I need a break anyway."

"It's freezing today." She looks at my bare arms. "Aren't you cold?"

I shrug and open my front door. "I don't mind the cold."

"You know, you should get a dog," Lola says as she hangs her coat in the entryway.

I snort. "Where is this coming from? And when do you think I'd have the time to take care of a dog?"

"Oh, come on." She rolls her eyes. "The gang could take care of him or her when you're away for work. It'd be good for you."

"I'm sure you guys would love to, but you don't need another excuse to come here more often." I open the fridge. "Almond or cashew?"

Lola sighs. "Neither. I'm going full black today. I'm too tired."

"Damn." I whistle. "I don't think I've ever seen you drink black coffee." I reach for the mugs on my wooden shelves, pour the freshly pressed coffee in, and nod toward the door. "Muskoka Chairs?"

"Heck yes."

"Bring the blanket!" I yell as I push the door handle with my elbow, the steamy mugs warming my hands.

I sit on one of the red chairs that faces the small natural lake bordering my cabin just as a heron dives into the water and emerges with its prize clutched in its beak. My gaze follows him as he flies off into the distance, his large wings engulfing the sky.

"I never get tired of seeing these magnificent creatures," Lola sighs, blanket in hand. "You're lucky; it's a perfect playground for them here."

"Did you know that although great blue herons possess some excellent fishing skills, they can sometimes choke trying to swallow prey that's too big? Because of their long, S-shaped necks."

Lola stares at me. "How do you think I would know that, Ols?"

"I don't know." I shrug. "I'm sure it's a well-established fact."

She takes a sip from her mug. Her mouth twists in disgust. "People are lying. They can't possibly like drinking this."

I shake my head and smile. "Not everyone likes two pounds of sugar in their coffee."

She can be so silly when she decides to be. Sometimes, I wonder how she and I came to be so close. We're so different, and to any outsiders looking in, our friendship probably wouldn't make any sense, but to us, it does. She's my oldest friend, my confidant, one of the few people on this earth who loves me for me.

The real me.

The boy who got laughed at his entire childhood for being too sensitive. Who spent his lunch breaks in art class by himself, nose buried in comic books and fantasy novels. That's where Lola found me. And when she did, she didn't make fun of me. No, she sat next to me and asked me what I was reading and let me bore her with stories about vampire slayers. I don't understand what she saw in me that day. Why she felt benevolent enough to listen to a kid she didn't know instead of having fun outside with her friends and simply ignoring me like everybody else did back then.

All I remember from our first encounter is the hope and fear that raged inside me. I didn't know if I was making a friend for the first time in my life or if it was the start of being someone's laughingstock once more.

But she hasn't left me since. She's always by my side, my fiercest protector and the sister I never had.

"Earth to Oliver," Lola says, and I focus on her scrutinizing brown eyes. "Are you going to tell me what you were doing in your woodshop?"

I pull the blanket closer. Everything has changed in the span of a week. And so fast. It's a lot to wrap my mind around.

"I spoke with Donna last week," I tell Lola. "She asked me to come to Vancouver out of the blue and told me that *Wild Planet* will be partnering with Movie Night Live to film a docuseries on the Great Bear Rainforest. A journalist from the Toronto office will be flying here, and she asked me to act as the Vancouver liaison since I know the place well. We'll stay in Pine Falls for a night since it's right at the border of the rainforest and head there the next day."

Lola's mouth hangs open. "You're shooting a series for Movie Night Live?"

I can tell what she's thinking, and she's not wrong. "Yes."

"How is that going to work for you? You hate attention."

I rub the five o'clock shadow that's been dusting my jaw for the past week. "Technically, I won't be in front of the camera. I'll just be there to make sure everybody is safe, guide them through the rainforest, and help the *WP* journalist with her storytelling if she needs me. Not my usual role at *WP*, but Donna saw a way to save money and took it. But Lola," I lean in and lower my voice, as if my next words will be so scandalous they shouldn't be uttered too loud, "I'll triple my annual salary just for the two weeks of filming. Do you understand what that means? I'll have enough to buy the restaurant back. I honestly don't care about what I'll have to do if I do end up needing to be in front of the camera. I don't care if I hate every second of it. Because I can buy it back."

I can pinpoint the exact moment realization dawns on my best friend's face.

"So that's why you've been in your shop," she murmurs, putting two and two together. "The project is back on!"

I laugh at her excitement and nod. "Yes, it is. I was working on the chairs when you showed up. I haven't felt this hopeful about it in a long time. It's like I can almost touch it, you know? I don't see how Rob can turn me down now. The place is rightfully mine. Jerry's made this town famous. Pine Falls is what it is today because of the sweat and tears my grandparents poured into this place. Rob knows that."

Lola's nose scrunches up at the mention of Pine Falls's mayor. "He might know that, but I see the dollar signs in his eyes every time that Oscar asshole from Lakeside Resorts comes to town with his shiny suits and that awful smirk. You need to tread carefully with this, Ols. He won't go down easily."

I sink deeper in my chair. "Maybe. But I have the money now. There's no way Rob can turn down reopening Jerry's. As attractive as Oscar's suitcases of money may be, nobody will book that hideous hotel if there's nothing to come here for."

"I know," Lola agrees, patting my knee. "Just make sure *he* knows that too."

I bring the mug to my lips as a gust of wind blows through the leaves and ruffles Lola's long black hair, sticking it to her face. I smile. "Trust me, I will. Oscar might play to win, but I won't give up easily either. Actually, I just won't, period. That building is my birthright."

And none of this would be happening if I had the money to keep it in the first place.

"So you *won't* be on TV," she says pensively. "That would have been fun, though."

"Not from what I've read in my contract. Mostly supporting the Toronto reporter and acting like the local guide and medic. And I won't be reachable for two weeks. I signed a pretty airtight NDA." Which reminds me. *Fuck*. I whip my head in Lola's direction. "You cannot tell a soul about this, you hear me?"

She makes a show of zipping her lips and throwing away the imaginary key. "Not even James and Matt?"

I shake my head. "Not even James and Matt. Please."

"What am I supposed to tell them when they ask where you disappeared to?"

I shrug. "Say I'm off for work. Just don't go into details."

"I can't believe you, of all people, have been chosen to do this. Only to you, Ols." She shakes her head, amused. "That shit only happens to you. Do you know who the other *WP* journalist is?"

"Not yet. Hopefully, they'll send someone with a bit of experience with nature. I don't think I can handle a city jerk."

Lola snorts. "I would pay good money to see you rip your hair out and bite your tongue if they come in high heels or in jeans."

I drop my head against the chair and close my eyes. "God, this is going to be two long weeks."

Two weeks of pushing past my safe and isolated bubble to be with complete strangers twenty-four hours a day, and probably putting up with more than I can endure.

Two weeks of hell for the dream of my life.

Hey, O.

No, no, please don't worry about smearing your writing. It made me smile when I saw it, and it's something that makes you, you. A little piece of information I'm tucking in the O folder.

Okay, pause. WHAT? This mail story is HILARIOUS. Talk about holding a grudge, hahaha. Now I'm picturing you on your porch fighting the letters out of his hands every morning and him leaving, stomping his feet. Gosh, I wish I could meet Emile. I like him already.

I would love to come visit one day. British Columbia has always been on the list of places I want to go to. Vast lands and gorgeous mountains, just me and the wilderness. The dream. Jerry's sounds absolutely delicious. You had me at burger, honestly. I'm not a fancy food person. Give me chips and a hot dog, and I'm a happy gal. Toronto has some amazing finger foods, and I know all the best places.

I LOVE that you chose to send me an article on the weirdest animals in BC. It's like you read my mind. Are you psychic? You'll understand why I'm asking when you see the drawing I'm sending you. Finding unusual living, breathing creatures is my thing. The weird, the imperfect, the ugly, the outcast. They all need some love, don't you think? And most of the time, they get rejected or abandoned because of a missing leg or crossed eyes. People are cruel.

Not just a cat lover. I love every animal. Through and through. Sometimes, I wonder if I wouldn't be happier if I could be surrounded by animals 24/7 instead of humans.

Anyway, I'm babbling for nothing, haha. Let me know what you think about this article. I wasn't very inspired, so give me all the feedback.

Talk soon!

C. (I'm liking the mystery of our names . . .)

Attached article
Looking to get lost around Toronto? We know just the (wild) places

Attached drawing
A cute spring softshell turtle

CHAPTER FIVE

I Hate It Here

Charlee

Riley

> Change of plans! We're having company tonight. Please dress appropriately.

I hold back a snort. My sister can be sassy when she wants to be. I *dress* appropriately. I just don't wear tight skirts or ridiculously high heels that could break my ankles any time I put one foot in front of the other.

But I guess my go-to worn-out shorts and too-large shirt won't be on Riley's "appropriate" list.

I throw my shirt on the bed, groaning.

Fine. *Fine*.

I know my sister well enough to have learned to pick and choose my battles over the years, and what she finds suitable for me to wear when it's not just the two of us isn't one I've decided to waste time on.

I rifle through my dresser and pull out a pair of black jeans and a dark-purple cashmere turtleneck. Then I run my fingers through my shoulder-length hair and try my best to comb the rogue auburn strands of my bangs.

I look at my reflection in the mirror. There. Presentable, right? I don't know who is crashing our sisters' night, but I hope Riley has a good reason not to spend my last hours in Toronto just the two of us like we planned.

So it better be the fucking queen of England visiting my dear sister tonight. Otherwise, I'm out of there.

"I'm sorry. I didn't know they were coming," my sister furiously whispers as she closes the door behind her, trapping us on her front porch. "They wanted to surprise Miles. Mission accomplished," she chuckles nervously. "I hope you don't mind."

I read the worry on her face as clear as day. Or maybe it's because she's my sister, and despite not being around her that much over the last few years, I know every single one of her expressions. And the way her brown eyes dip slightly, with her lips sealed into a thin line? She's scared I might run off.

Not far-fetched, I'll give her that.

"It's fine," I reassure her, despite not feeling particularly social. "The more the merrier, right?"

Riley makes a face, unconvinced. "Right . . ."

She opens the door, and before she can say anything, a mass of curly blond fur jumps all over me.

"Happy, it's good to see you too." I crouch down and bury my head in the goldendoodle's neck. I'm rewarded with three loud barks.

"Happy!" a deep voice booms from the living room. Miles. "Come here, boy."

Riley offers me an apologetic smile. "I'm sorry." She thrusts out her hand to help me get back up.

I take it, then dust off my pants. "It's fine. You know I love that dog. More than you or my brother-in-law sometimes, for that matter."

"Oh, I know."

The smell of Moroccan spices lures me from the doorway and into the living room, where Happy stands at Miles's feet. A young couple in their thirties sits comfortably on the couch with a baby in the woman's lap. They look familiar, although I've never encountered them before.

"It's good to see you, Charlee," Miles says as he brings me to his gigantically broad chest.

I hug him right back.

Riley knows I was kidding earlier. I love them both so much. The broken and empty shell my sister was a few years ago pales in comparison to the woman she is now. And although she put in the work on her own, I can't pretend Miles didn't play a big part in helping my sister regain the confidence she lost with her ex-husband. Everything he does, he does with her in mind. With him, it's always been Riley first, Miles second. I can't recall someone ever being that attuned to my sister's every need.

It's actually quite fascinating, when you pay closer attention to it, how his demeanor changes when he's around her. It's as if his body becomes aware of her presence and can't help but be drawn to her orbit. Scientists should study this shit.

"I'm sorry about the last-minute schedule change," Miles starts, turning toward the couple sitting on their couch. "My sister and her husband decided to make a pit stop here before flying to New York City this weekend."

"Very sorry to disturb your evening," the woman says as she stands, offering the baby to her husband before she walks toward me like a goddamn vision. Long brown waves frame her face and float around her shoulders, eyelashes to die for, hips I would spend nights dreaming about, and legs for days. I see that Miles's charm runs in the family. The woman pauses in front of me before leaning in and hugging me briefly.

"It's nice to meet you, Charlee. I'm Avery, Miles's sister, and this is Josh, my husband." She points to the man waving at me as he presses a kiss on the baby's cheek. Wavy brown hair, high cheekbones, and a sexy smile. Damn, where are these people coming from? "And this little nugget is our daughter, Margaux."

"I've heard a lot about you guys," I tell her. "It's nice to finally put some faces to names. What brings you to the East Coast?"

Josh rises, Margaux in his arms. "My beautiful and wildly talented wife is headlining a photography conference next week. She's been invited to guest speak on several panels. Very much in demand, this one." He grins at Avery, who blushes right away.

"Photography, huh? I'd love to see your work. I'm a wildlife reporter, so I'm around photographers all day, and I dabble in it too sometimes."

"Oh, I work mostly with people." Avery brushes her hair behind her ear. "Influencers and brands. Weddings, pregnancies. Landscapes aren't my forte."

I chuckle. "Well, props to you, then. I wouldn't be able to handle people and their lists of demands all day."

"Oh, we know that, Char," Miles retorts teasingly, walking toward Josh. When he's close enough, Margaux wiggles in her father's arms, stretching her tiny palms toward her uncle. Miles beams, picking her up, and something happens right before my eyes. His whole face melts like a marshmallow over a campfire, his crinkling eyes so alive with every smile he gives the kid, one wider than the next. The room falls quiet as we all watch him so naturally rest her on his shoulder, as if she were the most precious angel on the planet. *Meant to be* is what comes to my mind watching those two.

I glance in my sister's direction. She's as transfixed at the sight of Margaux, so small in Miles's arms, as everybody else, if not more. Riley shared with me how hard it'd been for Miles when he learned he couldn't have kids, and even though he's come to peace with it, even though my sister never wants children, I can still feel the outpouring of admiration and love she carries for him in this moment. It vibrates through her so fiercely, almost protectively.

As if feeling the weight of my attention, Riley snaps out of her daze and looks at me. She clears her throat. "Who's hungry?" she asks, breaking the spell Miles and Margaux cast over the whole room. As if life and time had stood still for a while.

"Depends." Josh's smile turns feline. "Did you cook?"

"Ha ha. I, in fact, did not. It's not like Miles would ever let me close to a knife again anyway."

Miles looks at his wife like she just said the most absurd words in the world. "Love, you've managed to almost cut your fingers not once, not twice, but *three* times this year. Forgive me for not wanting to spend fifteen hours in an emergency room on a Thursday night."

Riley rolls her eyes. "Ave, I'm sure you'll appreciate what your brother cooked tonight."

Avery pulls out a chair and sits down, gently unfolding her napkin on her knees. "Let me guess. By the smell of it, I'd say ... something flavorful and full of spice ... maybe a tagine?"

"Close." Miles settles Margaux in her seat and disappears into the kitchen. A few minutes later, he emerges with a large casserole dish, which he sets in the center of the table. "Careful, it's very hot."

He brings out two more dishes, then sits in the chair closest to the kitchen, leaving my sister at the head of the table.

"Start by taking a few spoons of the couscous," Miles tells us, taking off the lid. "Then choose the meat you want and add the veggies and sauce from this one here."

Riley lays her hand on top of his. "He spent all day in the kitchen trying out this new recipe."

"Hopefully, it'll have been worth it," he says, trapping her fingers with his and bringing them to his mouth.

Everybody gets started on their plates. The smells of olive oil, saffron, paprika, and other spices transport me to a warmer place.

"Mmm. God, Miles, this is fantastic," I moan under the firework of flavor happening in my mouth. "Definitely not Riley-made."

The men snort, and Avery hides her smile as she dabs her napkin on her lips.

"Okay, we get it. I suck at cooking," Riley quips, swirling the wine in her glass. "Can we move on to teasing someone else now? Aren't you guys curious to know where my sister is going tomorrow?"

I groan. Had that one coming.

"Not that it would matter," Riley adds, before throwing me a pointed glare. "Because apparently, she will not tell anyone. Not even her own sister."

"Can't," I rectify. "I *can't* tell you. I told you, I signed an NDA."

"Must be pretty important then," Josh chimes in. "Every time we get people to sign an NDA, that means we're cooking something big."

I shrug. "Can't say, really."

Riley puffs. "See what I'm dealing with?"

"If I could tell you, Ry, I would, I swear. But this is too important for me to risk it. All you need to know is that I'll stay safe and careful, and I'll be back in no more than two weeks, okay?"

It's my sister's turn to groan, pulling a chuckle out of me. If only she could see how ridiculous it is for her to always worry about me. I'm twenty-six, have been traveling the world for longer than I can remember, and have always come home. Granted, she often knows where I am, but doesn't she know by now that she can trust me to take care of myself? I'm not a little kid who needs to be protected anymore, but to Riley, I'll forever be the girl who needed someone to look after her, just in case she broke another bone while climbing higher than she was supposed to. Or the young woman who couldn't handle the grief of their mom's passing and has spent every waking hour since literally running from it.

I decide to spare her a few sleepless nights and give her one small detail. "I won't leave the country if that helps. Nothing dangerous, I promise."

"Thank you," Riley whispers, her chest deflating from the sigh she exhales.

I won't mention the potential presence of bears, wolves, or orcas. Or that I'll be basically lost in the woods with no cell reception for two weeks. She doesn't need to know that.

The night grows longer and warmer as our stomachs fill and our minds unwind. I find myself enjoying this unexpected evening, spent with two strangers who, by the time the night comes to an end, have become friends.

"Thank you for tonight," I tell Riley as I put on my coat. "It was surprisingly fun."

"I'm glad I got to see you before you leave."

I hug Miles goodbye, thank him for the delicious meal and homemade macarons tucked into my bag, and wave to Avery and Josh. Riley closes the door behind her, hugging herself against the chilly air.

"Please call and text me when you get there."

I sigh. "I will. I'll be okay, Ry. I can't wait to tell you all about it when I get back. You're gonna be so proud."

Her face softens. "I already am, you dumb-dumb. Have you met you? In what universe wouldn't I be proud of the woman you are?"

I smile and pull her into my arms. "I'm proud of you too."

Riley hugs me back tightly. "Don't forget to send me a postcard, though, okay?"

"Never."

I let go, squeezing her arm before starting to walk off. "You and Miles be good, okay?"

"Can't promise that!"

Laughing, I head toward my car. I still need to pack and stop by the office tomorrow morning before my flight.

And then it's two uninterrupted weeks alone in nature.

Well . . . almost alone.

Hey, C.

You have an O folder? What does that look like? I'm both intrigued and scared to know.

You're not too far off when you say I'm fighting my mail out of Emile's hands. Just this morning, I had to chase him in nothing but my underwear and my bathrobe flying in the wind because I didn't hear my "jerk mailman o'clock" alarm ringing on my phone. I swear, if he wasn't so old, I would shake some sense into him. I hope this won't offend you too much since you seem to have developed some inexplicable affection for the old grump. Plus, my grandparents have offered countless times to have him over at the restaurant for free, but he refuses because he's "not foolish enough to get diarrhea for days on purpose." Truly the highlight of my day, I tell ya.

I'm not psychic, no, but somehow, I feel like you and I share certain similarities, wouldn't you say? You strike me as the kind of person who could lose herself for hours in nature just contemplating what's going on around her, and I'm a bit like that too. And I get the feeling you've got a big, empathetic heart too. I don't know. There's something in your words, the way you write, the way you express yourself, that comes across that way. I like it a lot. It's too rare among humans these days. It's like I understand how your mind works because I think in the same way. And that's weird to say to someone I barely know. But the universe works in mysterious ways, or so the saying goes, and in our case, I believe it might just be true.

I love the drawing you sent me. You're very talented. Wow. The details in the lines and how much you focused on the eyes, the shell. I feel like I was right there with you as you sketched it. Why not consider a career as an illustrator? You could do funny children's books about weird animals talking to each other about their feelings of rejection. Pretty powerful stuff for kids.

Yeah, British Columbia is beautiful. That's what I love about Pine Falls. That's my town. (Do you know it? Probably not. It's not even a dot on the map.) It's small and lost in the middle of nowhere. If I need time to myself, I can go anywhere I want, and I'll find peace and quiet right away. No one to have to talk to or entertain. Pure silence.

Oh, and I'm a big burger guy myself. I was raised with food that felt like home and came straight from my grandparents' hands. Nothing was processed, the produce was always fresh, and they spent hours in the kitchen—either the one in their restaurant or the one in our small apartment above it—making it.

Your article was great, by the way! I like how you structured it and can tell you have a strong voice.

Already checking my mailbox, hoping to see your next letter,

O. (Any guesses on my name?)

Attached article
Where to hike in BC? Just a few of our favorite spots

CHAPTER SIX

The Sweet Sound of You

Oliver

I can't stop my leg from jiggling as I drive my electric pickup truck down Main Street. I will be meeting the *Wild Planet* correspondent from Toronto and the Movie Night Live crew later today at our offices in Vancouver, since Donna insisted on being present for the introductory meeting. It'll also be easier if I escort them back to Pine Falls since they don't know the area, then leave them at their hotel for the night.

But first, I park right in front of what used to be Jerry's and spot Rob rounding the corner. Right on time for his daily grocery run.

"Rob, hi!" I sprint in his direction before he gets the chance to dodge me. Again.

He turns his head my way, and I can feel his annoyance seeping through his imposing posture. Well, that makes two of us.

"Oliver, hi," Rob drawls as he stops. "To what do I owe this"—he checks his watch—"very early morning pleasure?"

I slide my hands into my pockets. "Yeah, I'm sorry about that. I'm leaving for Vancouver in a bit and thought I'd catch you before."

"Of course you did." He smiles, although his face is saying everything but "I'm happy to see you."

I ignore his tone. He's the mayor of this town, after all, and whether he likes it or not, he has to deal with his constituents. That's part of the job. "Listen, my situation changed recently. I'm up for a big bonus at work. Enough for a sizable down payment on my building."

"The *town's* building."

"My grandparents' building," I counter.

Rob sighs, pushing a hand through his graying hair. "We've been over this how many times already? The town took ownership of Jerry's when you couldn't pay for it."

"And we agreed I'd pay you the taxes and any maintenance cost as if it were still mine." Again, I force the boiling in my blood down to a mild simmer. Not today. Today is a good day, and none of his remarks will make me lose sight of that.

"Call it what you want; I don't care at this point," I add. "I came here to ask if you could hold off on the sale until the end of October. I know you're in talks with that business guy, but if the deal was closed, you would have told me. I don't know what's going on with that or what he's giving you, but I can guarantee you that what I have to offer you will top it. Maybe not with cash, but for the town."

Rob listens to me intently, one eyebrow arched.

"I can buy it back, Rob. I'm just asking for a month to get the money."

It takes him a few seconds that feel longer than the drive to Vancouver I'm about to embark on before he says, "Fine. I'll give you a month. But not a day more, understood?"

I nod curtly. "Thank you. I'll have the money to you by then, I promise."

He waves me off, grumbling, "Yeah, okay. Now let me get back to my peaceful morning."

No need to tell me twice.

I jog back toward my truck and can't help but smile.

After all these years, I finally get to go home. All my memories that still haunt those walls, the laughter and tears that resonate through the empty space that used to be my safe haven—it'll be mine again in a matter of a few short weeks.

When I arrive at the office around noon, the place is empty. Everybody must be in the break room or out at lunch. I don't know a lot of my colleagues since I mostly work remotely or am out in the wilderness. And it's not like I enjoy coming here anyway. Vancouver overflows with people and buildings, and there's no place to breathe or find the quiet calm you need. Everything reeks; I can't pick up the smell of nature through the thick clouds of pollution and exhaust fumes. Being here makes me uneasy, almost like my body doesn't know how to adapt or even survive in this foreign environment. Which is pretty comical, considering my survival skills in the wild.

I glance around, trying to find Donna. She and I agreed that I would come in early so she could brief me on the people arriving today and go over the filming and location schedules for the next two weeks. Since I'm also first-rescuer certified and will be largely in charge of the crew's safety while we're filming, I'm also going to be giving them a 101 training on what to do and, more importantly, what *not* to do while out in the rainforest. I'm happy to do it, even though the thought of public speaking never fails to make me nervous. She's lucky I got a certification a few years back and that I've given this exact talk more times than I can count. I'm saving her a ton of cash and trouble.

"Donna?" I poke my head into her office, but it's empty.

I stop by other offices. Nothing.

I check my phone. No texts.

She did say she would meet me here at noon, so where the hell is she?

I shoot her a quick text, and when, ten minutes later, I still don't have an answer, I start pacing the conference room a bit faster.

"Where are you, Donna—"

"I'm here, I'm here!" Her shrill voice comes through the door as she throws her bag on the chair next to me and sits down dramatically. "God, what a day."

Her face is red, and by the look of her graying hair sticking to her damp cheeks, I don't think it's because of the cold day we're having. I know Donna gets a bit stressed sometimes—she always has a hundred things on her to-do list—but seeing her winded like she ran after her bus, missed it, and walked the rest of the way to the office must be a new record.

I sit down too. "What's going on?"

"The journalist from Toronto is coming in less than an hour, and the hotel in Pine Falls that was supposed to lodge her bailed on me at the last minute. They double-booked the only room they had left. How do these things still happen nowadays? Doesn't your town know about computers and other intelligent machines?"

I chuckle at her joke, but the look Donna gives me makes me think she means business.

"I don't know. I'm sorry you're having to deal with that. Have you found an alternative?"

She pushes her thick glasses up her nose before folding her hands on the table. "Well . . . no. How am I supposed to find a decent room in a town of six hundred people with double the squirrel population and where the only bed-and-breakfast available is managed by a guy who is still sending faxes?"

Donna takes a deep breath and lets the air out slowly. "I know what I'm about to ask you is a lot . . ."

Oh no.

"And you're allowed to tell me no because I'm not paying you nearly enough for this . . ."

No, no, no, no. I'm not liking where this is going. And she knows it. She's been fidgeting with her nails since she arrived.

"I wouldn't ask you if I had an alternative. You have a lot of space. Could you house her while she's in Pine Falls? Just for that night before you leave?"

Fuck. There it is. The words are out, and I can't make her take them back. I can't pretend like I didn't hear them.

I slide a hand into my hair, pushing it away from my eyes. "Donna, I—"

"Please, Oliver. I don't know what to do if you refuse. She'll probably have to sleep on the streets, or worse . . . camp."

I make a face. "Camping isn't worse than the streets. Camping is my favorite thing to do. I would much rather go camping than live here."

Donna grabs my hands in what I can only describe as a death grip. Damn, this woman is strong for her age. "*Please.*"

I struggle to retract my hands from hers, but when I finally do, I let out a sigh. I can't say no, can I? I hate the idea of sharing my space with a complete stranger, but at the same time, what kind of person would I be, knowing I could have prevented her from being uncomfortable or freezing to death outside? I'm gonna hate every second of it, I know that, but I also know myself, and I'm not looking forward to the pinch of guilt poking me every time I'm with her if I say no right now.

"Fine, she can stay at my place tonight." It's like I'm getting my teeth pulled out one by one with each word. "I have a spare bedroom she can use."

Donna closes her eyes in relief. "Thank you. I owe you one."

"It's okay, really. Has the reporter heard about the change of plans?"

She shakes her head. "She hasn't landed yet, so I couldn't get a hold of her. I don't think she'll mind, though." Donna winks at me. What is *that* supposed to mean? "Let me forward you her details so you have her full name. Don't worry, she's not a serial killer. She's been with *WP* for about as long as you have."

My phone buzzes with Donna's email. I open it and skim over the unnecessary trip details until my eyes land on the name.

And I forget how to breathe. The only sign I'm still of this earth is the organ pumping blood in my chest with the speed of a hamster on crack.

I can't think; I can't speak.

That name. The name of a woman I knew five years ago. A woman I've thought about every day since my last year in college. A woman I haven't heard a word from since June 21, 2018.

Charlee Fletcher.

Toronto, September 29, 2017

Hello, hello!

My O folder contains strictly confidential information for my eyes only.

Don't worry, I'm not crazy. It's password protected. I wouldn't make it easy for anybody to find.

It's funny, I was thinking the same thing when I was telling my sister about our letters. I said to her that the more I read you, the more I get the feeling that we've known each other our whole lives. Not sure I believe in the universe talk, though. I prefer to think I'm in charge of my own destiny and that I forge my own path. But if there were any supercelestial powers at hand, then, yes, they're working very well.

I don't think I'd like to draw every day or make it my career. I'm just doing it for me, you know? Kind of an outlet for my mind to wander when I don't feel like staying in the real world. I wouldn't want to share my art with everybody, although looks like I made an exception with you . . .

What is it about isolating yourself that you like so much? Except the peace and quiet, of course. I think for me, it's when life gets too heavy and I'm too tired to support its weight. I got better as I grew up, but when I was younger, I had this unnecessary pressure to be as good as my older sister. "Get good grades like her, honey. Why aren't you as organized as Riley? If you were more focused on school rather than exploring and gallivanting everywhere, maybe I wouldn't have to worry so much." Riley represented the perfect daughter to my mom, and I get it, you know? Mom had enough on her plate without having to look after me on top of it all. She kind of expected me to do that on my own. I lived with this unattainable example in front of me, and all I could hear was "You're not good enough and you'll never be." So isolating myself in nature was my way of getting away from all of it. I much preferred missing a class or two in high school and challenging myself to discover a place where no one could find me.

Now things have changed, and even though I've learned to manage my life a bit better, my mom's recent cancer diagnosis has definitely put a damper on things, and I find myself craving solitude all over again. I know it's selfish, considering. But every time I think about the fact that my mom is fighting every second for her life, I feel like I'm drowning, and nobody can pull me out. But I know I need to stay strong for her and remain positive, so it's just a constant battle in my mind.

Anyway . . .

Wow, that was a lot of unpacking, huh? I'm sorry. You didn't ask for that much. Maybe this is a sign I should see a therapist? Ha! If you do read everything, though, and don't think I'm unhinged for sharing every detail of my life with a semi-stranger, then thank you. I guess I needed to talk, and you were there to . . . listen to/read me.

I wish I could relate to fresh produce and eating a homemade meal every day, but my mom didn't have time to cook for us, and it was perfectly fine like that. She did so much for Riley and me so that we could have the best possible childhood. She worked two jobs, and that meant she had to sacrifice some other parts, like spending quality time with her daughters. So my comfort food is Kraft Dinner. Yeah, I know, I know. What can I say? One bite, and I'm back at my kitchen table after soccer practice on a Tuesday night with my mom and my sister by my side.

If you made it this far, you're a saint. And I'm grateful for the friendship we're developing. More than you know.

Oh, and now I can't help but picture you in your slippers and bathrobe, running like a mad person behind an old and frail man so you can bully him into giving you your mail. Tsk, tsk, tsk. O. Tell Emile he has my vote.

Until next time.

G. No, you know what? As much as the mystery was fun, curiosity is getting the better of me, and I need to know your name. So I'll start, and I hope you'll indulge me.

Talk soon,

Charlee.

Attached article

Our hospitals need money and we're not listening—why is the Canadian government not increasing health funding?

CHAPTER SEVEN

Stranger

Charlee

When the plane lands in Vancouver, I'm reminded of why I love this corner of Canada so much. Mountains as far as the eye can see, the Pacific Ocean roaring on the coast, wilderness and nature at its finest. I could see myself living here one day. If I ever manage to earn enough money to rent or buy something other than a shed with these ridiculous prices.

I could have called this place home five years ago, if . . .

My heart pinches.

Thinking about him is always painful, no matter how many years have passed since I last read a word from him.

I sit down in the arrivals lobby, waiting for the Movie Night Live crew to join me. According to Ben, their plane isn't scheduled to arrive for another hour, which leaves me time to go over the schedule again.

We're supposed to meet *Wild Planet*'s Vancouver team this afternoon before we head into the wilderness tomorrow.

I don't know why, but I'm a bit nervous.

Actually, I know why.

A lot is riding on the success of these two weeks. Really, it's no big deal; just the future of my job—my passion and my career—and those of twenty other people.

I stifle a nervous laugh.

God, I'm exhausted. I woke up at four a.m. to catch my flight and spent the entire ride squished between a man-spreader and an old lady who used my shoulder as her personal pillow.

I get up, stretching my stiff limbs, and head over to the Tim Hortons a few gates away. Because coffee is exactly what I need to help with my buzzing nerves.

When I get there, I order a black coffee and a box of assorted Timbits to go.

The young man behind the counter chuckles. "Rough morning?"

If I had sunglasses on right now, I'd probably push them up so he could get the message. "Something like that. Oh, wait." I dig in my backpack when I see him grab a plastic cup and hand him my reusable one. "Here."

"Cute and environmentally conscious." He casts a long, deliberate look at me, which makes my eyes roll. "How can I leave you my number if I can't write it on the cup, though?"

Not only am I not in the mood, but it's also way too early for me to get hit on by a guy who is way too young if the two hairs fighting for their lives on his chin are any indication. And by the looks of it, they're both losing.

"Your dad is more my type."

This seems to do the trick of shutting him up. I pay and grab my mug, now filled to the brim with the hot, delicious black liquid, and the Timbits, then walk back to my seat, where my bags are waiting for me.

An hour later, the coffee has worked its magic. I'm pacing the arrivals terminal, vibrating with the desire to get the hell out of here and lose myself among the trees, when I spot a group of four people dragging huge trunks and crates behind them. I've been around photographers and crew long enough to recognize equipment when I see it. The woman at the front of the group sporting a black leather jacket and equally black short hair waves at me.

"Hi," she says, holding out her hand. "You're Charlee Fletcher, right? I recognize you from your LinkedIn profile. I'm Emma, from Movie Night Live."

I shake her hand. "Nice to meet you. How was your flight?"

Emma mouths "*awful*" to me before plastering a smile on her face as the guys approach. "Amazing! A bit long, but what can you do about it, eh? Let me introduce you to the guys."

Huh. Weird.

"This is Axel, Nick, and Trevor." Emma gestures to each man when she says his name.

Axel wears thick glasses. The one in the middle, Nick, continues to type something on his phone like he's already bored with this conversation. And Trevor looks to be in his late forties, if I had to guess by the graying hair on his temples. And he's impossibly handsome. *That's the type I was talking about earlier.*

"I'm Charlee. Nice to meet you all."

Axel waves timidly, and Nick offers a quick nod and goes back to his phone. Trevor's attention lands on me, a smirk stretching his lips. "*Very* nice to meet you, Charlee," he says, his voice deep. I hold out my hand, but instead of shaking it, he places it between his. "I'm a director at MNL, and I'll be directing this docuseries. *Wild Planet* went all out for us, huh?" He looks at Axel and Nick as if they're his personal audience. "A private chauffeur! Thank you," he drawls, exaggerating the bow of his head.

I laugh at his joke, but when I see Emma roll her eyes and Trevor looking at me like I lost my mind, I realize that he wasn't, in fact, kidding.

"I'm sorry. I didn't get a chance to introduce myself properly." I plaster the biggest fake smile on my face. I know exactly how to deal with this type of entitled guy. "Charlee Fletcher. *Senior* journalist at *Wild Planet*. I'll lead this project for the next two weeks."

Trevor's brows shoot up into his receding hairline. He lays a hand on his chest. "I'm sorry. I clearly read the room wrong; my mistake. I didn't expect you to be *the* journalist we heard so much about." He clasps his hands, making Nick jump. "Anyway, shall we catch a cab, then?"

I don't have time to ask what his fucking deal is before Trevor goes strutting off through the revolving doors, completely unfazed, followed closely by Nick and Axel, who haul the equipment behind them.

"Unbelievable," I seethe between my teeth.

"Don't waste your breath." Emma comes to stand next to me and, arms crossed, watches the men waiting for a cab outside. "He's not worth it, trust me. I've been working with him for years, and nothing will change his misogynistic ass. You get used to it."

"Sounds like we're gonna have fun," I quip.

Emma pats my shoulder and gets moving. "Oh, we are."

The upside of having to put up with an overconfident middle-aged man while being squeezed in one car for forty minutes is that Emma and I quickly bond during our ride to the *Wild Planet* office.

The downside is that I don't think I will ever be able to unhear the things I did. There are a limited number of cringy jokes I can force myself to laugh at, and I've exceeded my quota for the year.

"Thanks for the ride," Trevor says to the driver as he hands him a fifty-dollar bill. "Keep the change."

Emma and I get the bags out of the trunk while Axel and Nick grab the equipment. The ride to the seventh floor is silent, except for a loud ringing in my ears. *Just one more day, and we're off.*

The elevator doors open onto a bright lobby framed by glass windows. A reception desk stands in the middle of the space, a large *Wild Planet* sign behind it.

"Welcome to *Wild Planet*," the receptionist says. "How can I help you today?"

I rest my elbows on the counter. "We're here for a meeting with Donna? I'm Charlee from *WP* Toronto, and this is the Movie Night Live crew."

The receptionist—Sam, from his name tag—gets up and rounds the desk. "Right, I was expecting you. Charlee, Donna is waiting for you in the conference room, last door on the left." He points to the hallway behind me before turning to Emma. "Can you guys follow me? I'll show you where to store all this." Sam gestures toward the crates.

"Sounds good," Emma replies. "Lead the way."

They follow him while I make my way down the hallway in the direction Sam indicated. A voice rising behind the last door on the left—the one I'm supposed to get through—stops me dead in my tracks.

"I can't do this, Donna. I'm sorry, but I can't." The voice is deep but smooth, and there's a definite plea to it, a desperation bordering on panic that makes me want to know more.

I know I shouldn't, but I can't help it. I look around, making sure nobody will find me in a compromising position. After confirming the coast is clear, I step closer to the door and lean against it. It would be rude and embarrassing for me to interrupt whatever is going on anyway, so I might as well be entertained while I wait for the right moment to come in.

"You told me you would," a feminine voice comes through. Donna, I take it. "I don't have any other options. You can't bail on me right now!"

"It was before I knew who I'd be working with!"

Interesting . . . Are they talking about *me*?

I lean in further.

"Why does it have to change everything? You will *not* jeopardize this. There are a lot more people involved in this than just you and me."

"I'm sorry, Donna, I can't do it." The man's voice is shaking. "I can't work with her. I can't spend two weeks lost in nature with her and a camera crew. It's too much."

Her. So they *are* talking about me. What the fuck? What did I ever do to this guy to make him hate me so much that he can't even work with me? I don't even know any *Wild Planet* journalists in Vancouver, and I have never set foot in this office. Whoever he thinks I am, he's clearly mistaken. And even if, by some divine intervention, I happen to recognize his face, I will not give up this golden opportunity. No, sir. This man, no matter how his sexy voice is, will not get in the way of my future.

The woman sighs. "I'll call Toronto. I'll see if they can replace her and spare another journalist, but I doubt it because she's supposed to be here any minute now."

Oh, *hell* no.

I straighten and push the door wide open, coming face-to-face with the most beautiful man I have ever seen. Hazelnut eyes stare right into my soul with an intensity I can't put into words. His dark-brown waves, which tumble messily onto his forehead, make him look like he just rolled out of bed, despite the fact that I can tell he spent some time styling it just right. Dark stubble sprinkles the sharp angle of his jaw, and my fingers itch to touch it and find out if it's as soft as it looks.

The words that were about to come blazing out of my mouth are suddenly stuck in my throat. All the fury evaporates from my body in one whoosh, the eavesdropped confessions forgotten. This was clearly a mistake on his part, a misunderstanding. He must have me confused with someone else, because I don't know this man. I've never seen him in my life. If I had, I would sure as fuck remember it. With a face like *that*?

As I clear my throat, the man rises from his chair and stumbles backward, gripping the edge of the desk like his life depends on it. He looks at me with wide eyes, and his mouth falls open. His skin is as white as a sheet, the perfect portrait of someone who has just seen a ghost.

I frown. Do I look that awful? I know nobody looks their best after a flight, but come on.

Now I feel very self-conscious about not washing my hair this morning. If I'd known I'd be meeting the Canadian version of Sam Claflin, maybe I'd have thought twice about it.

The woman looks at me. "Can I help you?"

I smile, regaining my composure. "You certainly can." I hold out my hand. "I'm Charlee Fletcher. *WP* Toronto journalist. It's very nice to meet both of you."

Well, hello Charlee,

It's very nice to meet you and finally put a name to those words.

About that folder: Now I'm legitimately scared. At least now that I know your full name, I'll be able to rename the one I have on you.

I'm very sorry to hear about your mom. There are no words I can say that will make you feel better. But if you want to talk about it, if you feel like you're drowning, like you said, you know where to write to me. I think you could literally talk to me about anything, and I would gladly read you. You never bore me. I mean it. You're the highlight of my week, honestly. I wish I could talk to you every day. Sometimes, I see something that makes me think of you (like the amazing burger I had last week—god, you'd have loved it), and I find myself reaching for my phone to text you and remember that I don't even have your number. And I know it's not the goal, you know? This program is about writing, and exchanging numbers would spoil the fun. I don't even think we're supposed to write to each other this much, let alone share our names. I guess most of the people in the program send a "here is the article, bye." But somehow, we ended up here, and I'm not mad about it.

All this to say, never apologize or feel bad for writing me dozens of pages. Know that I'm always happy to receive them.

What do I like about being by myself? Ah, the unanswerable question. Like you, I guess it's changed and evolved over the years. But it's a need that's deeply ingrained in me now that I'm older. I wasn't always like this, actually. I grew up a very outgoing and social kid, always wanting to meet new friends, wishing so hard to one day belong to an inner circle. You know, those tight-knit friendships where you tell each other everything. Those that last a lifetime. So I went into each friendship with the same enthusiasm, giving it my all every time and ending up disappointed and confused when my eagerness wasn't reciprocated, or worse, when people made fun of me for being too sensitive, too intense, too weird, too eccentric. Too this, too that. You weren't enough, I was too much. Funny, right? We never were the right amount.

When you're just a kid, it starts to pile up. So I started to shut myself off and look for other ways to keep busy, ones that wouldn't require me to be around people. I never knew my parents. My grandparents raised me, so I asked my grandpa to take me on fishing trips with him on the weekends or go hike a full week when school was off. When he couldn't, I went to find peace alone in nature. There was no one around me to tell me how I was supposed to be. I would have given anything to be accepted for who I was and have friends like everybody else my age. I thought, "There must be something wrong with me."

One day, way later, I might have been fourteen or fifteen, one of my teachers asked my grandparents during a parent-teacher conference if I'd ever had a neurophysiological assessment. I didn't understand why she'd asked that at first. I was doing great at school, and my grades were excellent. She had even suggested at some point that I skip eighth grade. Turns out, I was diagnosed a few months later with what they called "giftedness." I know, sounds like I'm bragging, but I'm not. It basically means that my emotions are heightened, which leads to extreme sensitivity. It's easier for me to understand and retain information, which makes me even more curious about the things I don't know yet.

I'm sure you know kids can be pretty harsh and judgmental, and I find that even now, as a young adult, they're no better. But at least I have the tools I need to understand myself better and deal with uneducated people. And that's what matters: the knowledge that there's nothing wrong with me, that my brain is just not on the same wavelength as neurotypical people. You don't know how freeing it was to finally put a name to my feelings, my way of thinking and perceiving things. It's like everything that didn't make any sense suddenly did. Like I had been trying to put the puzzle pieces together for years, and they were finally fitting.

Those years spent finding ways to busy myself and learning everything I could about the outdoors made me realize that there is nothing I love more than being lost in my own world, between the trees and the sounds of living things around me.

That's a long story, but it should answer your question.

So I guess what is left to share with you is my name . . . here it is. The moment of truth. Drumroll, please.

Looking forward to your next letter,

Oliver

PS: Emile's answer was a nice middle finger. I didn't tell him you were supporting him in his crusade against my family, but when I opened the door at 8 a.m. sharp and saw him speed up, I stopped in front of him with my hands on my hips so he wouldn't be able to move past me. He raised his finger and shouted, "*Va te faire foutre, Reynolds.*" Which I believe translates to "Go fuck yourself." So there you go.

PPS: I was thinking of maybe submitting this article for my midterms. Do you think you could maybe give me some more in-depth feedback? Don't hold back.

<u>Article attached</u>
The gifted misunderstanding: Advocating for a better awareness of gifted individuals

CHAPTER EIGHT

Love of Mine

Oliver

The first thing I notice when my eyes land on Charlee, *my* Charlee, is the fire in her gaze. Nothing, not even the hours spent reading her every word and learning all her intricacies, could have prepared me for the feisty woman standing in front of me. The way her auburn hair brushes against her shoulders as she cocks her head, her hand still held out for me to shake. But I can't push my body to move, can't order my brain to send the signal to my arm to raise and take her hand in mine. Fuck, the mere thought of having her skin touch mine is sending me deeper into my spiral.

She's beautiful. No, the word doesn't even come close to doing her justice. How come the English language does not contain a single word to describe her beauty? That rosy tint that colors her cheeks and the tip of her round nose? Or what about a word for those full lips pressed together in a little smirk like she knows she has the upper hand?

How many times have I closed my eyes during classes and tried to picture her face? How many nights did I lie in bed, dreaming of those lips, the silky feel of her hair between my fingers, her head resting on my chest while I'd lull her to sleep? The sound of her voice?

Damn, her voice . . .

I wasn't prepared for any of it. Hell, I didn't think I would ever see her. Know the person she is beyond the words she shared with me.

Not after . . .

"Are you gonna shake her hand or . . . " Donna whispers in my ear, and I startle.

"I'm sorry, I need a minute."

It takes the strength of a bull for me to move my feet and push past her and through the wide-open conference room door. My strides are long as I rush to the bathroom and slump against the door once inside.

How can she be here?

In a heartbeat, I'm thrown back to the desk in my old room, smiling like an idiot as I write my answer to Charlee's letter. All of it rushes back to me—the memories and emotions, the indescribable ways in which she felt like the closest person in my life when I hadn't even met her yet. How she felt like she was *mine*.

I can't breathe. I'm falling, and there's nobody to catch me, nothing to grab on to.

That woman out there knows everything there is to know about me, and I know her better than anybody else. And yet she's a total stranger who hasn't figured out who I am, because how can she? I haven't told her my name. She doesn't recognize me.

She must think I'm the biggest jerk on the face of the earth, and quite frankly, when she discovers who I am, I'm not sure her opinion will change. Probably quite the opposite.

My body slides down the door. I dig my phone out of my back pocket and dial Lola.

"Ols?"

"She's here," I breathe.

"Who's here? Are you okay? Where are you?"

"Charlee's here, Lola." The words don't even make sense when spoken out loud. I sound like a madman.

There's a pause on the other end of the line. "Where are you?"

My head thumps against the door, and I rub the bridge of my nose. "I'm in the office. You know, for the training with the other journalist from Toronto?"

"Is she—" Lola's breath hitches. "Wh-what do you mean 'Charlee's here'? *The* Charlee?"

I nod, although she can't see my face, so I force the words out. "Yep. The one and only."

"Do you want me to drive down? I can take the rest of the day off."

"No, no, please don't. I'm okay." The hand gripping my knee trembles. "I think. I will be."

"I don't understand. How can she be there? Does she work for *WP* too?"

"Not only that, but she's *the* journalist from Toronto I'm supposed to train. And spend two weeks with in the woods. And . . ."

There's no point in telling Lola that Donna asked me to house Charlee, because I can't do it. And I doubt Charlee would agree to it once she puts two and two together.

But if Lola is anything, it's deadly stubborn.

"And?" she presses.

"Apparently, the bed-and-breakfast made an error with the booking. Donna asked me if I could host Charlee when we're in Pine Falls. I said yes when I didn't know who the journalist in question was, but now she'll have to find a plan C, because there's no way I'm agreeing to it."

"Okay, yeah, I can see how that'd be an issue."

I close my eyes. Maybe if I blink hard enough, it will all go away. Maybe I'll wake up from this bad dream and go back to my peaceful routine, as if none of this has happened. "What am I gonna do, Lola?" My hand slides across my face. "Fuck!"

"Oli, breathe. There's a solution somewhere, you know that. You just can't see it now because you're in the thick of it. Take a step back. What's in front of you?"

I do as Lola says and fill my lungs with air. "A dead end. It's either I say no and lose the money for the restaurant, or I say yes and have to deal with Charlee, and I don't have any clue about how anything will go down."

"Are you really ready to say goodbye to Jerry's, Ols? I know this is all kinds of fucked up. And I haven't even wrapped my head around it yet, so I can't imagine how you must be feeling. But this is your grandparents' place we're talking about. You can't back down."

"So, what?" I snap and regret it instantly. "I'm supposed to let her stay with me on top of everything? Do you know how long it's taken me to get over her?"

"*Are* you?"

"What?"

"Over her."

"I—"

There isn't really an answer to that question. None that would make sense five years later, anyway. The easy answer would be *yes, I am*. But the truth is far more nuanced, painted with many shades of *maybe* and *I don't know*. Because I still can't explain to myself how everything went so wrong so *damn* fast. How we went from having this overwhelming connection that made me feel like she was tethering me to this earth, to free-falling into utter silence.

"Look, Oli." Lola's soothing voice breaks the silence. "I'm not saying it'll be a walk in the park. I'm not saying you have to be at her beck and call while she stays with you. All you need to do is put up with it for two weeks. Two weeks. You've done harder things than that. Put on your most convincing smile, don't dwell on the past, and just do your thing. Stay professional. There's no need to hash things out if you don't want to. She's here for business, and so are you. Keep your eyes on the prize. And I'll be right there if you need me. You know that. Two weeks, Ols. Two miserable weeks to finally get your lifelong dream. What do you say?"

I push to my feet and stand. "I say I would rather become a finance bro who doesn't eat gluten because it's cool and works a nine-to-five job in New York City than spend two weeks with Charlee Fletcher with no cell reception." I walk to the sink and splash some cold water on my face with my free hand, then pull my reading glasses from my back pocket. And as I slide them on, I catch a glimpse in the mirror of the little boy who spent hours in the kitchen of Jerry's with his grandpa, preparing Christmas dinners for the whole town, his tongue stuck between his teeth and his glasses slipping off his nose as he focused on chopping the vegetables just right.

It's for that boy that I say, "You're right. Eyes on the prize." I lock my gaze on my reflection. "I'm doing this."

Oliver!

Wow, it feels so good to be able to call you by your name.

First of all, thank you for your words about my mom. I didn't know I needed them until I read your letter. Nobody has ever said that to me. Where have you been all my life? Ha!

Last night, I was working on a paper for my writing class. The teacher gave us this prompt: "Write about a place you've heard of but never been to," and I got this urge to write about Pine Falls. I was lying on my bed, my computer in front of me, *Red* playing in the background (please tell me you know what I'm referencing), and daydreaming about your town, how I imagined it, how it'd feel to walk its streets next to you.

You're not the only one wishing there weren't forty hours of driving distance between us.

Second of all, thank you (again) for opening up to me about your neurodiversity. I learned a lot when I read the article you wrote. I know it made you relive memories you probably didn't want to, so thank you for sharing this part of yourself with me.

If you ask me, I believe your sensitivity is a gift, even if it doesn't feel like it sometimes, especially in a society, with thousand-year-old stereotypes that men aren't allowed to be anything but tough.

How was it, growing up with your grandparents? Do you think about your parents sometimes? Oh boy . . . I don't know if it's insensitive or intrusive on my part. Aren't you glad you've been partnered with me? Haha.

I've talked to you about my sister, Riley, right? She's been like a mom to me all my life. Sometimes, she's a little overbearing, if you ask me, but she's there for me whenever I need her. Anyway, she's been married for six years to this guy from her work, Sean. Ugh, just his name makes me want to puke. Who do you picture if I tell you to imagine a guy named Sean working a corporate job in Toronto? Right?? Douchebag definition right there. Well, I hate him. He's always so nice when he's with us, but I don't know. I don't like how Riley acts when she's with him. She's off, not like I'm used to seeing her. And she always looks at him like she's waiting for his approval or something. But Riley is head over heels for him, and I don't know what to do. All I can do is watch him like a fox and make sure my sister knows I'm here for her if she needs me.

My midterms are next week, so I'm gonna keep this one short. I'm buried under study cards and running solely on caffeine, and I don't think I've changed out of the clothes I'm currently wearing in . . . oh god . . . three days. Please don't try to picture me right now; I'm so gross.

So you have a folder on me too, huh? Guess we're a good pair, then.

Can't wait to read you next week. You, but also your articles. You have a way with words. Your last piece might be your best work yet.

Oh, and give my best to Emile.

Xx,

Charlee

<u>Attached article</u>

It's a man's world: How do you navigate the business world when you have a vagina?

CHAPTER NINE

Regret Me

Charlee

W hat is his fucking deal?

First, he disrespects me, refusing to work with me for god knows what ridiculous reason, and now he's running away?

The nerve of this guy.

What? Can't fathom working with a woman? Is he that obtuse? I thought we left sexism in the past with the boomers, but clearly, between him and Trevor, I've been naïve.

Donna is still standing awkwardly in front of me, forcing an equally awkward smile onto her face. "Ms. Fletcher, I'm very sorry about that. I don't know what's gotten into him. Please, please, take a seat." She gestures toward the chair on my right, and I sit down while she rounds the table to take a spot in front of me.

"Thank you so much for making the trip all the way to Vancouver." She drums her fingers on the table and casts furtive glances at the door. "I want to make sure that you know your presence here means a great deal to us. We wouldn't be able to do this without you."

I quirk an eyebrow. "Are you sure about that? Because from the looks of it"—I nod toward the door—"I don't think I'm very welcome."

"Oh, that?" She shakes her head, and the white curls around her face jiggle. "Just a silly misunderstanding. He's *thrilled* to go off the grid for two weeks. Trust me."

I narrow my eyes, holding her gaze, and after a few seconds, Donna caves. "Okay, okay. I'll confess that I'm as much in the dark as you are. I don't know what that was about, but it doesn't matter, because we're going forward with the docuseries, whether he likes it or not."

"Knock, knock."

I turn around and find Emma in the doorway.

Donna stands. "Ah, Emma. I'm so glad to see you. Come here." She hugs the woman warmly. Seeing my confusion, Donna explains, "Emma and I have worked on a few projects before. Have you two been introduced?"

"Yes," I say, "we rode together from the airport, along with her crew."

Emma and Donna exchange a look.

I glance between them. "What?"

"Oh no, I'm just picturing you stuck with Trevor for forty-five minutes." Donna laughs drily. "Must have been fun."

As if on cue, Trevor walks in, flanked by Axel and Nick. "Donna," he booms. "Always a pleasure." He pulls her in for a quick hug before he comes behind me, one of his hands falling on my shoulder. I barely stop myself from gripping his wrist and twisting it behind his back. I exhale through my nose. "Have you gone over the assignment with Charlee yet?"

"Not yet," Donna replies. "We're just waiting for our reporter to join us. He's the one who'll give you the training today and assist you during filming."

Trevor claps. "Great, let's get started, then. Oh, Donna. Can you please grab us some coffee before we do? I don't want to snore in the middle of the presentation."

Yeah, because *that* would be rude.

He smiles an awful smirk before burying his attention in his phone, Donna completely forgotten.

Do I really need to work with that entitled fucker for two weeks? Because he's already on my last nerve, and it's only been three hours. Not sure I won't commit murder by the end of the job. Maybe we could turn the docuseries into one of the crime TV shows MNL loves so much.

Emma sits next to me, pulling a notebook and a pen from her bag, while Nick and Axel mimic her on the other side of the table.

"I forgot about this training session," I mutter so only Emma can hear. I don't want Trevor to know a single word that comes out of my mouth if he doesn't need to.

"I think it's cool we're getting one. It's not always the case, and it makes our job easier. Especially in places like the rainforest. So many potential risks."

"I love risks. I live for them."

Emma snorts, smiling. "You won't live long if you don't follow basic safety precautions." She looks around the room, searching for something. "Where is the guy who's supposed to give the training?"

"Oh yeah, I didn't tell you. It was the weirdest shit."

She focuses on me, and I have to swallow because the intensity of her stare is making me lose my train of thought. I notice how beautiful her eyes are. Gray with hints of blue as deep as sapphires that shine with her curiosity. "What happened?"

I snap out of it. "Yeah, um ... While you guys were dealing with your equipment, I came here. The door was closed, but I could hear voices arguing, so I listened in. The reporter for *WP* who is supposed to be our local guide during the trip was begging Donna to bring in a different journalist."

Emma's mouth hangs open. "*What*? Are you sure?"

I nod. "He said something like 'I don't want to work with her' and went on and on about how he wanted Donna to contact our Toronto office to send another person to replace me."

"*No*. You're kidding."

"But wait, I'm not done."

Emma straightens. "There's more? Oh my god."

I chuckle. "Yep. So when I heard this, I couldn't ignore it, you know? Enough was enough. I opened the door and introduced myself. I thought the guy was gonna drop dead. Never seen that man in my life, but he seemed to know *all* about me. He didn't even say hi. He just ran away."

"Charlee Fletcher, what have you done to this poor man?"

I hold my hands up. "Nothing! Although I wish I had, because the guy looks *good*."

"Uh-uh. Take it from me; it's never a good idea to mix business and pleasure." She tucks her black hair behind her ear. "Things can get messy real fast."

"Don't worry about it. I don't think I'll ever see him again. He's been hiding god knows where since."

As if my words had magically summoned him, the man in question walks through the door, his gaze high, looking everywhere but at me. He crosses the room in a few fast, determined strides, although I catch a glimpse of his fingers nervously playing with the hem of his shirt.

Emma leans in. "I see what you mean," she whispers, a smirk on her face. "Dorky guys get me every time."

I'm too focused on him to come back with a witty reply. It's true that he looks nerdy. I think the glasses he's now wearing add to that vibe, but his anxious demeanor and clothes fit the description as well. It's the way his shirt is wrinkle free, except for the part that's stuck between his fingers. And the way his hair falls messily on his forehead.

He makes his way to the front of the table, and Donna follows, coffeepot in hand.

"Here you go, Trevor." She settles the coffee on the table, and Trevor & co. fill their mugs.

"There you are." Donna pats mystery guy's arm. They exchange a long look, engaging in a silent conversation that only they can decipher. After what feels like several interminable seconds, the man curses under his breath and clears his throat.

"Good afternoon, everybody. Thank you so much for coming all the way to the West Coast." His eyes dart furtively to mine before settling on a random spot at the back of the room.

I frown and glance at Emma, who shrugs.

"Yes, so, um . . . I'll be with you for the next hour or so to go over the safety basics and first responder moves to adopt while out in the wilderness."

His voice feels like velvet, rich and deep, gliding down my skin with a softness that leaves goose bumps in its wake. His nervousness suffocates the air, and I wish I wasn't the cause of it. He's definitely confusing me with somebody else. If my twenty-third rewatch of *The Vampire Diaries* has taught me anything, it's that doppelgängers exist. Maybe I have my own evil Katherine Pierce somewhere.

"Are you okay?" Emma asks in my ear.

I whip my head in her direction. "Yes, why?"

"You're gawking."

I make a face. "I'm not."

Trevor clears his throat. "Ladies, please." He points to the local reporter, who avoids my gaze yet again.

"It's okay," the man stammers.

He turns to the whiteboard behind him, then picks up a marker and divides the board into two parts.

I'm not gonna lie, this view isn't bad either. He's all long legs and strong shoulders.

"The training will be split into two themes: first, we're gonna go over safety measures, and during the second half, we'll be doing a sensitivity training regarding the Indigenous communities living in and around the rainforest. It's important that we respect the communities and learn what to do and what not to do."

He switches the marker from his right hand to his left and writes down the themes, the letters smudging slightly as he goes. My heart presses uncomfortably against my ribcage as my mind grapples with unwanted thoughts. I've been so good at leaving them in my past, but the sight of those smeared letters on the board brings them front and center, as if it were just yesterday that I was writing letters to that college boy, spending every waking moment thinking about him and what it would feel like to be in his arms.

My eyes drop to the hand gripping my thigh. I loosen a breath and shake the thoughts away. Not today. He doesn't get to have another day of my pain.

"Excuse me," Trevor interrupts, pulling me out of the awful place I used to go to when thinking about him. "Before we get started, would you mind introducing yourself? I didn't catch your name. Since we're gonna spend two weeks together, might as well get to know each other."

"S-sure, of course, yeah." When the man turns around, his entire face is as red as a traffic light. He looks at Trevor, at me, then back at Trevor. Finally, he says, "I'm the local reporter for *Wild Planet*, and I'll be your guide for the next two weeks. Nice to meet you all."

"And your *name* is?" Trevor asks, bordering on annoyance.

"Ah, yes." He looks at me—really looks at me—for the first time since I set foot in the room, and that's when I notice it. The pain in his eyes. I frown, but he holds my gaze as he says his next words. "I'm Oliver Reynolds."

My heart stumbles and crashes to my feet.

Morning, Char,

I'm writing to you today before I get to class. It's 7:30 a.m., so I have thirty minutes before my daily fitness run after Emile (at least he keeps me in shape).

Hope you had a great week and didn't study too hard. When you get this, it'll be your midterms, so I'm wishing you the best of luck. I know you're gonna crush it! Side note: I know we've never seen each other, but I don't think you could look gross if you tried. Home fashion is a thing, and it's hot.

Today, I went to the post office to talk about the issue with Emile and to see if I could get a new postman assigned to my neighborhood, but they kindly declined. It felt like they were scared of him? Apparently, they have discussed his retirement with him before, and every time, he threatened to get the court involved for age-based discrimination. They're pretty heavily unionized too, so they told me their hands were tied. And then you know what they did? They handed me a bag of mail addressed to me and my grandparents. A bag, Charlee. Full of mail. For every morning when I must have missed him. They said they found it buried in his office under some old boxes. What am I going to do with him??? Maybe I should be the one to move so I can get someone new.

Oh, by the way, Sean doesn't seem like a great guy. Hopefully, your sister will see right through him soon enough. People's true colors often tend to come out on their own over time. If the guy is a manipulative asshole, he won't be able to hide for too long.

Growing up with my grandparents was probably the best thing that ever happened to me. I've never known my parents. They were young when they had me and didn't feel like they were up for the job. At least they were smart enough to leave me with my mom's parents. So no, I don't miss them, really, and I feel like if I had known them, I would have ended up resenting them for probably giving me a bad childhood. My grandparents <u>are</u> my parents. They raised me and have been by my side through everything: birthdays, school, heartbreak, and all the joys in my life. My grandma is my protector and the person who believes in me even when I don't. She taught me respect, to love myself, and to stand up for my beliefs. I remember her telling me one day: "Oliver, you don't have to make your voice loud to be heard when you're fighting for what you truly believe in."

I was, am, so loved, and I owe it all to them. I owe the man that I am today to them.

My grandpa taught me everything I know about nature. I don't think there's one thing he told me that I haven't memorized. We don't do it as often now that I'm in college, but we used to go on so many hiking trips, sometimes for days on end. He taught me how to survive in the wild, how to recognize what was good to eat, how to listen to the sounds around me, and that everything in nature has a place and a reason to be. My love of the wilderness comes from him. I remember the time we came home after four days of camping in the rain and my grandma yelled at us as soon as we walked in the door with our muddy hiking boots, telling us we smelled like fish that had spent too many hours in the sun.

Oh, Charlee, I have so many stories like this, and I want to tell them all to you. I want you to know everything.

Recently, I've been spending time with my grandpa in his shed. He's building a wood workshop next to where we plan on building my cabin, and he's making some wonderful wood furniture there. You should see how talented he is. I've been trying to follow in his footsteps, but my skills are nowhere near his.

Anyway, how's your year at uni going so far? Have you made any friends?

Waiting for your next letter impatiently.

Xx,

Oliver

Attached article
Demystifying procrastination: The benefits of knowing when to push to tomorrow what you could potentially do today

CHAPTER TEN

Can't Stop Loving You

Oliver

"I'm Oliver Reynolds."

I want to take my name back as soon as it leaves my mouth. I can pinpoint the moment understanding sinks into Charlee's brain. I see it in the way she grips the edge of the table as if she needs to hold herself up, her gaze fixed on me, full of questions I don't have the answers to.

Fuck, this is way harder than I thought it'd be. I expected her to be mad, to be shocked, I guess, and maybe resent me too, but I didn't expect the fury unfolding in her eyes. Didn't expect to watch her regain her composure two seconds later and put on an unreadable mask, lips sealed, shoulders squared, no emotion but utter disdain pouring out of her.

The switch catches me off guard, and I back up a step, lowering my gaze to my fingers nervously wrinkling the hem of my shirt.

Even like that, even with her hating me, she's still the most beautiful woman I have ever seen, and my heart gallops faster than a racehorse on derby day, aching to make things right between us.

Nails clicking on the table pulls me out of my stupor, and I turn my head toward the sound, finding Donna watching me intently with one eyebrow up.

"Yes, so, as I was saying," I rasp, "we're going to start with wilderness and survival skills. Nothing too fancy, just 101 knowledge." I swallow, but my mouth is so dry, it feels like sand going down my throat. I grab the glass sitting next to me and drain it.

"Are you okay, man?" Trevor asks and turns to Donna. "Is he really the best reporter you have?"

God, this guy isn't helping either. His whole attitude of feeling like he's above everybody in this room is getting to me. I want to punch him square in his smug face.

"Yes, sorry." I plaster a smile on my face before Donna can answer. "I was just going over everything in my head so I don't forget anything. Wouldn't want you to get eaten by bears or something."

A few chuckles echo in the room. I risk a look at Charlee, who remains as stoic as a rock.

"So let's start with the ten golden rules of hiking. Number one: research your routes in advance."

For the next hour or so, I cover all the safety bases, from food essentials to appropriate gear and what to do in case of bad weather. The familiar rhythm of my explanations eclipses my worries and almost succeeds in helping me forget who's in the audience. Almost.

Toward the end, tour guide Reece Marven from the Gitga'at First Nation steps in to give the crew sensitivity training on how to respectfully live on their land.

I can't help but look at Charlee from time to time and notice she hardly writes down anything I say. I'm not surprised. Most of this she already learned from me. How many times did I write to her and tell her everything I knew? I'm sure it feels as much as a déjà vu for her as it does for me. But when I glance at her, she never raises her eyes to mine. She doesn't move or let one shred of emotion past the iron wall she erected in front of herself.

"Thank you, Reece," I tell the man as he concludes his presentation. "What I want you folks to remember from this training is simple." I raise my fingers and start ticking them off one by one. "Pay attention to river torrents, always stay together, and never, *ever* interact with wildlife. This is the most important one of all and the one that will keep you and your teammates the safest."

"Got it, champ," Trevor says, saluting me. "I think we're good for today. We should start to head north so we can avoid traffic and arrive before it gets dark outside."

I nod. "That's probably wise. I'll be right over."

I look at Charlee, who's already packing her things, ready to fly out of the room. What do I do? At some point, she's gonna have to talk to me, right? Whatever happened five years ago, we'll talk about it and realize it was just a misunderstanding. If she ever agrees to listen to me . . .

Okay, Oli. No better time than the present.

I square my shoulders and force myself to move forward, one foot in front of the other. Once I'm just a few short feet away from her, I stop and clear my throat. Her eyes shoot to me like daggers. Great start. I haven't opened my mouth yet.

"Can I talk to you for a moment?"

"Oh, so *now* you want to talk?" she quips. "No, thank you."

I slide my hands into my pockets and rock back on my heels. "I didn't know you'd be here. I didn't plan it."

Charlee scoffs. "It doesn't matter. You don't want me here. I get it. I'm not thrilled to be here either now that I know who I'll be spending the next two weeks with. But I'll do the job I'm getting paid for. Nothing more, nothing less." She throws her backpack on the table with a loud thump. "Are we done here?"

"It's not . . . Charlee, listen, I need—"

"I said no thank you, *Oliver.*"

My name on her lips should have sounded like the most beautiful thing I'd ever heard, yet she said it like she was spewing venom. Like she couldn't wait to get rid of it.

I take the hit silently.

It's not going to be an easy couple of weeks, is it? Maybe I should have gone with my first instinct and ask Donna to take me off the project entirely. It was easy to guess that Charlee would react like this, and just the thought of putting her in that situation, of having to endure her loathing, makes my stomach turn.

"Charlee, Oliver!" Donna calls from her office next door. "Can you both please come over here?"

We exchange a look, hers so cold it freezes the blood in my veins.

"What did you do?" she spits.

"Why do you think I'm involved in this?"

"You're right," she mumbles and grabs her backpack, grunting as she exits the room. "Not a concept you're really familiar with."

I sigh and follow her, hoping that she won't bring the whole building down when Donna delivers the news.

Toronto, October 27, 2017

Oliver!

God, last week was EXHAUSTING. My midterms are finally over, and I can resume my life and be a functional human being who doesn't sleep with her head on her books. Thanks for your feedback on my last article, by the way. The change you made in the last paragraph really brings the whole story together.

Wait a second. Did you try to get an old man fired? Oliver! You heartless monster. Tell Emile I will riot with him if you succeed with your little coup. You can't see me, but know that I'm shaking my head and waving an angry finger in your direction.

My year at college is going okay. It's been a lot busier than I thought. This program is taking up a big chunk of my time, and *that* I didn't expect, haha. I'm happy, though. Getting letters from you is my favorite part of the week. I know I bitched about the program at first, but besides learning considerably on the journalism side, I've loved forging this super-special friendship with you. You're one of my favorite people now.

I don't spend a lot of time on campus, though. Mostly here for my classes and then I rush to my job. I hate it, but it pays the bills. Have you made any friends? I know you have a hard time with people, but I'm hoping students are more mature in college than in high school.

I could spend hours reading all the stories about your grandparents. I hope that we'll have the chance sometime to sit down with some hot cocoa so you can share them all with me. I didn't have the chance to spend time with mine, but your relationship with them sounds so beautiful and gives me major FOMO.

Although now you kind of piqued my curiosity, and I want to see how much you truly know about nature . . . hmm. Down for a quiz? Just ignore this if you're not. Also, how will I know that you won't google it before writing it down? We have to find a cheat-proof way for you to answer these questions . . .

Okay, they are:
- What is the rarest plant in BC?
- What do you do if you come nose to nose with a bear? Yeah, I know, the experts are divided on this one.
- Give me three bird species living in the Great Bear Rainforest.
- Last and probably most difficult one: What's the longest river in BC and how long is it? (Two questions in one—it's a win-it-all or lose-it-all situation.)

Hoping you'll get at least one right :)

Talk soon, my favorite little nerd. Xx.

Charlee

Attached article
It's science! Research shows that men who pose with fish on dating apps are most likely to get swiped left

CHAPTER ELEVEN

Closure

Charlee

How is *he* here? How is *the* Oliver the guy I'll be working with for two weeks? Out of all the wildlife reporters living in BC, for fuck's sake, I had to be paired with the one who ruined love for me. The very same one who destroyed my faith in men and relationships.

Of course.

Because that's just my luck. Or karma.

Actually, yes, it does sound like karma for all the guys and girls I've sneaked out on and never called back. If I had a dark sense of humor, I would laugh at the cosmic joke of the century, but even I am not that sarcastic.

Now it all makes sense. I get why he tried to get away from the assignment, to get *me* fired. The fucking nerve.

I drum my fingers on my thighs as we wait for Donna to come back from wherever the hell she went. We're seated so uncomfortably close to each other that I can feel the warmth radiating from him. I hope it's because he's nervous. Let him sweat his balls off. He can pass out from dehydration for all I care. All I want is for that woman to come back here and say what she wanted to say before she disappeared to god knows where.

Ugh. These West Coast people are in no rush, and I want to get the hell out of here ASAP.

"Are you okay?" Oliver breaks the silence, his eyes lowering to my jiggling leg.

I stop, crossing them at my ankles. "I'm perfect."

"You look nervous. It's gonna be okay. Don't worry too much about it."

I glare at him, and his cheeks turn that very cute shade of pink. *No. Stop it, Charlee. This guy broke your heart.* "Sounds like you know what this is all about, so why don't you fill me in?"

"I think it's better to let Donna handle this."

I shift in my seat to look at him, and for once, Oliver doesn't flinch. He holds my gaze, his chest rising a bit faster.

"Handle *what*, exactly?" I ask.

"Sorry for the delay," Donna says as she barges in. "Last-minute emergency with our team leaving for Madagascar tomorrow." She settles behind her desk and rests her hands on top of it, linking her fingers together.

Uh-oh. I don't like that look. I don't like it at all.

"Charlee, we're so happy to have you as part of this amazing opportunity for *Wild Planet*. I've heard such great things about your work and the kind of professional you are."

Oliver's hum is barely audible, but I hear it, nonetheless, and when I glance at him, he nods slightly, as if agreeing with Donna's statement. Like he didn't expect anything else from me. The thought fills me with something I've felt a few times before when we used to talk. Something gentle and sweet, like snow falling softly outside and hot cocoa with marshmallows sprinkled on top.

I shake the thought away. What does he know about it anyway? He never stayed around to watch me become the badass reporter I am today.

"Thank you, Donna."

"With that being said, I'm afraid I have some bad news. The bed-and-breakfast we booked made a mistake with your reservation and double-booked your room. They called us today to apologize and to tell us that the other person has already taken the room."

"Uh . . . okay? Did they provide another?"

Oliver inhales next to me.

"Unfortunately," Donna says softly, "they didn't have another bed available."

I shrug. "Okay. We can find another hotel, then."

Donna's smile tightens. "Pine Falls is a small town, you know. There aren't many hotels around. The nearest one is an hour away, and not in the same price range."

"Pine Falls?" I whip my head in Oliver's direction. "*That's* where the hotel is?"

"Well, yes," Donna replies, bringing my attention back to her. "Since the town is right at the border of the rainforest, we thought it'd be easier for the whole crew."

A rush of relief fills me when I realize that this error might actually be the best thing that could have happened to me. If I had to handle seeing Oliver for the first time *and* set foot in the town he loves so deeply, the one he promised to show me every hidden corner and all his favorite spots . . . a shiver runs through me at the thought of the vulnerable state I could have found myself in the moment I'd have crossed the town's line.

"We did find an alternative, though." Donna adds as she glances quickly at Oliver, who looks absolutely miserable. "Oliver has kindly offered his spare bedroom. It'll even be easier for you, as you two will be able to coordinate the rest of the trip together."

My stomach drops like a ball of lead to my feet. "No."

That's it. That's the only word that I can pronounce, but I think it's pretty clear. No way in hell am I sharing a house with him.

"Now, Charlee." Donna puts her hands up. "I understand the situation is less than ideal, but this will only be for one night, and then you guys are off to the rainforest anyway."

I shake my head. "No, I'm sure we can find another way. I'm not staying at the house of a guy I know nothing about." I stand, and the chair drags on the floor with a loud screeching noise. "Excuse me, I'll be right back."

What do I do, what do I do, what do I do? I pace in front of the office, trying to find a solution—*any* solution—that wouldn't involve me sleeping in the same house as Oliver. I pull my phone out of my back pocket, opening my hotel booking app. I scroll, looking for one in my price range that's located within a forty-mile radius of Pine Falls.

Come on, *come on*. There has to be *something* I can book. But everything I see is $450 per night at the lowest, and there's no way I can afford that. Not with my salary anyway. I love my job, but it pays the bills and that's it. I'm clearly not in it for the money.

I dial Ben. He picks up on the first ring.

"Charlee, hey! How's Vancouver? Did you make it to *WP* offices all right?"

"Yeah, yeah, listen, there's an issue with my hotel room, and I need you to get me another booking."

"What happened?"

I groan. "A double-booking issue. The bed-and-breakfast is full. I need you to pay for another hotel."

Ben chuckles on the other end of the line. "Fine, fine. Let me get my credit card." I hear muffled noises and a second later, he's back on. "How much?"

God, he's gonna freak. "$450."

His loud laugh blasts my ears. "Are you out of your mind, Char? Hell no. I'm not even paying that when I go on business trips, and I'm the manager. What did Donna say?"

"She . . ." I pinch the bridge of my nose between my thumb and index finger. This cannot be happening. "She suggested the local reporter could house me instead. But Ben, come on. I've never—"

"For free? Even better!" Ben exclaims. "Look, Charlee, you and I both know the financial situation of *WP* isn't good. We need to save money anywhere we can. So if you're asking me to choose between you getting housing for free or a $450 hotel room, this won't be a Cornelian choice for me. Please tell me you understand?"

I close my eyes, clutching my fists as I swallow my pride, for once. I hate it when he mansplains things to me. Like he thinks I'm too dumb to understand what he's saying. But there's a big difference between understanding and agreeing, and I *really* don't agree.

I inhale slowly before answering. "Of course I do. But I can't sleep in a stranger's bed. What about safety?"

Ben snorts. "Are you really playing the safety card with me right now? You? No. Nuh-uh. Will you have your own room?"

I sigh. "Yes."

"Then it's settled! He's a reporter for the same company as you, Charlee, not Jeffrey Dahmer. You've slept in worse places. I'm sure you can handle this for *one night*."

"Ben—"

"I gotta go. Don't be a jerk, Char. The guy's kind enough to let you stay with him. Okay, talk soon?"

He hangs up, not leaving me another chance to protest. *Ugh*, he can be such an asshole sometimes.

My back hits the wall. I slam my fists into it. "Fuck!"

I can't do this. It's too much to ask of me. I can't be in such tight confines with the man who slipped through m fingers five years ago, who held my heart in his hands bef my eyes ever landed on him. And now it's all coming ba big swoops, and I'm being pulled under the weight of the memories and the feelings I once carried.

But I can't tell anyone that. Not Donna, not Ben. No one understands why I'm being so single-minded about saying no. I wouldn't even want to explain why, or I'd look like a whiny sixteen-year-old. My professional integrity is, unfortunately, too precious for me to throw away with one single conversation.

It doesn't leave me with much of a choice, does it?

My dear Charlee,

You bet your ass I tried to get the old jerk fired. Emile gave me my mail yesterday by slapping it on my head. Spoiler alert: it really hurts.

I'm happy to read that you're liking the program and that I'm part of the reason why. I talked to my grandparents about you last night. Told them I've met this great girl who lives far away and whom I've never seen in my life but feel like I've known forever. My grandma said she had the same feeling when she met my grandpa. That feeling you have deep in your gut that you can be completely yourself with someone, that they will accept you, no matter how fucked up you can sometimes be. Her words, not mine. But I like to believe she's right. And the connection I feel to you is unlike anything I've ever experienced. Except maybe Lola, but it's different, you know? She's been my best friend forever.

We grew up together in a town of less than a thousand people. Her mom was employed at Jerry's, so when we were kids, we used to play all around the restaurant after school and get yelled at by Lola's mom for running into her while she was bringing empty plates back to the kitchen. During school breaks, we used to dress up as waiters and customers before the restaurant opened for lunch. I don't think anyone on this earth knows me better than she does, although I feel like you're becoming a close second. She's a sister to me more than *anything else. You're different. I don't know what exactly. You're . . . my Charlee. And, boy, do you take up space in my mind.*

So to answer your college question, yes, I did make friends. It's not super easy for me either, because I spend a lot of time at the restaurant helping my grandparents, but two guys, Matt and James, just moved to town and are super chill. I'm surprised we get along because of how different we all are, but they seem unbothered by my "intensity" and shrug it off. I've never experienced that, and sometimes I think it'll all go away. But for now, the three of us and Lola all hang out, and I love every minute of it. It's crazy how well everybody fits together, and my life is insanely better because they're in it.

I promise you, Charlee, that one day, we'll sit together next to a firepit outside with hot cocoa and a blanket, and I'll tell you all the stories you want to hear. And you'll tell me all of yours with your sister and all the trouble you got yourself into just to piss her off. I'm sure there were plenty.

I'm gonna answer your questions now, you smart-ass. There's not a lot I can do to prove to you that I didn't research the answers on the Internet, but I can give you my word that I didn't. The only question I have for you is: Do you trust me?

- *Easy. Who do you think I am? Knowing plants in nature is essential for survival. What if I eat the wrong one? The rarest plant in BC is scarlet gaura. It's not the rarest, but one of the rarest (pretty hard to narrow it down to just one).*

- Okay, this one is a long answer. You ready? I'll try to make it as short as I can. If you come close to a bear, you have to stay calm and never run away. It's best to speak softly while backing away slowly, without ever making eye contact. If a bear approaches you, have your bear spray ready (just like men, I know). Fun fact: I've met a lot of bears while hiking. They're not as bad as people make them out to be. They just want to be left alone, and if you do that, they won't bother you. Like all wildlife. Better to never interact with it.
- You're gonna have to make this harder, Char. Three bird species: bald eagles, marbled murrelets, and water ouzels.
- Okay, the longest river question took me some time. I'm not gonna lie. I was debating between the Fraser River and the Columbia River, but if I remember correctly, only the Fraser River has its full body in BC. Now the length, I don't know. I would say somewhere between 1,000 and 1,300 kms.

Did I pass? If it makes you feel better, I'm sure you know way more about Ontario than I do. I've never been to Toronto, or Ontario, for that matter. Never been outside BC, actually. It's pretty crazy when you think about it, since one of my biggest dreams when I was younger was to travel the earth and discover every nook and cranny our planet has to offer before nature as we know it disappears.

All right, I'm gonna wrap this letter up. It's 7:50 a.m., and Emile is coming in ten minutes. Gotta have it ready, or you won't get it in time. I don't feel like running in boxers again today. The weather is turning pretty chilly. And I think Mrs. Miller, who lives down the road, was scarred for life when she left her house to grab her newspaper and saw me running around half-naked. I heard her huffing and puffing about decency and manners.

Talk to you next week, my favorite wild girl.

Xx,

Oliver

<u>Attached article</u>
When deep human connections have an effect on our brain chemistry

CHAPTER TWELVE

When We Drive

Oliver

"Right over there." I nod to my pickup as Charlee walks beside me, keeping a good distance between us. She hasn't uttered a word since she miraculously agreed to stay with me.

Stay with me.

I'm still struggling to grasp that the girl I've been thinking about for all these years will be sleeping a few feet away from me tonight. That she's standing right here next to me, within reaching range . . .

I chase the thoughts away, my body growing restless, not knowing what to do, how to act, confused at having her here and not being able to touch her like it has always craved.

Part of me is terrified to spend so much time with her, especially with how she's acted so far. But another part, a dangerous part, one that has lain dormant for years, is stirring awake at the thought of having her so close. It's contemplating the possibility of a second chance, a do-over at something I fucked up years ago.

"Here," I say when we get to my truck.

She struggles to open the door with all the bags she's carrying, so I round the vehicle and grab the door handle at the same time that Charlee sets her stuff down and reaches for it too. Her hand lands on mine, and the touch shoots a spark up my arm. She jerks back as if she too felt the jolt. Or perhaps she just can't handle contact with me. Either way, her hand is gone, and only the aftermath lingering on my skin is proof that it used to be there.

"I got it," she quips, low and cold.

"I'll put your stuff in the truck bed, then."

"Fine."

I grab her backpack and suitcase. *Fine*. The same word she used when she said she'd stay with me. So much contempt in such a small word. I shake my head. I knew she had some fire in her, but I didn't expect it to burn this hot.

I load her luggage into the truck bed and shut the hatch, then settle behind the wheel. I spare a glance her way, but I'm met with a mass of wavy auburn hair.

I sigh, turning the engine on and putting the gear in reverse. If that's how she wants to play it, fine. I let out a bitter chuckle. There's that word again.

"What's so funny?"

"Nothing," I reply, doing my best to sound as unaffected as I can, despite every nerve ending in my body being aware of her proximity. "I was just thinking about something."

Charlee sinks deeper into her seat, her body angled toward the passenger door. "Care to share?"

My eyebrow rises, but I control my surprise before she gets a chance to see it.

I shrug. "It's nothing, really."

Charlee mumbles something I can't hear and goes back to the silent treatment, looking out the window. The warmth coming from the heater starts to melt the icy space between us, and I relax my fingers around the wheel, settling my focus on the steady rhythm of the highway.

For the next two and a half hours, only the radio playing nineties rock music fills the silence in the car. Charlee doesn't move from her position: legs tucked underneath her, her body turned completely toward her door. At some point, her breathing changes, growing slower until she exhales deeply.

She's sleeping. At least the silence is less awkward now than it was when she was openly brooding.

God, what am I going to do with her?

She seems so . . . *stubborn*.

She wasn't as hardheaded or closed-off before, even if a part of her enjoyed being in her own bubble back then. I don't know where this toughened-up side of her is coming from, whether I played a part in fortifying her defenses, or if other moments in life have shaped her this way. Whatever the reason, the next time I want to attempt a conversation with her, I'd better be armed to the teeth and ready with a battle plan. Otherwise, she'll never let me past her guard, and I'll never be able to explain to her what happened on June 21, 2018.

"Charlee."

I lay my hand on her arm, squeezing it lightly. She stirs, groaning as she frees her arm from my hold. A second later, she's back to her soft snores.

I shake my head, a smile stretching my lips for the first time since I've been in her presence. Even asleep, she's a little grump.

"Charlee," I say again.

This time, I shake her with a little more force.

She opens her eyes slowly, then looks around, frowning. She removes her arm from under my hand like a feral cat about to get caught and crawling out of reach.

"How long was I out?" Sleep clings to her voice, giving her a soft, soothing edge. Such a contrast to earlier. It leaves me breathless, begging for more. This is the voice I imagined her having when I used to think of her. Being able to hear it outside of my fantasies sends my heart tumbling in my chest. It takes me a second to remember she asked me a question.

"Almost the whole ride," I manage to get out. I glance through the windshield at the sun starting its descent below the horizon. We're in Pine Falls, parked on the street in front of Lola's boutique. "I need to make a quick stop. Do you mind?"

Charlee shakes her head and grabs her phone. I gather this will be her only answer.

As soon as my feet hit the ground and I slam the truck door shut, I inhale fresh air, and my chest expands for the first time in three hours. I allow myself a few seconds of respite before heading into Lola's store.

The doorbells chime when I walk inside *One Last Chapter*.

"We're closed!" Lola shouts from the back, probably finishing some last-minute paperwork for the day.

"It's me," I call, picking up a book tastefully placed on one of the display tables. *Love and Other Words*. I turn over the hardcover in my hands, studying the beautiful gold-sprayed edges and all the small details decorating the spine.

"Have you read this one?" Lola asks when she comes out of her office. "It's the tenth-anniversary edition of the book. Just . . . beautiful."

I put the book back. "I've heard of it, but, no, I haven't read it."

She nods toward it. "Take it. Early Christmas gift."

I laugh. "Christmas isn't for another three months."

"Come on, take it. I have a feeling you'll love it."

She's like that, Lola. Generous beyond belief, even when it comes to the store she just opened a few months ago. It's the final milestone in her lifelong dream to open the first bookstore in the entire province dedicated to the romance genre.

She picks up the book and holds it out, waiting for me to take it. So I do.

"Thank you, Lols."

I hug her briefly and drop a kiss on her temple.

"What are you doing here?" she asks.

"I'm not staying. Charlee is waiting for me in the car."

Lola's mouth forms an O. She leans against the table and crosses her arms, as if she has all the time in the world and is about to hear the most interesting story of her life.

"So you talked to her. And she agreed."

I nod. "She did. Not without trying to get out of it first, but she did."

Lola hums but doesn't say anything else. She just watches me, which in Lola's language means that she's trying to figure out how I feel about having Charlee here with me.

I don't want to think about it.

I don't want to start exploring the rush that surged through my body when I drove past the town's sign and realized she had finally arrived in Pine Falls.

No, I can't open that can of worms right now.

"What?"

"You can't hide from it forever, Oli."

"I know."

Lola presses her palm to my arm. "You're gonna have to forgive yourself at some point. Maybe now's the time to face your demons."

"I don't know." I let out a sigh and run my hand down my face. "I finally turned the page and put this behind me."

"Did you, though?" She looks so smug with her cocked eyebrow.

I shake my head, chuckling. "This isn't what I came here to tell you anyway. Charlee is waiting for me. I should head back. I don't want to put her in a worse mood than she's already in."

"If she's here, I'm guessing you came to tell me you wouldn't be able to make it to tonight's dinner."

"You guessed right."

Lola puts on a shocked face, one hand on her heart. "I can't believe your first time missing our Friday night dinner is for *a girl*. Matt and James are gonna have a field day with this when I see them later."

I groan. "You know I'm already feeling guilty as shit, Lols."

She straightens, patting my arm. "I'm teasing. Relax. Go now before she rips your head off and I have to find myself another best friend."

I hug her goodbye and walk back to my truck, where Charlee is still sitting in the same position, her nose buried in her phone. When she sees me approaching, she locks it and looks away.

"Sorry about the wait," I tell her as I slide behind the wheel.

"It's fine," she mutters, and I can't help but wonder if "fine" and anger are her two default modes I'll have to put up with for the rest of this trip.

We ride in silence for fifteen minutes before we reach the thick pine forest. The trees swallow up what little daylight remains, plunging us into near-total darkness. The road twists and turns like a snake around the trees, giving me little visibility of what lies ahead. Out of the corner of my eye, I notice that Charlee's curiosity has gotten the better of her bad mood. She pulls herself up, taking in the sights as we drive deeper into the shadows. Minutes later, I put my blinker on, then pull my truck onto a narrow dirt road.

"Sorry," I say when Charlee's head hits the passenger window. "The road's a little bumpy."

After a while, the pines disappear, giving way to a large clearing with a view of the lake. My cabin stands at the far end. I park my truck and switch off the engine.

"Home sweet home."

Charlee doesn't laugh, doesn't even break a smile at my absurd attempt to lighten the mood. Instead, she says *thanks*, opens the door, grabs her luggage from the back, and strides briskly toward my front door.

Meanwhile, I'm still sitting behind the wheel, watching her and wondering how the hell I'm gonna get through these two weeks unscathed.

Hey Oli,

Today, I miss you more than ever.

My mom isn't doing well. Since the beginning, I've been to every chemo appointment, poured countless glasses of water to help her swallow an endless number of pills, and waited while she was having her double mastectomy. But I can't do it anymore, Oli. I can't be the strong daughter she needs me to be.

We got news today that her breast cancer progressed to stage IV. Can you imagine? She did chemo, radiotherapy, meds, and surgery, and still, the cancer found a way to get worse. Doctors said that seeing her current condition, Mom isn't a good candidate for clinical trials. Those are for patients who still have a fighting chance, and in her case, we've apparently reached the stage of keeping her comfortable.

I lost it, Oliver. I ran out of the room and slammed the door behind me. Riley was there too, so she took Mom home. I drove straight to the Bluffs (it's a park near the city). I can't believe what's happening to her. The prognosis seemed so promising when they diagnosed her three years ago. She's only fifty-four. She's so young, and she has so much to do and see. She can't die now. There are so many things I still want to do with her, so many places I want to show her.

If you were serious about that promise, I'd take you up on it right about now. I need a friend like you. It's funny how someone can become so close to you despite not having met them in "real" life. I can't remember opening up to anyone like I do with you. It's always been so hard for me, but with you, it comes naturally. Maybe you're asking the right questions, or maybe you're just . . . magic. So, to answer your question, yes, I trust you. It feels weird to say, but if my life depended on it, I'd trust you in a heartbeat.

I wish you were here today. I'd lay with my head on your shoulder, and we'd just sit in silence, watching the sun fall below the horizon instead of being alone. The view from the park is beautiful, though. I know you'd be able to make me feel better just by being here.

Would it be crazy if I said I wanted to meet you in person? Do you think we could do it? We've joked about it here and there, but I realize now that I'm actually serious. Because when things go awry like today, it's you I turn to in my mind. It's you I think about, and it's you who soothes me, if only a little, even if you don't know it. Can you imagine what it would be like if we were next to each other? I get shivers just thinking about it. Thinking about you.

And maybe I could meet your grandparents too, and your friends and Lola. You guys sound like quite the crew.

Hope all is well on your end. I'm sending you so much love.

Xx,

Charlee

Attached article
Going out with someone you've never met? The dangers of online dating

CHAPTER THIRTEEN

Motion Sickness

Charlee

There is something very strange about standing in Oliver's house. Even after all these years and knowing so much about him, I still feel like I'm in a stranger's home. Everything makes sense but also doesn't. It's like I can reconcile some pieces of him with what I see, while some parts just don't want to fit into that mold.

I'm still in the doorway, Oliver's footsteps coming closer. I can feel him behind me before he says, "You can go in, you know."

I nod and step forward, dropping my bag next to a row of shoes and shedding my coat. I hang it next to his flannel jacket before I move out of the way.

The cabin is made of wood, with large windows taking up an entire wall. Two brown leather sofas on a cream-colored rug sit in the middle of the large space, a wooden coffee table in front. I look up, but the ceiling blocks my view of the pointed roof I saw from outside. Some part of me wants to explore his entire house, look through those bookshelves that line the living room walls and see what he's been reading lately. See what kind of man he turned out to be.

"Do you want something to drink?" Oliver asks from behind the kitchen bar, startling me out of my thoughts.

"No, I'm fine. Thank you."

I hear him whisper, "Okay."

I study him, the blush on his cheeks, his sharp nose, his wild hair falling on his forehead, the defined lines of his jaw under his stubble.

It hurts to look at him, so I avert my gaze. Anywhere that doesn't remind me of the pain I feel when I think of him. But here in his house, I can't escape him. He's everywhere I look.

Oliver clears his throat. "Do you want me to show you to your room?"

I nod. "Please."

"This way."

I follow him down the hallway on the right until he stops in front of a door and opens it. Inside, the bedroom is simple: a queen bed and two nightstands.

"I'll bring you towels in a moment," Oliver says. "The bathroom is at the end of the hallway. If you need anything, I'll be in the kitchen cooking dinner. Help yourself to anything you want downstairs. Upstairs is just my room."

"Thank you." I try to mean every word of it. I'm grateful he's offering me a place to stay, but my mind can't wrap itself around *where* it is I'm staying—and with *whom*.

I should call Riley. She'll know what to do.

"Char, if I can just . . ." Oliver starts, but he stops short when he realizes what he just called me.

His eyes meet mine.

I cross my arms. "Well, don't let me stop you, *Oli*. Say what you want to say."

It comes out way harsher than I wanted, but maybe I'm more pissed than I thought I was. Although when our gazes meet again and I see the pain in his, something in me caves a little. I was in love with this man for a while. Of course some small part of me is going to feel something if I see him hurting. Him more than anyone else. Now that he's standing in front of me, in all his beautiful and tangible ways, I'm realizing that my body and mind can't stay impartial when it comes to him.

His hand on the door handle, Oliver shrugs. "I'm sorry. That's all I wanted to say."

I narrow my eyes. He wanted to say so much more. I can tell. He was probably about to address the one thing I have no interest in talking about: why we haven't been in touch in the last five years. But old wounds are better left alone. Reopening them would only make me remember how alone he made me feel.

So I stay perfectly quiet as he walks out of the room and closes the door behind him, and I'm left feeling like the biggest jerk on earth.

I wake up to the smell of cheese tickling my nose, the sheets sticking to my cheek.

Shit, I must have dozed off while I was emptying my suitcase.

My stomach growls.

I pat the bed and find my cell on the edge of the mattress. No reply to the quick message I sent Riley after landing. No text from Ben. It's just me and my lonely self and . . .

Oliver.

And that smell . . .

My stomach twists, not from hunger this time. If I were a betting woman, I'd put all my money on what Oliver is cooking right now. I can't believe this. What is he trying to do? Does he really think that cooking me my favorite childhood meal will suddenly make everything right again?

I jerk up, grab my burgundy hoodie, and slip it on before I tie my hair into a short ponytail. When I open the door, the smell intensifies, making me more upset with each step that takes me closer to the kitchen.

"I need some air," I blurt when I get to the open space where Oliver is cooking, an apron wrapped around his body.

My steps falter as my brain tries to compute what my eyes are seeing. It's a lot, especially when I'm not thinking clearly, when anger, pain, and curiosity blend into a racket within my body and become indistinguishable from one another, leaving me feeling defenseless. And I fucking hate feeling like this. Hate that he's the reason why. Anger it is, then.

Oliver gazes at me over his shoulder while stirring the contents of the pan with his left hand, corded muscles lacing around his forearm as he does. "Dinner will be ready in a few."

"I'm not hungry." My stomach chooses that exact moment to betray me. "Is there a coffee shop or a bar in the area?"

Oliver stops stirring, turning to look at me like I'm deranged. "You want to go out? *Now?*" He looks through the window as if to prove his point. It's pitch-black. There's not a lamppost in sight.

Probably not the smartest idea, but I'm beyond that point. "I just need a breather."

"Okay, well, let me at least drive you." He wipes his hands on the cloth on his shoulder. "The Fir Café is closed, and the bar is two kilometers down the main road."

I shake my head, pulling my eyes away from his fingers pressing into his biceps as he crosses his arms. "I'll walk. So, down the road?"

Oliver frowns. "Charlee, it's late already. It's not safe to walk alongside the road at this hour, especially when you don't know the surroundings."

"I have my phone. If anything happens, I'll call you."

Oliver stares at me. "On which number?"

Right . . . I forgot about that. We've never exchanged numbers. Gosh, I can't believe now is the first time I'm going to enter Oliver's info in my phone.

Once our numbers are exchanged, I put on my hiking boots and pull my socks up to my shins. "Don't wait up for me," I say when I open the door.

Oliver doesn't even bother to answer.

"And so I told her, 'Miss, this is not how we do business in the real world, but with skirts like that, you'll make one hell of a secretary.'"

Raucous laughter erupts around the man in the suit standing at the bar.

All guys, of course.

The man, with his hair slicked back with a shitload of gel, takes a sip of his drink. He's basking in the attention, a wry smile on his face. I shake my head from where I'm sitting in my booth and take another swig of my beer. What a load of bullshit.

"Everything okay here, honey?" the waitress asks, a tray of drinks in hand.

"Can I have another one, please?" I point to my empty beer bottle.

The waitress smiles at me, and I detect the hint of pity. I can't blame her. If I were looking at myself, I'd pity me too. I've been drinking alone for the past two hours, reveling, for once in my life, in the discomfort of my loneliness.

I bring the glass to my lips again. I've had, what, three, four beers? Plus a shot, courtesy of the bartender himself. I'm slowly losing my control.

My head weighs less than feathers, as if gravity has lost its hold on it. My bad mood, my fears, my anxieties, and even my regrets slide easily down my throat with every sip I take.

I've almost forgotten where I am. With whom.

It almost doesn't matter.

Almost.

If Oliver were here with me, I'd have enough drinks in me to face my fears and tell him how hard my heart broke when he left me on my own the day we were finally supposed to meet.

The promises made, the weeks spent writing, opening up and confiding in each other, growing feelings, and becoming one another's person . . . *Poof*. It all went up in smoke in the space of a day.

Doesn't he know what that does to someone? To lose such a vital part of oneself? Did he suffer from the loss too? Or was it just me? Was I the only one who almost broke their own rule every damn day that followed to not reach out to him?

"Need some company?"

The man in the suit is standing in front of me, pulling me out of my spiraling thoughts. Up close, his skin shines with sweat, likely from all the alcohol he's swallowed since I arrived. Although his heavy build probably makes him more resistant to alcohol than me.

It takes a lot of concentration to make sure I don't roll my eyes all the way to the back of my head. "It's okay, thanks."

Clearly not getting my cue to fuck the shit off, the man sits down on the opposite side of the booth. "You seemed lonely from up there." He nods toward the bar. "Thought you might prefer to spend a bit of time with me instead of sulking here all alone."

I narrow my eyes. *Shut up, Char. You're drunk, and he's just an asshole. Don't waste your breath on him.* But my mouth opens without my consent. "Is this you flirting?"

He wiggles his eyebrow. Gross. "Maybe. Is it working?"

I snort. "Fuck no."

His drink stops halfway to his lips. "You shouldn't be talking to me that way. Not with that gorgeous mouth of yours."

"Get a good look at it, then." I stand and lean over the table, making sure my lips are plump as I say, very slowly, "Go fuck yourself, asshole."

His gaze darts from my mouth to my eyes with the hint of a threat. It's like he's finding some twisted pleasure in my rejection. What a sick pervert.

"Do you know who I am?" His voice raises the hair on my arm.

I grab my beer. "I don't know who you are, and I don't care. Now leave me the fuck alone."

I turn, but the man grabs my wrist and pulls me toward him. I lose my balance and catch myself on the edge of the table. Anger grips me faster than the man can release my arm. With my free hand, I clench my fingers into a fist and land it right in the middle of his pathetic face with as much force as I can muster.

The sound of cracking bones echoes as blood sprays from his nose and runs down his upper lip.

"Fuck!" I cry out, shaking my bruised hand.

"You little bitch," the greasy man seethes. He tries to extricate himself from the booth, but he's wedged in. He lunges for me instead, and I ready myself to plant another punch right in his crotch, but a strong arm pins my fist against my side.

"Hey, hey, knock it off!"

I turn my head to see Tom, the bartender, behind me. Two other employees have the asshole restrained.

"All right, get off me!" I demand.

"None of that in my bar," Tom warns.

"She assaulted me!" the man yells, pointing at me.

I scoff. "Who touched who first, asshole?" My words come out garbled, barely intelligible.

Tom releases me, firmly motioning for me to sit at the bar while the man retrieves his belongings and storms off. "Is there someone who can come pick you up?"

I shake my head.

Tom fills a glass of water and sets it in front of me. "Where are you staying?"

"What makes you so sure I'm not from here?" I slur. My arm hangs heavy on the counter, and my hand throbs like hell.

He shakes his head. "Because I know everybody in this town, and I'd remember a redhead brave enough to punch Oscar like that."

"Oliver's," I mumble, not having enough strength in me to get another word out.

I faintly hear the bartender say, "Ah" before he swipes his phone open.

I really don't care. I just want to go back to his place and sleep. My head is already pounding against my skull. Tomorrow's not going to be pretty.

I fold my arms on the sticky counter and rest my head on top, closing my eyes. Maybe in a few hours I'll be sober enough to walk back to the house. If I remember which way to go. Or I can just stay until morning and wait for someone to point me in the right direction.

Maybe I'll just lose myself so nobody can find me again.

I hold on to that last thought, so tempting and seductive, as I drift into my slumber.

My dear Charlee,

Words can't express how sad your last letter made me. My heart aches for you and for what you're going through. I'm so, so sorry to hear about your mom. I can't imagine how hard it must be for you and Riley, trying to be there for her and handle all of this yourselves too, while also trying to continue to live your lives as if everything were normal. I don't blame you for having lost it. I would have too.

I wish I could be there with you too, holding your hand and helping you through this awful time. I wouldn't be able to do much, but I'd never leave your side, just in case you needed me for a hug or to help you navigate what's coming your way. So if you ever feel down again, just imagine it. Close your eyes and imagine that I'm right there with you. That you can lay your head on my shoulder like you wanted, while we sit in silence, just content in each other's company.

Would it be crazy if I answered that I'm dying to see you already? I'd love to meet in person, but with all you have going on now, and with it being the end of the semester, I don't think now is the right time. Trust me, it pains me to write this. I'd fly to see you in a heartbeat. How about we plan on meeting before next summer, after we're done with college? The restaurant season really picks up in July, so I won't be free after that. But June would be perfect. Does that sound good to you? God, just thinking of having you in the flesh in front of me is sending my mind into a frenzy of delirious thoughts.

Maybe after that, if you're free and feeling up to it, you could come back to Pine Falls and spend the summer here with me. No pressure, but I'm still offering.

I'm sending you something unusual in this week's letter. I hope this small gift will bring you a bit of light in moments of darkness, and if I'm lucky enough, a little smile on your face. I've been working on it for a while, but now seems like a good time to send it to you. See, in BC, we have what we call the Great Bear Rainforest. It's paradise, one of the planet's most beautiful jewels. There is so much wildlife in this rainforest, but there's one I love the most: the spirit bear. What makes the spirit bear so special is the fact that its fur is white, despite it not being either an albino or a polar bear. It's, in fact, a black bear with a recessive gene that causes its fur to turn white. They're beautiful creatures, rare and unique. They make me think of you. My very own spirit bear.

I hope you like the pendant.

Sending you my love and hugs from a distance I wish I could make disappear.

Xx,

Oliver

Attached article
The spirit bears of the Great Bear Rainforest: One of nature's most beautiful mysteries

CHAPTER FOURTEEN

The Alcott

Oliver

"What happened?" I say when I barge into the bar and my eyes land on Charlee dozing on the counter.

"She punched Oscar," Tom replies from behind the bar. "He must have said something inappropriate, as usual. You know how he gets when he's had a few drinks."

I take a long inhale through my nose. The fucking bastard.

"How is she?" I cross the distance separating us and rest my hand between her shoulder blades. She doesn't flinch like I feared she would, which tells me she must really be out of it.

Tom wipes the counter around Charlee. "Pretty drunk."

I brush a few copper locks away from her face and tuck them behind her ear. She groans, but her eyes stay closed. "Can you give me a glass of water, please?"

"Sure thing." He grabs a glass and fills it up, then hands it to me. "I gave her one already, but she hasn't touched it."

"Thanks." I massage Charlee's neck. "Char, come on, it's time to go home." She lifts her head and opens her eyes, and I slide the water to her, dropping my other hand from her sweaty skin. "Drink."

She takes it, mumbling something I can't understand. I stay next to her while she downs the glass and regains a bit of consciousness. It takes a couple of minutes for her eyes to change from the glazed-over state they were in moments ago.

I try again. "Let me drive you home. Come on."

"Home. Your house isn't home," she mumbles.

Oh yeah, she's better, all right.

"Let's go." I help her up, and she grabs my arm to stabilize herself. "Thanks, Tom," I say over my shoulder before we head outside.

We walk—stumble—to my truck. I open her door, holding her hand as she scrambles to get into her seat.

"I'm fine, I'm *fine*." She snatches her hand from mine.

I close her door, then round the hood and settle behind the wheel.

"Thanks for picking me up," she says in a whisper.

I nod and start the drive back. "Don't mention it."

"I'm not usually like that," she slurs.

I smile, keeping my eyes glued on the road. "You know, the guy you . . . punched tonight. He's not a great guy. He probably got what was coming to him."

I take my attention off the road for a second to find Charlee watching me with a hint of curiosity. "He put his hands where he shouldn't have."

My fingers curl around the wheel, grasping it tighter. In retrospect, it's a good thing I wasn't there. I don't think Oscar would have walked out of the bar in one piece.

"You know him?" Charlee asks.

I glance back at her. She frowns when her eyes settle on my hands. I relax my grip and let them fall to the bottom of the wheel.

"Sorta. He's not from here, if that's what you're asking. He's a real estate guy who owns the Lakeside Resorts luxury hotel chain. He's been in town for a few months now, trying to convince the mayor to sell him some buildings." *My* building. *My* family history. "He has big plans for this town, but people won't go for it."

At least that's what I keep telling myself. But even I have to admit that the offer is enticing.

"What kind of big plans?" Charlee asks, wiggling her fingers in front of her in a spooky way.

I scrub my jaw. "I don't know all the details, but from what Rob has told me—Rob's the mayor—Oscar wants to transform Pine Falls into a huge hotel complex for tourists looking for an 'authentic nature experience with all the luxury Lakeside Resorts has to offer.'" I air-quote the last part before I bring my hands back to the wheel. "The whole thing is absurd. We don't need an all-inclusive concrete resort to attract tourists. We're the last town before the rainforest, and we already have everything we need. You should see how packed the town is during the summer."

Charlee's breath catches, and I dare a quick look at her. Her eyes are trained on the road, but the rise and fall of her chest is giving her away. "So you've said once . . ."

I peel my eyes away, something pressing against my chest. I should be surprised that she'd remember such an insignificant detail, but then again, I memorized everything too.

There's a beat of silence before she adds, "He did look like the biggest asshole I've ever seen. He's lucky I didn't punch him with my good hand." She lowers her gaze to her bruised hand folded on her lap.

Shit, it's already swollen. I press the gas pedal a little harder. Hopefully, we'll arrive in time for her to ice it and keep the damage to a minimum.

"I'm so over men like him, who think they can just own whatever they set their eyes on," she continues, her voice rising, sharpening. "Like they're playing some giant game of dibs where the ones with the biggest cock will get what they want without caring for a single second if what they're claiming ownership of is theirs to take."

I hum but don't have time to say anything else before she adds, "And what? He's gonna convert this whole town into a mega-concrete center full of malls and spas and bullshit like that? The entire charm of Pine Falls is how embedded in nature it is. That's what tourists are coming to see. Not some hideous all-inclusive resort."

I hide my smile. She spat everything out in one breath. The fire she's been aiming at me since she arrived has shifted toward something I loathe just as much as she does, and I'm seizing the reprieve it gives me.

"Trust me, I'm fighting this as hard as I can. I've got a small group of business owners who can be swayed into opposing the project, should Rob go forward with it. I think he's starting to feel the pressure from the Pine Falls folks." I turn onto the small path that leads to my cabin. "I'm not in Rob's good graces these days," I add, chuckling.

"That's good you're involved," Charlee mutters.

From the corner of my eye, I see that she's back in her curled-up position, staring out of her window.

I swallow my defeat.

Did I say or do something I shouldn't have?

How stupid of me to think that a short car ride would be enough to make her forgive me and open up to me again. But still, hope was there, and she just blew it out like a gust of wind on a candle flame.

After I park the truck and we head into the house, Charlee wobbling a safe distance behind me, I grab a bag of frozen peas and my first-aid kit and wait for Charlee to join me in the kitchen.

"I see you're well prepared," she says when she slumps on one of the stools.

"Have to be when you live where I do." I nod to her hand when she grabs the peas. "I can help you with that, if you want. It looks swollen and a bit red on the side. I can take a look at it, see if anything's broken."

She blinks. "I'm fine. I can do it myself."

"I know. I was just offering."

"And I answered." Her eyes show no mercy when they land on me.

I bear the blow without flinching, but some part of me feels like giving up already. She's too damn stubborn, too damn hurt, too damn furious for me to even bring up the subject. I know her, despite what she might think. I know her so deeply, it sometimes feels like her reactions, her emotions, are my own.

What I did was the highest betrayal of all, and in her mind, there's no coming back from that. But still, some foolish part of me is holding out hope that there's a way forward, however hidden it may be right now.

When I open my mouth, it's that part of me that speaks out. "I meant it when I told you I didn't know you were the journalist they were sending, Charlee. But I'm glad you pursued your dream and became as successful as you are today. You deserve every bit of it."

She stands up a bit too quickly and sways, but she manages to keep the pea bag resting on her left hand. "You don't know what I deserve or don't deserve. You don't know me anymore, and you have no right to have a say in my successes or failures. You don't get to waltz in here and tell me whether I'm worthy of my own career when you didn't even fucking bother to stay in my life."

Her words are slurred, barely understandable, but they hurt all the same.

She doesn't leave me time to answer, not that I would have found anything to say to that anyway. She closes the bedroom door behind her, and I stand alone in my kitchen, shattered to my bones.

Toronto, December 1, 2017

Hey Oli,

Reading you was like a hug around my heart. Thank you.

Oli, I can't believe that you made the necklace yourself. This is the most beautiful pendant I have ever seen. The details??? How?? This must have taken you days to create. And for me? You don't even know how much it means to me.

I snapped a photo while wearing it, but I didn't show my face. I like the mystery between us. I love having this idea of you in my mind and keeping you a surprise until the last moment. It makes this whole thing so unique.

So here you go, just my neck. I wanted you to see how well it fits me. Thank you so much for this beautiful gift, Oli. I love it so much.

June works for me. College will be done by then too. How should we do this? Maybe we could meet somewhere in the middle. Although there's nothing really exciting about Manitoba . . . I'd be down to go to Alberta! I've never been, and the Canadian Rockies are begging for me to come and explore them. We could make a whole trip out of it too, maybe go hiking? I don't think I'll be working next summer, so if you drive to Alberta, don't mind me jumping in the car and going back with you to Pine Falls. A full summer there sounds like a dream. I'll go hiking and exploring every single day and could help you at the restaurant too. Maybe I'll even spot a few spirit bears and say hi. Have you seen any?

Gosh, I can't wait! I'm already thinking about all the things I can bring with me.

In other news, you won't believe what Riley did. I want to strangle her. One of Sean's friends has a single younger brother, and Riley thought it'd be the best idea in the entire world to set me up on a date with him. Apparently, he loves to be in nature, and that character trait was somehow enough for her to be like "Ah, yes! Perfect for Charlee."

Sooo, I might have a date tonight. I hate it. I don't want to go, but I told Riley I'd make an effort for her. Since Mom's health has been going downhill, Riley's been worrying about me like crazy. She's always been motherly with me, but right now, she's smothering. She worries that I'll just close myself up—and to be fair, she's not wrong—but there's really nobody other than you I'd want to spend my time with. We'll see. Maybe I'll be pleasantly surprised? I doubt it, but who knows.

Anyway, I'll let you know how it goes. If I make it out alive.

Thinking of you always.

Your Charlee

PS: Your article inspired mine. Let me know what you think of it. I took a more editorial tone for this one.

Attached article
We're watching species going extinct, and nobody is doing anything about it

CHAPTER FIFTEEN

I know it won't work

Charlee

I wake up the next morning with a lingering headache.

"Fuck me," I groan, massaging my temples.

Great. Just . . . great. I twist in bed and hiss when my weight comes down on my hand.

"The fuck?"

I raise my arm and stare at my hand, the bruises around my knuckles. What—

Oh. Right. I punched someone last night. Just before Oliver came to pick me up . . .

Fuck.

I can't believe I pulled him into my mess. What must he think of me? Nothing good, I'm sure, but again, I don't think he's had a very high opinion of me since meeting me yesterday.

Snippets of last night in his kitchen, our exchange, the words that came out of my mouth, everything rushes through my mind as clear as day, and I pull the covers over my head.

Shit. I was harsh. They say alcohol brings out the truth, and I suppose that in my case, it did not take much to coax it out of me.

I regretted the words as soon as they were out of my mouth. Poor guy was just trying to help. *Did* help. And all I had to do was to thank him for the kindness he'd shown me and go to bed.

But *nooo*.

Charlee had to do what Charlee does best: Run. Put up walls and barricade herself behind them. Leave no survivors.

But the worry in his hazelnut eyes made me weak like a kid in front of a treat. *Just one candy, I promise.*

It was the soothing notes in his voice when he talked to me that almost did it, the way his body seemed to angle itself in my direction, as if he was holding himself back from touching me, checking me, making sure I was all right.

Red alert.

I came so close to caving in. *That's* what scared me shitless.

I'd almost forgotten that the man my heart raced for every time I saw his handwriting on an envelope had never shown up in Calgary five Junes ago.

That I'd stood at the airport terminal, alone, for hours, hoping he was just running late.

I never got an explanation. Never received another word.

Only silence.

Loud, screaming silence.

It was as if he'd vanished into thin air and the person I'd been communicating with for almost a year was nothing more than a figment of my imagination.

That was a good reminder to have last night. Maybe too good? Because add to that his sweet and caring attitude toward me, and it was enough to trigger my fight-or-flight response—actually, my fight-*and*-flight response.

Two birds, one stone. Putting a necessary distance between us, drawing a clear line that cannot be crossed.

I stretch my tired limbs and check the clock. Oliver would hate my guts—if he doesn't already—if I woke him up at four a.m. when our departure time isn't for another four hours.

Today marks the start of our two-week journey. And my feet are aching to get moving. A long, hot bath. That's what I need to quiet my jittery nerves and enjoy some last-minute luxury before I spend the next two weeks washing my body in makeshift showers.

I walk softly to the bathroom down the hall and pull my tank top over my head as I open the door to a distraught voice.

"Occupied!"

My eyes land on Oliver. In the bathtub. Naked. With barely enough soap to cover his body.

His gorgeous, *dripping-wet* body.

"*Oh my god*, what are you doing in here?!" I wheeze.

I avert my eyes, cheeks flaming hot, and turn around to face the door as sounds of water splashing reach my ears.

Please don't tell me he's getting out while I'm still here. I don't have the strength to endure that sight.

"I-I'm so sorry," he rushes to say. "I didn't think you'd be up at this hour."

I cross my arms over my very see-through bra. Great. Even my nipples aren't immune to the brief glimpse I caught of his defined muscles. "Don't you have your own bathroom or something? I thought this one was mine to use."

From the corner of my eye, I see him reach for a towel. "It is," he says. "I just—mine doesn't have a door, and I thought maybe you'd be . . . more comfortable if I used one that locks."

"*You didn't lock it.*"

"Habits. *I'm sorry*, Charlee. You can turn around. I'm half-decent."

I do, and frankly, I wish I hadn't. Because now I know what Oliver looks like in boxer briefs in the morning, his hair damp and floppy on his forehead, his skin still glistening with water.

His eyes dip to my chest before his cheeks turn the same shade as mine must be, and he looks away.

"Sorry," he whispers. "I didn't mean to look."

I roll my eyes. "I'll go make breakfast."

"You don't want to take a bath? I can be out of here in a minute."

I retrieve my shirt from the floor. "It's fine. I'm not in the mood anymore."

I close the door behind me and stride toward my room.

Well, there goes my one chance at relaxing before we leave.

One night. I only had one night here, and I have to deal with this bullshit.

I'll never be able to get rid of what I just saw. It's etched in my psyche forever. And that annoys me even more, because the last thing I want to think about is how fucking hot Oliver is.

I yank on a pair of dark leggings, slip into some warm socks, and throw on a thermal top that clings to me like a second skin, tucking it into my leggings.

Then I make my way to the kitchen and open the fridge. It's as if I've just opened a portal door and walked straight into a Trader Joe's or something. It's stocked to the brim, filled with fresh produce, locally sourced milk and meat, and even farm-fresh eggs. Not a surprise, given his upbringing, but impressive all the same. I didn't expect him to be the kind of guy who spends hours in the kitchen, and now the images of him cooking with an apron tied around his waist are burned even deeper into my retinas.

"Add those to the list," I mumble and grab the box of eggs. I crack three and hesitate.

Would it be such a bad thing if I added a few for him? Maybe he would see it as a gesture of good faith. A *professional* olive branch.

I add four more, whipping the mixture until the yolks and whites are combined. I cut a few tomatoes and add some baby spinach and cheese. Grabbing a pan, I turn on the heat and pour the eggs and other ingredients into the sizzling butter while bacon cooks in the pan next to it.

There. I think this says, "I'm sorry about last night; let's be professional," doesn't it?

I wash my hands and wipe them when my phone chimes.

Emma

> Are you awake?

Charlee

> Yep. The question is more what are you doing up already?

Her answer comes straight away.

Emma

> Would love to be sleeping, but Trevor is already up and asked us to have a team meeting before joining you guys later.

I roll my eyes.

Charlee

> Clearly in the running for Boss of the Year.

Emma

> Try Asshole of the Year. What's up with you? Does it have anything to do with a certain dorky boy with cute, ruffled hair?

Oliver's body—his face—flashes through my mind.

Charlee

> Do you want to know how my day started?

Emma

> Please.

Charlee

> I walked in on him taking a bath.

Emma

> What???? Holy shit. And? *eyes emoji*

And? And . . . I sigh.

Charlee

> He's fine. Not gonna lie.

Emma

> Yeah, he is. Wow, your morning sounds so much better than mine.

I snort.

Charlee

And it will only get better. I can't
wait to go running everywhere.

Emma

It's gonna be epic. But you'll have
to stay close. I won't be able to
run after you with the camera on
my shoulder.

Charlee

Okay, I'll take it easy on you. Won't
promise anything for Trevor, though.

Emma replies with a devil emoji, just as Oliver emerges
from the hallway.

"Hey."

I set my phone down. "Is that your official good
morning?"

He chuckles, sliding his hand into his pockets. "Listen,
Charlee, I'm really sorry about earlier." He throws a thumb
over his shoulder. "If you want to take a bath now, I won't
disturb you, I promise."

I wave him off. "It's okay. I'll take a quick shower before
we leave."

Truth is, the minute I set foot in that bathroom, I'm going to picture him right there in the tub. A quick shower is the safest bet. I wouldn't be able to relax anyway now that we're so close to leaving.

Oliver walks up to me, eyeing the plates on the counter. "What's going on over here?"

I shrug. "Peace offering."

His eyes find mine, and it's irritating how much they throw me off every time. They're tentative, cautious.

Well, good. Because as much as I'm waving the white flag, by no means am I forgetting. Or forgiving.

Just learning to coexist.

"Peace offering, huh?" Oliver's mouth tilts upward slightly as he walks to the kitchen counter and pulls two mugs out of the cabinet.

I scoop the egg mixture onto two plates. "Don't get too excited."

"I'm not, but you're talking, and that in itself is progress."

God, have I been that awful since yesterday? *You know you were*, a little voice says in my head, but I tune it out.

I pick up the plates and settle them on the dinner table, plopping in one of the chairs with a frown.

"Coffee?" he asks.

"I think I should stick to caffeine-free drinks today."

He hums, and it unnerves me. He does that often, I've noticed, but he never follows it with an explanation, so I'm left to wonder what his "hmm" means.

"I'll make you an herbal tea, then."

I watch him as he prepares my tea, tracking every movement he makes, so thorough, so meticulous. How strange is it that, after all these years, I can finally understand what it's like to be in his presence? To experience firsthand what I knew to be true about him when he existed only as words on paper?

Oliver comes to the dinner table, setting two steaming mugs down, and starts digging into his plate. "Thank you for breakfast. It's delicious. I didn't know you cooked like this."

"I manage. Nothing like you, I'm sure."

He smiles. "Still, I appreciate it."

We lock eyes for a second too long, enough for me to read more than what he says out loud.

I take a bite of my eggs, then swallow. "Listen, Oliver . . ."

"Charlee, there's so much . . ." he blurts at the same time.

We both chuckle, and he waves for me to go first.

"I admit I came on a bit rough yesterday," I say carefully. "To be fair, you were the last person I expected to see. I've slept on it, taken the time to process it." I keep my gaze focused on him. I want him to know I'm not afraid, even though my body is screaming for me to flee. I clear my throat, my right leg bouncing. "Look. I'm not here to rekindle the past, or to dwell on it, or even get an explanation from you. I'm not looking for one, nor do I want you to feel like you need to provide any level of clarification. I'm here because I have a job to do, and so do you. It just so happens that we've been chosen to do the same one. I don't know about you, but I can't let this project fail. I'm under a lot of pressure to get it right, and it needs my entire focus for the next two weeks. I can't be distracted by the past. So I'm offering a truce."

His eyebrow lifts.

I shake my head. "Not a truce, but you know what I mean. I want this to work—I need this to work—and whether I like it or not, that means doing it together. I promise I'll be on my best behavior going forward. No more bitchy comments or attitude or getting drunk and having to make you come pick me up. But in exchange, at least for the next two weeks, I need you to stop trying to bring up our history. With me or with anyone else. Deal?"

Welp. There, I said it. It's out of my mouth and out of my hands.

Oliver studies me, nothing on his face betraying what he's feeling inside.

It drives me insane.

But it's okay. I let him take the time he needs to think about my offer. I know it probably wasn't what he wanted to hear, but I can't deal with that right now. I need the filming to unfold perfectly, and the what-ifs will only get in the way of that. I may have moved on, but the painful memories of the months it took me to get him out of my system still linger right under my skin.

Oliver straightens in his chair, putting both elbows on the table and lacing his fingers together. "Deal. You're right. We can't mess it up."

Something strange flickers through his voice, an emotion I can't quite put my finger on, and it rattles me a little. Is that . . . resolve in his eyes?

I exhale a relieved breath. Now that's said and done, the rest of the trip should go smoothly and without a hitch.

I hold out my hand, and he grasps it, giving it a firm but gentle shake.

Big, big mistake.

I should have known better than to willingly give this man a chance to show me just how delusional I am.

I retrieve my hand as quickly and discreetly as I can, but his soft huff as pink creeps its way up his neck is a dead giveaway that neither of us is in for a walk in the park.

"We're flying in *this*?" Emma yells over the strong gust of wind that blows through our hair as we approach the propellers of the smallest airplane I've ever seen. The runway is hardly large by any standard, barely a thin strap of damaged road in the middle of the forest that surrounds this tiny local airport.

I wince.

Few things scare me, but flying at two thousand feet above sea level while crammed into a small tin box with six other people is not on the list of things I look forward to. No matter how many times I've been in this kind of situation in my career, it doesn't get easier. Especially in these conditions. But only light aircraft have access to where we're going.

"Come on, Emma, don't be such a wuss," Trevor mocks. "If you can't handle this, you should probably stay here."

Emma throws me a look that would have made Trevor run away, and I laugh softly. She can handle herself all right.

A man standing in front of the cockpit waves for us to gather around him. "Welcome, everybody. My name is Austin, and I'll be your pilot for today. Fair warning, this is going to be a bumpy ride." Austin looks at the sky, the gray clouds growing darker with each minute. "We expect some crosswinds and low visibility, but we should still be able to fly through. I hope you guys have strong stomachs," he laughs.

I swallow hard, my insides already in knots. Axel and Nick let out a few nervous laughs that echo my own. I glance at Oliver, who's standing next to the pilot, focused and serious. He doesn't exude even an ounce of fear. He must have done this hundreds of times, and that thought eases some of the tension in my body.

I study him a few seconds longer than necessary, appreciating the way his thermal pants cling to his thighs. There's no denying how good he looks dressed in hiking gear, which leaves no room for doubt as to how fit he is under those clothes. Not that I had any after this morning. He catches my gaze, and I glance away.

"Equipment and bags in the back," Austin continues. "People in the front. Takeoff's in five."

Everybody hurries to stack their things as best as they can before we all hoist ourselves into the small aircraft. Emma goes in first, sitting in the back next to where our bags are securely fastened. Axel and Nick claim the middle seats, while Trevor settles in front with Austin. Oliver and I climb aboard last. I crawl as best as I can behind Trevor's seat, which leaves me wedged between the window and Oliver, whose right leg rests flush against me.

"Are we sure this plane can fit this many people?" I ask.

Austin twists and surveys the aircraft. "Yes, miss. We're at full capacity." He sets his eyes back to the front, turning a bunch of buttons on. "We're ready for takeoff. Buckle up!"

I groan and grab the headset in front of me, putting it on. Oliver gently nudges my thigh, and I turn to him. He points to my headset, then to his own, indicating the power light. I turn it on.

"Are you okay?" he asks, his voice crackling in my ears. His eyes slide to my clenched fists.

I barely manage to nod before the plane picks up speed, rocking from left to right with the bursts of wind. The end of the runway is approaching dangerously fast, and the plane's two wheels are still firmly on the ground. I jerk my hand and clutch the first thing I find. Oliver's gaze slides to where my fingers curl around his with bone-crushing strength. He doesn't say anything, doesn't complain. Just squeezes back just as hard. And in that moment, I forget that I'd like to be anywhere but next to him. I forget my spite, and shrug off the little voice in my head screaming at me to quit being so damn vulnerable.

At last, the plane lifts off, and we shoot into the gray sky as Austin tries his best to stay on course.

We tilt to the right, the plane leaning almost perpendicular to the ground. The view rips my breath away. Below is Pine Falls with its charming houses and bustling main streets. Ahead, I catch a glimpse of the Pacific. And

Trevor gripping the sides of the aircraft as if his life depends on it.

I snort. Who's laughing now?

My anxiety eases and yields to trepidation. This is it. We're on our way. The call of the wild roars in my bones, my nerves, my muscles. And strange as it may seem, I can also feel it radiating from Oliver's body, still pressed tightly against me.

And through my hand, which I keep locked in his for the rest of the flight.

"Welcome to the Spirit Lodge," the man at the desk reception says when we arrive.

The lodge, composed of several cabins, is nestled right in the heart of the rainforest, surrounded by some of the oldest and largest trees I've ever seen.

Oliver sets his phone on the counter, smiling a broad but tired smile at the receptionist. "Hi, we're the *Wild Planet* team?"

Emma leans toward me and whispers, "Where's Trevor?"

"Just outside, still puking his guts out," I tell her with a grin.

He ran out of the plane so fast it was hard not to laugh. He struggled the whole hike here and for the rest of the afternoon as we prepped tomorrow's first day in the lodge common area while our cabins were being readied.

"Here are the keys to your cabins," the man starts, handing Oliver four keys. "I can see here on the file that *Wild Planet* has one, and there are three for MNL. Do I have the correct information?"

I frown. One?

"Yep, that's correct," Oliver nods.

I move forward and stand next to him. "What do you mean by 'that's correct'?"

Oliver shrugs. "Tight budget." He thanks the receptionist and grabs his bag. Then he looks at me over his shoulder with that damn upward tilt of his lips. "You coming?"

How he can find this situation amusing is beyond me. I jog to catch up with the fast pace he sets with his long legs, despite the tiredness in my bones.

A thousand questions scramble to push their way past my lips. "You knew about this and didn't think to tell me?"

Oliver keeps his speed and doesn't bother to answer. Only the sound of leaves and twigs crunching under our hiking boots echoes through the air. It makes me want to plant my foot right in his strutting ass.

"Oliver!"

Oliver whirls around and throws out his arms. "What, Charlee? Would you rather I told you before or after you wouldn't talk to me yesterday, except for when you were telling me to fuck off? Or maybe when you wanted to drop the whole thing because you couldn't handle sleeping in the same house as me *for one night*? I couldn't risk telling you and have you walking out of this for good. I need this too."

Well, that's new.

Surprise must be painted all over my face, because he sighs, dropping his head. "Sorry, sorry. It's been a long day. Look, can we just focus on what's important? You said it yourself this morning. We'll make do. All right?"

"Fine."

"Always fine, huh?" He shakes his head and resumes his walk to the cabin.

Our cabin.

I cringe.

I'm not entirely certain of the real reason I'm bothered by the prospect of sharing a cabin with him. The most rational explanation is that I have no interest in spending any more time with him than necessary, and sharing a cabin undermines that goal.

As if wanting to prove me wrong, my brain starts rolling images of my thigh pressed up against Oliver's on the plane, my hand clasped in his. My whole body snaps awake at the memory of the heat that swept through me and how much I struggled to rein in the urge to press myself even closer to him, the craving and the shame of wanting him in that moment—him and no one else.

"Okay, point made," I mumble to myself as I quickly get rid of those thoughts.

After five minutes of trudging through a dark forest, the air damp and cold from the night settling in, we arrive in front of a modest cabin made of logs. It's no wider than three of Oliver's long strides. A pile of chopped wood sits on the wraparound deck, just to the right of the door, and a single light flickers over the entrance.

The whole thing looks like something out of some fairy wonderland. A Hobbit or any other magical woodland creature could stroll past me, and I wouldn't even raise an eyebrow.

There's a soft click when Oliver turns the key in the lock. Inside, there's not much: a queen bed in the back of the room next to a door that I assume is the bathroom, a fireplace, two chairs, and a table. On the left, French doors open onto a small patio, and I'm already picturing myself enjoying a nice cup of tea in the middle of nature.

"Uh . . . okay." His eyes search the room. "I thought there would at least be a couch or something . . ."

I can't contain my nervous laughter. Oliver turns to look at me, brows furrowed.

"I'm sorry," I blurt, clasping a hand over my mouth. "It's just so . . . Of course. Of course there would only be one bed."

Oliver walks back to me and closes the door. "We don't need to blow this out of proportion. Take the bed. I can sleep right here." He points to the narrow space on the floor next to the table.

"You're not going to sleep on the floor."

"I've slept in worse places." He shrugs. "I have my sleeping bag, and maybe the front desk has a cot to spare. It'll do just fine."

"Okay, then. That's settled." I don't argue, because there's not a world that exists where I would agree to share the bed with him.

He offers me a faint smile. "Perfect. I'll start working on warming the place up."

"What?"

"There are logs out front and twigs. I'll start the fire for the night." He nods toward the door, his hazelnut hair brushing his forehead.

"Oh. Thanks." I rein in my desire to sink my fingers into the mass of strands that look as soft as silk.

Treacherous, treacherous mind.

While Oliver busies himself gathering what he needs for the fire, I slip into the bathroom, power through a quick shower, and put on a pair of old shorts and a too-large shirt.

When I come out, the fire is already crackling and warming the room. Oliver is sitting at the table, a book in his hand.

"Good night," I murmur, pulling the blanket off the bed.

He looks up from his book, his gaze tripping on my legs before he clears his throat. "Good night, Charlee."

I open my eyes to the early morning sun streaming through the cabin, casting the place in gentle honey light.

I stretch my limbs out wide. I can't recall the last time I slept this well, and a teeny-tiny part of me feels guilty for having made Oliver take the floor. Maybe we can switch tonight.

I make a move to get up, but when I do, I notice the number of covers piled on top of me. There must be at least three. No, four.

Did I get up during the night to grab them? I have a vague memory of a dream where I was reporting from Antarctica and freezing my ass off, but I don't recall waking up and getting these.

I look around the room for clues, but I only find Oliver standing by the bay window, his back to me. He's leaning casually against the windowsill, coffee in hand, staring off into the distance.

He mustn't have noticed that I'm awake. It gives me time to lose myself in his tousled hair curling in big waves at the nape of his neck, just above the white T-shirt he's wearing. It outlines the edges of his back, working around the solid muscles of his shoulders before it falls to his hips. My eyes glide lower over the simple gray sweatpants he's sporting, stopping at his bare feet. That sight has more of an effect on me than I can explain.

I feel as if I'm intruding on a private moment I have no business being a part of. Like I shouldn't know how he looks when he gets out of bed in the morning unless I've woken up right next to him. The thought pulls at something in me. And just like the past few days spent with him getting frustrated and feeling a thousand things at once, it's hard to understand what exactly, but it keeps pulling and pulling until it feels impossible to breathe. I mourned the loss of this love and never looked back. I did that already. So why do I have to welcome him back into my life? How am I supposed to act like I'm totally indifferent to him?

How? How am I supposed to do that?

How am I supposed to ignore the deepest connection I ever made? How can I pretend that my body isn't aware of him sleeping just a few inches away from me when memories of the intimate letters we shared flash through my mind and heat my skin?

My frustration rises, and I throw the covers off. I still don't understand how I ended up buried underneath them.

Oliver hears and turns. I look at the covers, then at him.

He takes a slow sip of his coffee. "You were cold," he says, then turns his gaze back outside.

Hey Char,

I wasn't expecting the photo you sent with your last letter. It left me all kinds of speechless. Not to sound like a creep (probably gonna sound like one anyway), but I might have stared at it for a solid ten minutes after I opened the envelope.

You want honesty? I might have committed it to memory so, wherever I am, I can close my eyes and imagine the soft lines of your collarbone with the pendant I made resting on your neck.

I'm glad you liked it. How did your date go?

Talk to you soon,

Oliver

PS: Your last article? Brilliant. I wouldn't change a thing.

<u>Attached article</u>
The negative effects of climate change on our planet are worse than we thought

CHAPTER SIXTEEN

Colour Me In

Oliver

I should be focusing on where we're about to go. I should concentrate on the day and the paths we're planning on hiking, the spots we should be resting at, and the ones where we could potentially do some spirit bear sightseeing.

But nothing is working to take my mind off Charlee.

Not when I'm still haunted by her beautiful face from this morning, sleep still clinging to her eyes. A low curse pushed past my lips as I felt myself harden, desperate to discover her touch, to join her and peel the covers from her warm body, to rake my hands down her sides and explore what I'd dreamed of for so many nights, her flush against me in bed, not leaving the place for the whole two weeks.

I've thought about this. So many times. So many sleepless nights. What would she feel like in my arms? Is she as soft as her words or as wild as her spirit? Would my world finally tilt on its axis the day I get to hold her? Would she give me her everything too?

I would have. Oh, I would have given her the sun and everything she'd ever wanted back then. I would have traveled the world with her, followed her anywhere she went.

I shake my head, lacing my boots. When it mattered, when it came down to my actions matching my words, I failed. I didn't show up.

And now, here I am, with all these unanswered questions that still haunt me every day, even more so now that she's here, a walking reminder of my mistake and the dream I had to let go of.

But I can wait. I've waited five years. What's two more weeks?

It was stupid of me to try to bring it up yesterday morning. She's right, we need to keep our minds sharp. Not only because every day we venture into bear territory is a day we put our safety on the line, but also because the success of this shoot holds the key to my life's dream. Now is not the time to unravel our shortcomings.

It killed me a little to make the deal, but it was the most sensible choice, and when it comes to her, I need to be smart. Always one step ahead. I'll give her those two weeks. Two weeks where my sole focus will be on finishing this docuseries and supporting the crew so I can cash in my bonus and buy the restaurant back.

But once that's done, once we are back in Pine Falls and her mind is clear, she'll have no choice but to listen to me. No more excuses. I'll explain everything to her. I'll go all out, recreate the first date we never had. Tell her everything I never got to say. Show her the places I always wanted to take her.

Two weeks for a chance to get everything right where I failed five years ago.

"You ready?" Charlee stands next to me in her hiking gear. "The MNL crew is waiting for us at the reception."

"Yep," I say, clearing my throat and chasing away the hope that forced its way into my mind. "Let me grab my bag, and we can head out."

We walk in silence to the reception desk to meet the rest of the crew.

We couldn't have asked for finer weather on our first day of hiking. It's all bright sunshine and mild temperatures that'll leave us sweating during our efforts without freezing to death.

"Morning, reporters!" Trevor booms, making Charlee jump next to me. "Ready to play adventurers today?"

I chuckle. "Easy, Trevor. Safety first, okay, guys?" I climb a little rock to gain a bit of height and face the group. "All right, everybody, listen up."

Everyone's attention swivels to me. Axel and Nick hold the sound equipment, and Emma rests the heavy camera on her toned shoulder, not breaking a sweat or looking uncomfortable in the slightest.

"Today is our first day in the forest. I just want to reiterate a few important rules: no interacting with wildlife, be sensitive toward the communities we're going to meet, and always stay together. Am I clear?" I make my voice sharp and final on purpose. Where we're going, we cannot afford risky behavior and unpreparedness.

Heads bob up and down. I glance at Charlee, who watches me like she's trying to understand something.

"Any questions, Charlee?"

She jolts, her cheeks tinting pink. "No. Nope, all good."

I clap my hands. "All right, then. We're starting on the Hagensborg Loop Trail today. It's a moderate six-kilometer hike that should take us to the west falls. With this weather, we should cross paths with some bears along the way."

I jump off the rock, and Trevor comes forward. "Thanks, Oliver. For my team, instructions are pretty simple. We're shooting as much as we can: environment, wildlife." He winks at me. "At a reasonable distance, of course. Charlee, you'll be in front of the camera, while Emma will be asking you questions. Nick will hook you up with a mic. Just be yourself and speak your thoughts out loud, what you see, what you hear. Don't hesitate to ask Oliver questions too, assuming he's comfortable getting in front of the camera?"

Am I? "I don't remember it being included in my contract."

Trevor shrugs. "No, but it can add a more authentic touch to it. If you're up for it, of course."

I glance at Charlee. I don't know why.

Absolute lie, my inner self says, calling me out in my head.

I know why I look at her. It's because her opinion matters to me, but also because I detect her discomfort when Trevor mentions the mic and talking to the camera. It's as if the thought kindled her nervousness. Which doesn't make any sense, because the Charlee I know has only been nervous on so few occasions, I could probably count them on one hand. She's confident and sure of herself in everything she does. But I can read her body language, and if she is nervous, then maybe she could use someone by her side. No matter how uncomfortable and awkward it might be.

"Sure, I'll do it."

Her shoulders relax an inch when I agree, leaving me pleased with my decision.

"Perfect! Nick, can you mic Oliver and Charlee? Oliver, let's give Charlee the most airtime, okay? You can chime in here and there."

I nod while Nick wraps wires around me and hooks the device onto the waistband of my pants.

"Push this button to turn the mic on and back to turn it off. Pretty straightforward," Nick instructs.

"Thanks," I say.

He goes and does the same with Charlee.

My feet ache to start walking, to lose myself in this beautiful place that I know like the back of my hand. My muscles tremble with excitement I can no longer contain, the smell of the wild already overpowering my senses and begging me to explore.

In this moment, I am no longer worried about the docuseries, the safety of the crew, or the disdain Charlee holds toward me that leaves a gaping hole in my chest.

No, in this moment, I feel at peace.

"Watch your steps," I warn Charlee behind me. "The path gets slippery here."

We've been walking for two hours now, getting as many shots of the luxurious green all around us as we can. Moss covers every nook and cranny of the forest, from imposing western red cedar trunks to rocky boulders. Evergreens stretch as far as the eye can see, and I breathe deeply, inviting this vivid nature to take root deep in my lungs.

A few feet away, I point to a tree looming larger than the rest. "This one is an ancient western red cedar. From the looks of it, I'd say it's at least two hundred feet tall."

Everyone looks up, and Emma follows with the camera.

"These trees play a vital role in the rainforest ecosystem," I continue, "as they help stabilize the soil. They can live for a few thousand years. They're also central to the First Nations' spirituality here on the coast, often called the Tree of Life."

"How old would you say this one is?" Charlee asks, her head tossed back to peer at the sheer size of the tree.

"Hard to tell. But the trunk is pretty large, so I'd say at least five hundred years old."

She looks at me, her brows disappearing under her bangs. She rests her hand on the cedar as she closes her eyes. "He must have seen so many things," she murmurs.

The moment seems to stretch and stretch and stretch as everything around us disappears except for the sound of birds chirping and leaves rustling.

My hand burns to rest on top of hers, but I don't know if she would jerk away as soon as she felt my touch, so I keep it safely at my side, where my feelings can't be bruised even more.

"Let's get moving, guys," Trevor says, snapping me out of my enchanted daze. Charlee offers me a hint of a smile, as if she too has been pulled back from that place. She retrieves her hand and walks away.

It's not until early afternoon that I hear movement in the leaves ahead of us. I slow my pace and signal the crew behind to do the same.

"Emma, zoom in over there," Trevor hisses.

"Keep your voice down," I snarl at him.

His eyes dart to me, storming, but I couldn't care less. If he wants his shot, he will shut the fuck up when he needs to.

In front of us, two gorgeous brown grizzlies are getting their afternoon snacks from low tree branches.

I join Charlee, who's getting ready for the shot. Her shoulders are tense, her brows furrowed as she absently brushes some strands of hair off her face and tucks them behind her ears. I clear my throat softly, and she turns to me.

"You don't want to be too quiet," I tell her. "Otherwise, they'll get spooked when they see you, but don't make too much noise or they'll attack, okay?"

She nods once, and I step to the side, away from the camera. Axel and Nick position themselves and their sound equipment around Charlee. She's standing as straight as an arrow, and her posture somehow confirms my morning suspicions: the great, fearless Charlee Fletcher suffers from stage fright. She looks like she might puke any minute now.

But then Emma nods, counting down from three on her fingers, and when she gives Charlee the go, all signs of fear disappear. Her features loosen, and her eyes gleam with pure excitement.

"We found our first two grizzlies of the day, young teenagers judging by their size," she says, her voice flawlessly calm. "Grizzly territory once ranged across most of western North America, but we're a long way off from that estimate today. According to the latest studies, grizzly bears living in coastal British Columbia are now a threatened species."

Charlee continues to recite what we went over during our prep meetings, quoting scientific studies and statistics, changes in their habitat, and the effects the transformation of the forest has had on their population. She's a star. Her ease and professionalism are a sight to behold, and I can't get enough. Her shoulders have loosened up, and her stance appears more natural as she guides the camera through her thorough analysis and captivating storytelling.

She's a natural. All signs of her previous nervousness evaporated the second she began speaking. It would be easy to defer my admiration to my history with her, but the truth is she knows how to command the space and make the viewer feel as if they're standing right next to her, next to the grizzlies.

It's here and now that I know, without a doubt, that the show will be a massive success.

People will eat this up, just as I am now.

Emma signals to Charlee that the camera will turn off in three, two, one . . .

Charlee exhales. "Oh my god. That was so stressful."

Emma smiles. "You did great."

"Incredible, even," I add before I can stop the words from coming out of my mouth.

Charlee mutters a small "thanks" before walking away, and I curse myself for scaring her.

Once they're done with their spot, the grizzly bears head off in search of their next meal. Maybe a river with some salmon flapping around.

We do the same and continue our trek through the woods, though we don't come across any other bears for the rest of the day. I pause often, providing Charlee with explanations she can easily recite when the camera is rolling. I keep it simple and professional, and she keeps her attitude neutral, as if we're doing nothing more than exchanging useful information and platitudes.

Though I don't miss the glances she steals at me as I talk. She thinks I don't notice. She should know better than to think I'd be indifferent to her attention, but I keep it to myself and pretend I don't see her intrigued, curious.

After a few kilometers, Axel stops in front of a hiking sign. "Are we already at the lake?"

I nod. "Straight down the path."

"Anybody game for a quick swim?" Trevor asks, mischief in his gaze.

"The water will be freezing," I say.

"Yeah, and nobody brought swimsuits, Trev. Or towels," Emma adds.

"Come *on*, wusses. We're almost back to the lodge, the sun's out, birds are singing, and we're done for the day. Let's live a little."

"I'm down."

I turn and glare at Charlee, eyes wide. "You are?"

"Yeah," she says and shrugs. "Anyone who doesn't want to go can just head to the lodge. We're not that far."

I hold her gaze. "No, we cannot separate the group, Charlee."

Who does she think she is? She has training. She knows nature is dangerous and unpredictable. What game is she playing? And leaving her alone with Trevor? No fucking way. Has she met him? The guy has been ogling every woman he crossed paths with and is waiting for the perfect moment to pounce, and she's gladly giving it to him.

"Fine," she drawls. "So why don't we all go, then? Those who don't want to have fun can just stay dry on the shore."

That fucking attitude. I clench my fists. "Fine. Let's go."

Emma looks at me, then at Charlee. Let her think whatever she wants. I'm done caring about it. Charlee talks a big game of wanting to stay professional, but then she pulls shit like this? I don't know how to act or how to be around her, and it's driving me crazy. Every second is a confrontation I don't want to have. And I'm tired of fighting a fight I can't win.

As we move through the lush forest, the trees grow sparse, revealing a large meadow with a crystal-blue stretch of water at its center, and just like the times I've come here before, I'm left breathless.

"Not gonna lie, I feel like if I go in this, I'm gonna come up ten years younger and have eternal beauty," Emma says, blinking. She lays her windbreaker on the grass, then carefully sets the camera on top. "All right, I'm in."

"Yesss!" Charlee cheers while unlacing her boots.

She's not going to . . .

Charlee doesn't even pause as she slides her leggings down her long, toned legs, uncovering a black sports thong and flashing her gorgeous ass in front of me. And I don't waste time dwelling on it, because her top comes off next, leaving her in nothing but a bra and thong, her smooth, sculpted back just begging for me to run my fingers over it.

Emma follows, and I look away. Trevor, on the other hand, doesn't miss a thing.

"You girls ready?" Trevor asks, a grin on his face.

They stand on the ledge, and on three, they all jump into the lake. Droplets of water splash everywhere, and for a moment, I'm spellbound by the smile on Charlee's lips. Maybe Emma was right and the water is magic, because the woman who shrieks from the cold and laughs like a kid isn't the same one who hardly says a word to me.

My heart sinks, my throat knots, my eyes sting. It's too much.

I'm swept up and pulled down into the depths of the emotions that I've tried so hard to control since Charlee came back into my life. But what's the point? If my body is screaming at me to release them, what's the point of resisting?

So I stop.

And everything rushes in: my feelings for her when we wrote each other all those long letters; her attitude toward me over the last few days; the memories of that dreadful day I can't bring myself to forget; her smell, her smile, the sound of her voice; the things I never thought I'd be lucky enough to discover one day.

Dampness collects at the corners of my eyes, and I turn away.

"You okay, Oliver?" Charlee calls from the water. "Give us a few. We'll get out in a bit."

It takes all I have in me to push the words out, and even then, they come out shaking. "Take your time. I think I'll just head back to the lodge."

Worry grows in her voice. "I thought you said no separating the group."

"It's okay. The lodge is thirty minutes this way, and the path's wide and clear enough." I point toward the trees ahead of us. "You'll be fine, but keep your phone with you just in case."

"Are you sure? Oliver!" Charlee yells.

But I'm already walking away, my long strides taking me as far as possible from the reminder of my biggest mistake.

Toronto, December 15, 2017

Hi Oli,

Are you okay?

I was surprised by how short your last letter was. I hope everything's okay with you and your grandparents.

My date was A-W-F-U-L. I was right, by the way. He was 100% a douchebag. Full of himself. He didn't even pay for the super fancy restaurant he picked. Most of the time, I'm fine paying for myself, but if you choose a place that costs my monthly rent, you better pick up the bill.

I thought about you the whole time. Which, honestly, made the two hours go way faster than they would have otherwise. I was wondering what you were up to and if you were thinking about me too. My guess was that you were probably in your grandpa's woodshop, working on something with him. I like to picture you there. I don't know why. Maybe you were just snoozing in bed with a book splayed on your chest. How's _that_ for honesty? (Also, when have I ever made you think otherwise? I always want your most honest self—I love how blunt you are.)

I wish I could say that my date was the only time I've thought about you, but gosh, your last letter is burned in my mind. The first time I read what you wrote, I think I blushed for three days straight (and that _never_ happens). If you memorized my collarbone, then what would you do if I sent something else? Would you memorize other parts of me, too?

I don't know how many times I read it, but at some point, one night, I ended up falling asleep and woke up to your letter on the pillow next to me and your words in my memory, as if I'd dreamed of you the whole night. You know that feeling when you wake up and it feels like your dream really happened? It was just like that. I woke up and patted the place next to me, sure I'd find you there. But my hand only grazed your letter. I suppose, in a way, it was almost as if you had slept beside me. But you didn't. Because if you had, I wouldn't have felt so lonely.

I can't believe Christmas is already here. And that I won't be hearing from you for the next two and a half weeks. Not looking forward to *that*. What are you doing for Christmas? Do you have any special traditions with your grandparents? First of all: Do you like Christmas? Who am I kidding? Who doesn't love Christmas? (Please don't be a grinch.)

This year is a bit different for us. With Mom sick, she won't be able to decorate the house with us or go pick up a tree like she used to. So it'll just be Riley and me, but I'm still excited about it. I want the house to look good and festive for Mom so she feels like everything is just like every other year. Riley will be cooking (don't worry, I already ordered plan B from a caterer) and I'm in charge of getting our mom's presents. Have you gone to a store during Christmas time? It's lawless. People are crazy, and I'm scared every time I go. Lucky for me, I'm a morning person, so I usually succeed in avoiding the big crowds.

Anyway, this isn't the Christmas we would have hoped for, but the three of us are still celebrating like we usually do, so that's what matters, right? My only wish is that I'd get to spend a few more with Mom before I have to say goodbye.

Since I won't hear from you before, I wish you a Merry Christmas, Oli, and a wonderful time with your grandparents.

I'll miss you so much.

Your Charlee

<u>Attached article</u>
Shop local during Christmas! Holidays are a crucial time for small business owners

CHAPTER SEVENTEEN

Cardigan

Charlee

"Oliver?"

I wait behind the bathroom door for a response. I'll even take a sound, something, *anything* that would let me know he's alive and well. All the proof I have is his backpack lying against the bed, his jacket on top of it.

There's a rustle behind the door. "Yes, I'm here." I quirk an eyebrow at the strain in his voice. "I'm in the shower. I'll be right out."

There's no sound of water whatsoever.

"Okay. Well, I'm having dinner with Emma in the common room if you're looking for me."

"Sounds good!"

I close the front door and head to the main building. I used to pride myself on knowing Oliver like the back of my hand, but his sudden shift this afternoon has left me wondering what happened to make him run away like that.

He's not your problem, Charlee. I groan as I increase my pace, tucking my head into my jacket against the evening chill. *He's not.* But it doesn't stop me from worrying. This internal war will drive me over the edge. If only I weren't so damn stubborn, so damn proud. Maybe then I'd be able to get over my fears and stop oscillating between hot and cold when it comes to him. But every kindness he offers triggers my fears. Every time he brings out a side of me I haven't seen in years, I panic and revert back to mean-girl behavior.

When I arrive at the main building, the room echoes with chatter from amazed travelers and nature lovers. I locate Emma, who waves at me while holding a burger.

I plop my ass down on the seat across from her, grabbing a fry from her plate. She swats my hand away. "Excuse you! I don't share food. Especially when it's this fucking good." She takes a chomp out of her burger.

"Fine." I laugh. "I'm not that hungry anyway. Where is everyone?"

Emma looks over my shoulder. I turn around and catch Trevor talking with big gestures and laughing his head off. Everybody around him, Axel and Nick included, drinks up his words as if he were God himself.

I roll my eyes and turn back to Emma, who sports a similar exasperated look. "Are they always like this with him?" I nod toward Axel and Nick.

"Yep. Two good little boys who just love to do and say everything Trevor does or says."

"How can you stand working with them?"

She shrugs, her black hair shimmying with the movement. "You get used to it. I usually tune out the noise, you know? What they say doesn't affect me because it doesn't reach me. You learn to toughen up real fast in this industry when you're a woman."

"When *don't* you have to do that when you're a woman?" I muse. "I have yet to find somewhere I don't need to battle for my rightful place."

Emma raises her beer. "Amen, sister." She looks around. "Where is Oliver?"

"In our cabin. I don't think he's coming."

She takes a sip of her beer. "He acted a bit weird earlier. Never seen anybody leave that fast."

I focus on a point behind her. "I don't know either . . ."

She eyes me suspiciously. "You do know."

"I don't!"

"Your cheeks are redder than your hair, and you can't look me in the eye. Worst liar ever. What's going on?"

I really don't want to get into it, but maybe I can keep it short and sweet, enough for Emma not to ask a thousand follow-up questions. "Oliver and I have a complicated history. We knew each other when we were in college and had a falling out." More like he broke my trust and my heart, then ghosted me. "It's the first time I've spoken to him since."

She lets out a long whistle. "Damn, I didn't see that one coming. You and the hot nerd, huh?"

"Nothing happened." I sink deeper into my seat. "Just two lonely college kids who needed each other at the time, I suppose. It's just weird to be here with him. I'm not looking forward to spending all this time together."

Emma hums, lost in her thoughts. After a while, she looks at me. "You know, I had someone like that once. We went to high school together but lost touch over the years, and suddenly, three years later, here he is on my Instagram followers suggestion list, looking hot as hell. Next thing I know, he DMs me and we grab some drinks. Everything is magical, we decide to start dating, and two years later, I learn that he was cheating on me."

Fucking idiot. Cheating is unforgivable, but to cheat on a once-in-a-lifetime woman like Emma? "You are so much better without him."

I can't figure out what she's getting at. It's not really a happy story, is it?

"I know, I'm fine. It was a long time ago. But that's not my point. Point is, had the asshole not done what he did, had I not agreed to go out on a date with him, I would never have understood that I was strong enough to handle losing him, handle him betraying me. I would never have discovered the woman I became after that or the lines I decided to draw for future relationships."

If only she knew the losses I've already endured. I know who I am and what I'm made of. Oliver made sure of that. And so did losing my mom when she was still so young. It left indelible scars.

"I'm glad you found yourself after that jerk, but I don't need Oliver to help me do that."

Emma quirks an eyebrow. "Are you sure? Don't you believe that people come into your life at certain moments for a reason? Don't you think you deserve to find out why? Why now? How did you end up working on this project with someone you hadn't spoken to in years? Aren't you the slightest bit curious about the meaning behind it?"

Her flurry of questions makes my head spin with questions I've never allowed myself to ask before.

I lower my eyes to my hands folded on my lap. After a while, I whisper, "I don't know."

"That's enough for me."

When I look at her, Emma is grinning like she knows she got me right where she wanted. Questioning just enough to have me doubting.

When I open the door to the cabin an hour later, I'm met with absolute silence. Except for the million questions screaming in my head, courtesy of Emma.

"Oliver, you here?"

Nothing but those damn questions.

Fine. If he wants to hide all night, he can be my guest. I won't be crying a river about it.

I grab the hat and gloves from my backpack and wrap a long cotton scarf around my shoulders and neck. By the time I left the common area, the evening had slipped into cold twilight, the frosty sky twinkling with all the stars I can't see from Toronto.

I open the patio door and step outside. The crisp air instantly chills my cheeks and nose, and my lungs expand as I take a deep breath, my mind cooling and my thoughts calming under the musky scent of the forest.

It's been a long time since I felt like this. Lost. A compass with the north arrow pointing south.

I gaze up at the sky. Looking at this immensity, I feel insignificant. Nothing matters in the grand scheme of things, does it? We're just specks of dust floating around, giving ourselves a purpose before we're nothing but a glimmer in the sky.

Is my mom one of those glimmers up there, looking out for me? What would she think of me and my life? Always traveling, running away. Never settling for too long in one place at the risk of everything else catching up with me.

I rest my tired limbs against the deck's guardrail and breathe out. "Do you remember when we talked about this place, Mom?"

The cold breeze sweeping gently through my hair is my only response. "I wanted to come here so badly." I let out a chuckle laced with melancholy at the memory. "You couldn't bear hearing me talk about it for another second."

I furiously brush away the tears pooling in my eyes and groan. Every fucking time my mind has space to quiet down, this is where it wanders to. To the past I can't extricate myself from. To my mother, to Oliver.

And when I'm not paying attention, the tears rise, and with them, my anger.

I won't allow it. I won't allow myself to be weak again.

I need a distraction, something to help me take the edge off. Maybe if I smooth my mussed-up hair and put on a touch of mascara, I can head back to the main building and find someone lonely enough to spend the rest of the night with me.

I snort. How pathetic have I become?

I start marching toward the main building in hopes of catching Emma when a faint orange glow behind the cabin draws my attention, tugging my feet in its direction.

Oliver is there, sitting on a massive log next to the campfire. A blanket is draped over his body, and he holds a travel mug in his hands, his gaze lost somewhere in the roaring flames. From where he sits, he doesn't see me approach, so I make sure to stomp my feet as I draw closer.

He raises his eyes to me. "Hi."

I smile lightly and nod toward the space next to him. "Can I join you?"

"Of course." Oliver scoots over to give me more room.

"I've been looking for you." I glance at the steaming mug he's holding. The sweet aroma tickles my nose.

"I needed some time by myself." He takes a sip. "It's been a day."

The questions burn my tongue. Some that popped up in these last hours, some that I've been rehashing for years. But I can't open that door. If I do, if I ask the questions I've been craving the answers to for years, my heartbreak will drown me just as hard as it did back then, and it would be like it happened yesterday all over again. I'm a tough woman, but I'm not sure anyone would be tough enough to go through that twice in one lifetime.

So instead, I focus on matters that won't wreck me. "I'm probably the last person you want to talk to, but I'm here if you want to tell me what happened earlier."

After my behavior these past few days, it'd take a miracle for him to share whatever is on his mind. But to my surprise, he chuckles, stretching his long legs in front of him. "You want honesty?"

"When have I ever made you think otherwise?" I ask.

We lock eyes.

It's not the first time he's asked me that. And it's not the first time I've given him that answer.

We both let out a laugh that breaks the tension, if only for a small second.

Oliver rakes his free hand through his already messy hair. "It's been hard. Being here with you. It has . . . stirred some things up." He inhales, as if it took all the breath he had to push out those words. "I never thought I'd actually meet you one day."

"Me neither," I say, my voice trembling. And then I decide to push my luck. "How is it?"

"What?"

"Meeting me."

The light of the campfire dances across his face, a tango of orange and red flickering on the edges of his cheeks, his jaw. His eyes glow like liquid gold.

He stares into the flame, a smile tugging at his lips. "I mean, it hasn't exactly been the easiest week so far. You've made sure of that. But if what you're truly asking me is if you were like the person I've spent entire days imagining, then my answer is no. I wasn't even close to how beautiful, fierce, and smart you are. It's one thing to know it through your words. It's another to experience it in person when I never thought I would."

I must be gaping at him, because he laughs, and the sound warms me up better than the fire in front of us.

"Why are you looking at me like that?" he asks.

His eyes glide to my heated cheeks, and I can almost see the faint amusement in them.

My face burns. I straighten, even though I know Oliver sees right through me. "Your honesty unnerves me sometimes."

He shrugs and brings his mug to his lips. "If you ask me something, I'll answer it. It's hard for me to hide anything."

"I know," I whisper, and the way he looks at me when I say that shouldn't fill me with pride, but it does.

Not a total stranger, then. There are still some parts of him that I remember.

"What about you?" he asks. "Am I close to how you pictured me?"

How could my imagination have even come close to the man sitting next to me? It's always been easy for me to get swept away by someone attractive, get physical, and never see that person again. I can't say it hasn't worked well for me so far.

But I need more than sex to feel a connection, a spark, that our souls resonate on the same wavelength. Oliver and I had that from the start. That's what drew me in five years ago. And now, if I paused to think about it, if I dared to look deep within my soul, something tells me I'd still be able to tug on that string tethering us to each other.

But I'm not blunt like him, and there are things I'm not ready to share with him just yet. Or even to admit to myself.

"Something like that," I say softly.

If he's disappointed with my response, he doesn't let it show.

Oliver curls his other hand around the mug and rests his arms on his knees. "So where does the intrepid Charlee Fletcher travel to these days?"

I tuck a smile in my scarf at the sound of my full name on his lips. "I'm lucky to have been around the world many times in the past few years. I've discovered isolated places, seen more beauty than I could ever imagine seeing at my age—and more than most of my colleagues combined." At that, Oliver raises his brows. "I pretty much jump on every assignment. If I'm not already out on a project."

He chuckles. "Always on the run, huh?"

It's more of a comment than a question really, but it still startles me that he can read me so well.

"So many things to see and so little time."

Oliver hums as if he too knows the feeling well. "What was your favorite place?"

I ponder his question before answering. "I don't know about *favorite* because there's always something unique wherever I go, but I was in Australia last year during the fires, and I accomplished my most impactful work there. I'll remember it till the day I die."

A shadow crosses his face. Or maybe it's my imagination and nothing more than the flames crackling in front of us. "Must have been pretty dangerous."

I shrug, pulling the scarf around me tighter. Even if the fire is still burning brightly, the night is growing colder and colder by the minute. "It was, but it doesn't mean we shouldn't have been there. My articles were read around the world, and the photos that accompanied them were shown on the news. My work got people to pay attention. I participated in rescue missions with teams that were sent to help wildlife escape the flames and find shelter. I will never forget what I saw."

His eyes drift to meet mine. "Sounds like such a Charlee thing to do."

I hold his stare, my heart thundering in my chest. I swallow. *How is my throat so dry?* "What do you mean?"

"You've always been so . . . unafraid. About everything. Bold. You dare anyone to stand in your way when you have your heart set on something."

I want to tell him that he couldn't be more wrong, that I'm scared all the time. I'm just not afraid of the same things most people are terrified of. I would gladly dive off a cliff into shark-infested water, but I can't drop my bags and stay more than a few weeks in the same place. I suppose, over time, I got good enough at pretending. But I don't want him to know this is all for show. I like that he thinks of me like that. That thought settles heavily in my chest. Since when have I ever cared about what people think of me?

I don't, I remind myself. But Oliver isn't most people.

"Thank you for that," I whisper before I clear my throat. "How are your grandparents doing? Still holding down the fort at Jerry's?"

He stares into the fire, but I still see the dimness in his eyes when he says, "They passed away a few years ago."

"Oh, Oliver . . . I'm sorry."

I take one of his hands away from the mug and try to ignore the warmth that spreads when I squeeze it. Oliver takes an uneven breath, a muscle in his jaw ticking. He moves his hand, lacing his fingers with mine. I don't say anything.

"It's okay. It's been a while now. I miss them like crazy, but most of the time, I'm okay."

"I get that." More than he knows. Back when we exchanged our last letters, my mom was still battling her illness. "I wish I could have met them. They sounded like people you'd want to know in your lifetime."

Oliver lets out a chuckle heavy with sadness. "I wish you could have met them too. They would have adored you. They already did, from what they knew about you."

I look down at our intertwined fingers, not wanting Oliver to see what his words are doing to me, how hard they tug at my heart.

There's a thin scar drawn on his skin, running from the base of his thumb to his index finger. "What happened?" I ask, stroking the white line.

He lowers his gaze there too. "Woodworking accident."

"You're still doing that?" I murmur, not trusting my voice not to falter.

"I am. Do you . . . Do you still have . . ?"

I release my hand from his and unzip my jacket. Oliver follows my movements with deadly precision, his Adam's apple bobbing along the column of his neck as I pull the necklace from under my sweater with trembling fingers.

Even after all these years, after all he's done, I've never been able to bring myself to part with it. Oh, I've tried, but it was like ripping out a part of myself. I felt so hollow without it.

"Charlee . . ." Oliver stretches his hand toward my neck as if he doesn't trust that the pendant is really there but stops just inches away from touching me. He closes his fingers around thin air before letting his hand land softly on the log. "I thought you'd have thrown it away the first chance you got."

I stroke the bear. "Oh, I did." I look down at the places that have worn away over time. "But then I always picked it back up."

He lets out a hushed laugh, his hair swishing across his forehead with the movements of his head. "I didn't think I'd see it again."

He reaches out again, and this time, he doesn't pause. He brushes my hair away from my collarbone with a gentleness that squeezes my throat and leaves me breathless. Slowly, he curls his fingers around mine, his eyes riveted on the pendant, as we're both holding the small wooden bear.

"I spent hours crafting it, perfecting it," he murmurs hoarsely. "And just as many imagining it around your neck, what it would be like to see it with my own eyes."

"And?" I rasp.

"It's mesmerizing."

He raises his eyes to mine.

For a breath, I'm enthralled by the intensity of his gaze, and I can't look away, sucked in by his effortless magnetism.

I want to lose myself in the rich brown of his irises, surrender to his warmth, and ask him to tell me what else he imagined when he thought of me and if he spent as much time doing it as I did.

But something passes on his face, too quick for me to catch it, and I'm released from his hold with a snap.

The spell is broken.

I let go of the pendant and clear my throat for the millionth time tonight. Oliver retrieves his hand, and I swiftly tuck the necklace under my sweater again. A shiver runs down my spine.

"Are you cold?" His voice touches my skin like a soft caress.

I nod, not trusting myself to say more with the charged air flowing between us.

He opens the blanket wrapped around him, his arm extended in an invitation to join him. Sensing my hesitation, he says, "You're cold. This is just that and nothing more. I promise."

I look at the small space next to him, and after a moment, I slide across the log, my leg grazing his as I come to his side.

It's barely a touch, yet it feels like it's burning a hole through my clothes. When I'm fully tucked against him, Oliver drapes the blanket over me, even though it doesn't even feel like I need it anymore.

Every place my body touches his, my skin is burning, and his pine and musky scent does nothing to soothe my mind from his intoxicating grip. My muscles tense as I try to resist the call to lean against him. If I yield, I'll never forgive myself. But I can't help it. His solid, sturdy frame brings me a comfort I've never needed before.

What else would I discover if I allowed myself to indulge just a little more . . .

"You know what?" Oliver snaps his fingers, and I jump out of my reverie. "They sell s'mores packages at the lodge." He picks up a package next to him and offers me a cheeky grin. "Want to make some with me?"

I wonder if he can see the steam coming off me as the coldest bucket of water douses over my scorching body.

Good, good, *good*. I needed that.

I shift on the log, repositioning myself to create some space between us. "Sure. Why not," I rasp.

He opens the box to reveal marshmallows, graham crackers, and chocolate bars.

"Have you ever done this?"

Oliver snorts, grabbing two branches lying next to his feet. "Haven't you?"

"Not really."

His laughter vibrates through my body. "You either have or you haven't. You can't say 'not really.'"

He turns to me, and because I'm still tucked under the blanket with him, the space between our faces disappears. We're close. So close that his breath mingles with mine in an electrifying blend of softness and longing that compels me to lean closer.

Oliver's breath hitches, and I blink.

"Here." His voice is hoarse as he hands me the small twig. "Push it through the marshmallow. And hold it close to the fire."

I mimic his movements. In a matter of seconds, the marshmallow turns brown and starts to melt.

"Now." He gets two crackers out of the package and breaks off a piece of chocolate. "Place the marshmallow between the two crackers and press gently."

The white mush melts into the chocolate, sticking everything together.

Oliver smiles. "Ready to eat."

I bite into the treat, and sweetness coats my tongue. "Oh, this is good," I half moan.

Oliver chokes on his s'more before laughing. "Isn't it?" He holds out his stick. "Cheers."

Chuckling, I tap mine against his just as I notice him looking at my lips.

"You have chocolate on your face." He points to the left corner of his mouth.

"Oh." I rub my right side, but he laughs, shaking his head. "Let me."

Oliver reaches out and gently rubs the corner of my mouth with his thumb. He lingers for a few seconds, his thumb pressing softly on my lower lip, his eyes riveted to the point of contact, his lips parted and his breath shallow.

He's about to kiss me.

He's about to kiss me, and I don't know if I want him to or if I never want to know what it's like to be kissed by Oliver Reynolds and his gorgeous lips that look so, so soft.

Panic swells, clawing at my throat until breathing becomes hard. "I-I have to go. Long day tomorrow."

It takes everything I have in me to not break down right in front of him.

My dear Charlee,

You must be crazy if you thought I wouldn't find the time to write to you before Christmas. I even got up extra early today so I could make sure to catch Emile at 8 a.m. That old bastard threw the cookies I made for him in my face, plate and all. Everything went splattering everywhere. Wouldn't even be able to tell you the French words he let out, but they sure as hell didn't sound pretty.

I'm not sure when you'll get this letter, but hopefully before Christmas. Hope this will be a nice surprise for you.

Would I be horrible if I said I'm relieved your date went terribly? Don't get me wrong, I'm sorry you had to sit through that, but reading that you were out having a romantic dinner with another man . . . I'm actually happy you weren't here to see me. All your guesses are wrong, though. I wasn't reading, wasn't with my grandpa. I was sitting in my bed, going crazy thinking about you and all the scenarios that could potentially happen. I even thought that the next letter I'd receive from you would be you telling me that you'd met the most incredible guy ever and we had to go back to being friends and sending articles only. Not that we're more than friends, but you know . . . sometimes it does feel like something more.

And reading your last letter . . . Charlee, if I ever see you one day in the flesh, trust me when I say I'll spend hours, <u>days</u>, mapping every inch of you like I did with your neck, just so I can go back to you in my dreams when you're not with me. I'd breathe in your smell and live on it for weeks until I could get my next fix. Do you know what I imagine you smell like? Something sweet and warm. Something that, in the dead of winter, would take me back to summer days spent basking in the sun. I know you have a tough shell when you're around people, but deep down, I like to think your spunky personality hides a gentler side of you. And when I think about what it'd be like to have you by my side, my mind goes exactly to that. How easily I'd be able to coax out your softness because you'd know you can be truly yourself around me, just like I am with you. You make me want to be so gentle with you, Charlee.

I'm not delusional, right? I don't know when, and I don't know how, but at some point, we became way more than just friends, and you can't convince me otherwise. And I say that with so much certainty because I know you feel it too. I dare you to tell me you don't. This whole journalistic exchange thing has become so secondary to reading your words that I sometimes forget that I'm still supposed to send you articles I've written. Although the article I'm sending you today makes me think of us in a way, so even with the assignment, I find ways to connect it to you.

So yeah, while you were out on a date, I was miserably hoping he'd be the biggest dick. I can't believe he didn't pay for the restaurant, although I'm not that surprised. Any guy who doesn't treat you like a queen doesn't even know how lucky he is to be in your company. I would never waste a chance like that.

Would it be a deal breaker if I told you I was, in fact, a grinch? I'm kidding. Christmas is my favorite time of the year. My grandparents and I have a unique way of celebrating. We have a big homemade dinner on the 24th, just the three of us. We open presents on the morning of the 25th, and then we head to the restaurant where we serve a Christmas meal for everybody who's alone on Christmas Day or for those who want to come and celebrate with us. It's my favorite part of it all.

I know Christmas isn't the same for you this year, and I'm sorry about that. There's not much I or anyone else can do, but I hope you'll still get to enjoy it and all the moments spent with your mom and your sister. I'm sure your mom will be happy with her girls taking on the family traditions this year.

I miss you too, so much.

Until I get another letter from you, I'll imagine what it'd be like to have you here, in the same room as me. Maybe even waking up next to you, if I could ever be so lucky.

Merry Christmas, Char,

Your Oli

Attached article
The science of romantic gravity: The universal law with a love twist

CHAPTER EIGHTEEN

Fire and the Flood

Oliver

*B*y the fifth day of filming, it feels like every dent in the floor has been molded into my skin, the cot from the lodge hardly making any difference. I get up, stretching my sore thighs and arms, and hear a crack in my lower back. But the stiffness in my body isn't the reason my legs refuse to move.

No, that'd be because of the woman lying in bed in front of me.

She looks so soft and small in the white sheets, one leg draped over the duvet. She's not wearing much, just a simple T-shirt and shorts, but the way she's sleeping makes her shorts ride up her thigh, giving me a glimpse of the curve of—

What am I doing? I turn around. I'm not a fucking creep.

I pinch the bridge of my nose and close my eyes, trying to chase away the images settling in my mind: Charlee breathless under my palms, Charlee soft and pliable as I knead my fingers into her skin, Charlee slick and warm from the fervor of my lips.

Erase, erase, erase.

All I'm left with is a growing headache and an uncomfortable bulge pressing against the front of my pants.

I've been waking up with thoughts of our almost-kiss by the campfire for the past four days, though it isn't helping the situation. But how can I not when the hot brush of her breath still lingers on my thumb? When her scent still clings to where she was pressed against me under that blanket, the sweetness of peaches and vanilla floating all around me?

When she dared to look at me for the first time, stripped of all animosity, something flickering in the depths of her green eyes, I felt it too. The tug between us. That thin thread wrapped around my soul and connecting me to hers. I thought that it had snapped over the years; at one point, I realized I couldn't find that comforting, grounding feeling I used to have every time I read her letters.

Until four nights ago.

Until we started talking and reminiscing, falling back into that steady, familiar rhythm.

A soft click. That's how it sounded in my mind, how it felt in my bones, when Charlee burst into one of the goofiest laughs I've ever heard. That's when the realization sank in that, despite the years stretching between us, that thread is still there. Brittle and frail, but still there.

That was enough. Enough to make me stare at the ceiling every night since, wondering if she felt it too and hoping like hell that I won't lose that feeling again. If Charlee was affected by it, she didn't let it show. And it's her soft snores that have been lulling me to sleep just when night turns into morning, the blanket smelling like her warming my body.

I inhale deeply and grab my coffee mug off the table, padding across the small space to reach the counter where the kettle is. I fill it with water, turn it on, then dump two spoonfuls of instant coffee into my cup and wait for the water to boil.

I glance out the window and frown. Despite the early hour, I can already see the thick clouds darkening the sky.

Fuck. Today was supposed to be clear.

From the look of it, they don't look like passing clouds that'll just make the day a little grayer. No, those are rain clouds, and if my calculations are right, we should be under a solid downpour right in the middle of one of the hardest hikes of this trip.

This complicates things. We've been trudging through the forest for the past four days and haven't seen a single spirit bear. Trevor is growing more impatient with each passing hour that brings us closer to the end of the first week of shooting.

I pour the water over the coffee, and as silently as I can, I grab my jacket and open the door. I zip it up to my chin when a cool, damp wind ruffles my hair. Yep, it's gonna rain, all right. Just stepping outside for two minutes turns my skin sticky and frigid with the dampness clinging to the air.

Heavy rain will make the hike planned today highly dangerous, if not impossible. The path is narrow, steep, and tricky, even on a dry day. It's not worth the risk of going up and cracking our heads open on a slippery rock.

I rub the nape of my neck. I'm not sure the news will go over well, but staying in is the safest option for today. We'll postpone the hike till tomorrow if the skies clear.

The strong winds send a shiver down my spine, and I hurry back inside to find Charlee awake and standing in the kitchen-living-room-bedroom space, rubbing the sleep out of her beautiful eyes.

"Morning," I say softly.

"Good morning," she yawns. Cuteness embodied. "What are you doing up already?"

"I could ask you the same thing. Although if I remember correctly, you're more of an early riser, right?" I hide a smile as I sip my coffee when I see the surprise register in her eyes.

She stretches her arm above her head, rising up on her tiptoes as if to distract me from her reaction. Even then, she's still a good head and a half shorter than me. A thin strip of skin just above her hip bone catches my eye but disappears as soon as her arms fall back to her sides. I swallow and dart my eyes away.

"Right." She looks out the window. "Doesn't look like we're gonna have a lot of sunshine today."

"No. And to be honest, I don't think we should head out there. Won't be safe."

Charlee grins. "When have I ever backed away because things got risky?"

"I'd venture to say never, but this is too dangerous. Even for you. We'll be soaked to our bones, and we'd also risk damaging the equipment. It's a bad idea."

She seems to think about it before she nods. "You're right, we should hold off. I trust your judgment, but it's not me you'll have to convince."

I sigh, pushing my fingers through my hair. "I know."

"Absolutely not." Trevor slashes his arm through the air in a definitive way. Next to him, Charlee smirks, looking very smug.

"Trevor," I start, holding my hands up, "I get that we have to follow the schedule but—"

"We can't skip a day, Oliver," he cuts in. "Especially because time is ticking, and you can't seem to get us in front of one of those oh-so-special bears. I don't care if it's sunny, raining, or snowing. I don't care if there's a thunderstorm and aliens are upon us. I understand the risks, and that's why you're here. We'll manage just fine as long as you stay ahead of us, showing the way."

I don't even know where to start with how wrong he is, how none of it makes sense. Charlee looks at me, one brow raised, as if waiting to see my next move.

I shake my head. I could use a little help here. This isn't a game. "Listen, man, I can't in good conscience sign off on this. Everyone's safety should come before some stupid schedule.

I'm sure we can find some wiggle room somewhere and rearrange."

Trevor moves toward me, coming up so close that the smell of his menthol breath cools my face. "If I'm not mistaken, the one holding the purse strings is me. So if you want to see that nice, fat check at the end of this, you'll do as I say."

His voice is low, a threat from a man who wouldn't dare step into my space like that if he didn't hold that bargaining chip. Because like it or not, whether he knows it or not, the bastard holds my future in his hands. A gamble for him, but as it turns out, a paying one.

Still, I stand my ground. I won't back down because some city exec thinks he can do my job better than I can. Not my style. "Fine," I seethe, barely more than a whisper. "You want to go? Go. I don't care if you're drenched, if your teeth start chattering, or if you catch the worst cold of your life. But if one of them," I say, pointing to Charlee and the crew behind him, my eyes not leaving his, "if one of them gets hurt because of the unsafe conditions you're dragging us into, this will be on you. Understood?"

Trevor breaks the tension with a short laugh and slaps the side of my arm. "Hey, Oliver, come on, man. I was joking, relax."

I hold his stare. "I'm not."

His smile falters, but he schools his features before anyone else notices. "Okay. If anything happens, I'll assume responsibility."

I nod and walk past him, grabbing my bag. "Let's go, then."

Nobody, not even Charlee, dares to hazard another word.

Turns out, my prediction wasn't completely accurate. The rain started pouring earlier than anticipated, about an hour after we had started our trek through the dense trees. We climb for hours on a steep and muddy path, water dripping from my hair and clothes and creating rills in the soil, despite the hood of my jacket being tied tight around my head. Time and again, Axel slips and has to catch himself on a rock or tree branch. Emma struggles with the camera, which is covered by a plastic tarp, the cumbersome gear slowing her down considerably. Everyone's miserable, although no one admits it. Only Charlee is able to match my pace in the front, walking silently beside me.

"How long till we get to the spirit bears?" Trevor shouts above the roar of the rain pounding on the leaf-covered ground.

I slow my pace to let him catch up with me. "If you keep screaming like that, probably never. But we still have a solid two hours before we get to their territory, and even then, I'm not sure our chances are good. Too much rain."

Trevor grunts. "I'm not gallivanting in this weather for nothing. You better find us the bears."

I'm tempted to reply *I told you so*, but I don't think that'll go over well, so I say, "If we find a river, we'll have a better chance of catching one while they're hunting. There's one a little bit more to the west."

"Lead the way, then."

This is too dangerous. Every bone in my body is screaming at me to turn around and walk back to the lodge, but I resume the hike and head west. I carefully navigate the narrow path, pushing aside branches as the trail becomes increasingly narrow. The last stretch to the river dwindles into a vertiginous descent littered with rocks as sharp as knives, and with the mud, it's practically impassable.

I test the terrain, my boot slipping instantly. I land ten inches lower than planned. Securing my position at a forty-five-degree angle, one foot down, my other high on the slope, I extend my palm toward Charlee. "All right, let's go slowly, one by one, and always perpendicular to the descent. Never face it forward, or you'll be sure to end up on your ass at the bottom."

Charlee nods, stretching her fingers toward me. I grab them, ignoring the now-familiar tingling sensation in my nerves every time her skin meets mine.

I tighten my hold around her small hand as she starts her descent, but her left foot lands where I slipped, and she loses her balance. My arm flies around her waist, yanking her tight against me before she tumbles onto the rocks below. Her hands clutch my shoulders, her fingers digging into my soaked vest. She looks at me with wide eyes, surprise or panic at what might have happened, I'm not sure. Her cheeks, on the other hand, have a red hue they didn't have seconds before, and I can't help but wonder if my proximity is to blame.

"Thank you," she wheezes, her breath caressing my mouth. Just the slightest movement, and our lips would brush.

"Are you okay?" I flex my fingers where they're still firmly curled around her waist. She could have hurt herself very, very badly. Or even worse.

She nods.

I lift the hand that isn't holding her against me and gently wipe a smear of mud off her cheek. Her eyelids flutter, and I swear it almost feels like she's nuzzling further against my palm.

"Are you hurt anywhere?"

So many thoughts I can't read rush through her forest-green eyes. "No, I'm fine."

"Okay." I loosen my grip, leaving it up to her to take whatever space she wants. She tears herself away from my arms and resumes her descent. Slowly and carefully, she makes her way down like a pro, her body locked and alert until she's at the bottom.

I let out the breath I was holding, then signal for the next person.

Axel and Nick go down without a problem, while Emma holds my hand in a death grip as I try my best to stabilize her with the camera. When it's Trevor's turn, the man just ignores my extended hand and handles the slope by himself.

A heartbeat later, I join everybody down the hill. Behind us, the river flows wildly, the rain pattering on the water. And right there, across the swollen riverbank, are two white bears.

"Emma, look." I point toward the spirit bears, who are working hard to catch salmon. "Looks like a cub and his mom."

Emma angles the camera in their direction as Trevor signals to Charlee to turn her mic on and get in the shot.

The spirit bears catch our movement and raise their heads with curiosity in our direction. The promise of food is too great to make them dangerous, though, and the river too wide for them to cross safely, especially in this weather.

Still, I come to stand next to Charlee. "Don't get too close to the river. The bears look hungry, and a mom would do anything to feed her cub. Even if it means putting herself in danger. No harsh or threatening movements, okay?"

I don't know if she notices the fear in my gaze. I trust her—god, in that moment, I realize how much I do—and if I had the time to explore that thought, I would probably spend hours trying to understand how quickly I've come to blindly place my faith in her. But there's no time to linger, and despite that trust, the poor conditions could make even the smallest of mistakes fatal.

"I understand," she says over the racket of the river. She looks across the water. "They're beautiful. I could sit here for days watching them. Drawing them."

I hum my approval. "They're quite the creatures. Rare and unique."

I've said those words before—said them about her—and I see on her face that she remembers. *My very own spirit bear.*

"Charlee, get in front of the camera!" Trevor shouts, and my warning look shuts him up.

Emma holds out her fingers, counting silently from three to one before she points to Charlee.

"Our adventure today takes us to meet some Kermode bears, more widely known as spirit bears. Indigenous tribes living in the rainforest decided on that name, as they saw these rare bears as sacred animals. And, no, the two you're seeing right now aren't polar bears, nor are they albinos. They have pigment in their skin and eyes, which wouldn't be the case for albinos. So why are they white, you ask? It's because they have a recessive gene that causes their unusual coloration."

I listen, mesmerized by how easily she captures her audience's attention. She could be reading me her grocery list, and I'd be sitting with my face in my hands, drinking in every word that pours out of that gorgeous mouth of hers.

"The only place you'll find these beautiful creatures is here, in Canada," she continues. "We estimate the population to be around four hundred individuals, but that number is slowly dwindling due to the numerous threats they're facing. Before we get to that, let me show you how they hunt for dinner."

Charlee waves at Emma to come closer as she slowly backs up and stands next to the river. She shouldn't do that. She's being reckless, inching closer to the torrent while the rain is still beating down. I *told* her not to get too close, and now the distance between her and me is too wide. If something happened to her, I wouldn't be fast enough.

I grit my teeth. Shouting at her would only make matters worse with the bears right there.

"Yes, Charlee, that's it. Get me that shot," Trevor urges. He's standing next to me, but I'm too busy monitoring her footing to smack his stupid face.

"Look how focused the mother is on the fish sputtering out of the water," she tells the camera. "Bears aren't known to be graceful, but their determination is unmatched. It's only a matter of time before mama bear catches dinner for her cub."

She sucks me right back into her spell, and I'm too wrapped up in her poise and confidence, hanging on to her every word for just a moment too long, to notice the surge of water heading straight for her.

"Charlee!"

I'm too late.

The water crashes into her.

I watch in horror as Charlee scrambles to grab hold of something, anything, as she loses her balance and tumbles into the rushing water.

Toronto, January 4, 2018

My Oli,

Happy New Year! I'm sorry I couldn't get back to you sooner. The holidays kept me pretty busy.

Getting your letter on the 24th was the best Christmas present I got this year. I'm sorry you got cookies thrown in your face, though. Hope Emile didn't leave you with crumbs and bruises!

I hope you had a wonderful Christmas with your grandparents and everybody who joined you guys at Jerry's.

Mine was surprisingly good. We spent most of our time lounging in our PJs with Mom, watching rom-coms and drinking hot cocoa. And thank god for the caterer, because Riley almost burned down the kitchen. Twice.

Would I be horrible if I said that reading that you felt awful while I was on my date makes me feel all kinds of ways? Honestly, maybe I could have given the guy a chance if I didn't have you on my mind all night, but he was done from the start because he just wasn't you. Picturing you brooding while I was on my date makes me laugh. And . . . it also makes me realize that I'm not going crazy and that maybe I'm not the only one who feels this thing between us. Whatever it is, whatever the word is for what I feel for you, it's strong enough to make any other man irrelevant to me.

I don't have any words to describe the way I feel every time I read you. It's both surreal and impossibly logical at the same time, like everything makes perfect sense. But it shouldn't, because what's happening between us would be crazy to anyone outside looking in. And your last letter . . . Oliver, I've never felt so . . . <u>wanted</u> in my life. Not in that way, anyway. There have been plenty of men and women who've been attracted to me for my body, but with you, it's different. You don't know what I look like, and yet you make me feel like the most beautiful woman on this earth through your words. I am drawn to you in a deeper, more meaningful way than I've ever been drawn to anyone. You make me feel seen and valued and cherished. All this without ever having touched me or laid eyes on me.

So yeah, you're right. It'd be delusional to think we're friends and nothing more, and the fact that you see right through me, even about something like this, is enough proof of our bond. There's something about you that pulls me in, and I don't want to resist. Just like the last article you wrote on the laws of gravity.

I talked to my sister about you during the break. I told her everything. She said that I should go with my gut and do what feels right, even if I haven't met you in person yet or even know what you look like. But why would any of this matter when it feels like nobody on this earth understands me better than you?

If we were living in the same city, would you take me on a date?

Let me tell you what we would do if the planning was up to me. First, I would take you camping at my favorite place. I've only been there a few times because it's so far from Toronto, but the magic from the red and white pine forest at Caliper Lake Park is like none other. You can camp under the most beautiful starry skies, surrounded by centuries-old pine trees. We'd set up the tent in a meadow where there's enough space to gaze at the sky, and we would build a fire to roast marshmallows. (Can you believe I've never done that before? Maybe I'm just waiting now to do it with you). We could hike all day, and when night falls, just warm ourselves next to the fire and drink hot chocolate (yes, I love it, sue me). And maybe the day would be warm enough for us to not even need to sleep in the tent, but under the stars. Next to each other. Or even bundled up together. And we would wake up to the sound of wind rustling in the leaves and birds singing to the new day. Yeah, that would be my perfect date with you.

I hope we get to do it.

With love,

Your Charlee

PS: If we're imagining things, I imagine you smell just like the forests you spend your days in. If I remind you of warm summers, you're my cozy days during fall.

PPS: I don't know why I chose this theme for my article because I hated every minute of writing it. Please, critique away. I'm sure you'll have plenty to say.

Attached article
Not your regular camping: Glamping popularity is growing faster, and it's all thanks to (or because of) the internet

CHAPTER NINETEEN

This Is Me Trying

Charlee

The ice-cold water is the first thing I register. It's cold. So, so cold. The swift current pushes me in and out of the torrent, and I have to grip a jagged rock to stay clear of the rapids. Searing pain shoots through my hand, and I swallow a cry as blood trickles down my palm before washing into the water.

"Charlee!"

It's the second time Oliver has screamed my name in the span of a minute. The first time was just a heartbeat after I started falling. This time, it's as he scurries through the vegetation surrounding the riverbank and plunges knee-deep into the freezing water.

"Char, take my hand."

I hoist myself as best as I can onto the sharp rock, my hands screaming with the strength of my grip against the roughness of the surface.

"Come on, Char." The panic in his voice overrides the deafening sound of the water roaring all around me. It's enough to make me push through the pain in my ankle as I use the rock to haul myself and my backpack up.

Stifling another cry, I extend my hand to him, and just like that, I'm hoisted up and slammed into a wall of muscle before we fall onto the riverbank, Oliver's body cushioning the landing.

Not a second later, his hands are cupping my cheeks, his gaze roaming my face frantically. "Are you okay? Charlee, *are you okay?*"

Our chests are rising and falling hard, both of us struggling to catch our breath.

I nod. "Yeah. Yeah, I think I'm okay."

But Oliver doesn't let go, as if he's afraid I'll break into tiny pieces. I'm not sure I won't. I'm still lying on top of him, too scared to move and take stock of the damage to my body.

His thumb brushes my cheek softly, tentatively, his eyes fixed on mine with so much worry, it threatens to make me sob. "I thought you—"

"Charlee, oh my god, are you all right?" Emma pants as she rushes toward us.

Oliver's hands fall to his sides as he lays his head back on the grass.

I clear my throat. "I'm okay, I think."

She braces her hands on her knees, breathing hard. "Fuck, you scared the shit out of me."

"That'll make for good bloopers," I wheeze harshly, forcing a smile. Slowly, I move off Oliver and roll onto my side, then push myself up on my knees. I wince at the sharp sting in my left hand. "Ow!"

Oliver is at my side in a heartbeat, lifting me to him effortlessly. He takes my hand in his and turns it over so he can examine the wound. The slice in my palm is pretty deep. I'll probably need stitches for it, and now that the water isn't washing the blood away, red oozes between my fingers and stains the grass, my clothes, my bag.

"Wrap this tightly around your palm for now," he says as he rips—*rips*—a part of his shirt like he's tearing a paper towel. "Emma, can you get the med kit from my bag, please?"

"Sure thing." Emma runs toward Trevor and the rest of the crew as Oliver waits for me to grab the piece of his shirt.

I shrug him off. "It's okay, Oli, I—"

"Charlee."

One word, low and sharp, as if his patience is hanging by a thread. Not a warning. No, he's past that point. A command. The crackle of his voice grates over my skin like a match on the striker.

His eyes bore into mine, as if growling my name wasn't enough. I don't know what lights the fire in my core more: the unexpected roughness he emanates or the worry marring every inch of his face.

I grab the ripped fabric and roll my eyes. "Whatever." Better he think that I'm a brat than let him see the effect he has on me.

I tie the scrap around my palm in a secure knot, and instantly, the blood soaks through the material.

"This is not working."

"Let me."

"It's okay," I protest again. "It'll stop eventually."

"Yeah, when you've passed out from losing too much blood."

Oliver takes one step closer, hesitating for a breath before sliding his fingers along my cheeks again, his eyes roaming my face, worry still etched in those beautiful hazelnut irises. "Please, *please* let me take care of you right now. I know you're a stubborn, proud woman, but just this once, let me make sure you're okay. I can handle you being mad at me for the rest of our lives, and I can handle not talking to you for years, but what I won't be able to do is survive if something happened to you. Do you understand?" he asks, his breath ragged. He looks at me like he's a second away from being torn to shreds with panic. "I need you to let me help you. Can you do that for me?"

I'm too tongue-tied to say anything. Too stunned to draw the connection between the half confession he's just made and the meaning behind it all.

I won't be able to survive. The words echo in my head, my brain trying to make sense of them, but to no avail. But why? Why wouldn't he be able to survive? Since when does he care what happens to me? He left me behind once. So why now?

Why, when he's the one who ghosted me, and I was the one who had to figure out how to survive without him?

I must have been silent for a while, because he tries again. "Please, Charlee."

I nod tightly, not trusting that I won't burst into a tangle of incoherent words when he looks at me like that, his hair drenched and soaking his face.

Oliver lets out a shuddering exhale and gets to work on my hand. Gently, but with a meticulousness and care that only years of practice can hone, his fingers work around my palm to secure the cloth so that the necessary tension is applied just above it.

"Can you move your arms okay?"

I rotate my shoulders. "Yeah, they're fine. A bit stiff."

"To be expected with how strong the current is." Oliver glances at my left foot, one eyebrow cocked. "Can you put weight on it?"

I shake my head. "I think it's broken or something."

"Let me see," he says, more to himself than to me. He crouches down, raising his eyes to mine. "Can I?"

"Yes."

Delicately, he rolls my pants up to uncover my ankle. It's swollen and purple. I swallow, trying to ignore how my body reacts to the brush of his fingers on my skin and the way his broad and sturdy shoulders brush against me as he explores my bruised flesh.

I hiss the moment he presses a bit too hard. He gets back up, mud dusting his knees. "I don't think you'll be able to walk on that. I'm not sure it's broken, but it's too swollen for you to put your weight on it."

I glance back at Emma and Trevor, then meet his gaze again. "Well, I'll have to suck it up."

The glare Oliver gives me would make more than one person scurry away. "You're not continuing the trek like that. With the rain, you'll hurt yourself even more. And put everybody else at risk too."

I don't even try to argue, because one, he's right. It's not just me on this project, and everybody would need to wait for me, support me, or worse, carry me. And two, even with all my willpower, I don't think I can stand on my foot.

Trevor walks toward us, Emma in tow with the med kit in hand. "Everything all right over there?" he shouts. "Are we ready to continue?"

He's not asking if I'm okay, and there's not even a hint of worry in his eyes. Such a contrast to the man who was kneeling before me a few moments ago.

I square my shoulders, ready to headbutt him. "I can't walk."

"Well, that's unfortunate." He throws a glance at Axel and Nick, as if looking for backup. "We need to get going, though."

"I can't." I blink, making sure I enunciate every word.

"We're on a tight schedule, Charlee."

My brows shoot behind my bangs. "Really?" I quip. "I didn't know that. Must be the first time you've told us."

Trevor snarls. "I see you haven't lost that attitude of yours. Where's the mighty Charlee I've heard so much about? I should have trusted my instincts from the moment I saw you at the airport. I knew you didn't have the spine for this."

I take a step forward, half limping, and come as close as I can to him. "I would watch what I said if I were you."

I feel Oliver coming closer to me.

"You have a contract," Trevor seethes. "You're legally obligated to fulfill your obligations, or you can say goodbye to your jobs."

I try not to let fear sweep through me at the sound of his threat. Stupid, stupid ankle. I didn't work my ass off to get where I am to let this stupid mistake—or this stupid asshole—take it all away from me.

"I'm taking Charlee back to the lodge." Oliver's voice is barely above a whisper, but it's full of warning. "It's my professional assessment that she is in no condition to continue this trek and needs medical attention right away."

"And what about us?" Trevor scoffs. "What about all your rules and safety now, huh?"

"Just go back to where we came from. The path is tricky but pretty straightforward. You have your phones with you. Call someone if you're lost. I don't care, honestly. I tried avoiding this exact situation this morning. *You* deal with it now. Charlee and I will make our way back as fast as we can, considering how much pain she's in."

"You'll hear from our lawyers."

Oliver shrugs, but I don't miss the shadow that crosses his face. "Fine by me. Come on, Char. Put your arm around my neck."

The sharpness of his tone doesn't fool me, and I would feel sorry for anybody else on the receiving end of it, but I don't flinch at it. Instead, I pick up on how softly he said my name. Oliver must feel my eyes on him, because he comes closer and slides his arm around my waist, holding me securely against him so my left foot barely grazes the ground.

I dare a glance at Emma, who nods slightly and mouths, *I'll be fine*.

I smile, mouthing, *I'm so sorry* back.

"Unbelievable," Trevor scoffs, walking off.

Because he's a solid head and a half taller than me, Oliver has to look way down at me when he says, "Are you okay?"

I nod. "Did we just fuck this entire thing up?"

He presses his lips into a thin line, and again, that dark cloud passes over his face. "I don't know."

"Ben will be furious."

Am I going to lose my job? I don't know what I'd do if that happened. I have no savings, and nothing to come home to. I've made my work my whole life, and it seems like it's just a matter of time before it's taken away from me.

Guilt punches my stomach. *The Toronto office.* Did I just cost twenty people their jobs?

"So will Donna," Oliver adds, interrupting my downward spiral. "A problem for another day. Let's get you home safely first."

I look up, breathing in his scent of pine and earth, made stronger with the rain. "Do you think we made the right choice?"

Oliver squeezes my waist once. "It wasn't a choice. More like our only option. You can't go anywhere like this. It'll already be a challenge to get you back."

I ponder his words. As much as I hate it, he's right. I've been doing this gig for years, and bodies of water are always fickle under these conditions. This could have been avoided if I had paid more attention to my surroundings.

"I'm sorry," I whisper above the rain. "I should have anticipated it."

He offers me a tight smile. I don't know what he's hiding, but I can tell there's something he's not telling me. "You couldn't have seen it coming, Charlee. This is not your fault. Nature is unpredictable, and even the best-trained person can't foresee every possibility. The important thing is that you're safe." He eyes the fabric wrapped around my hand. It's already tinted red. "Let's clean your hand before we go."

He drops his bag, digs for the med kit, and pulls out a clean bandage and some antiseptic. With infinite gentleness, he loosens the piece of his shirt tied around my wound. I hiss.

"Sorry."

"No, no, it's okay."

Oliver wastes no time disinfecting the gash, then he wraps it in the new, clean bandage. "Good as new."

"Thank you. Good thing you're here."

He clears his throat as he stows the kit in his bag. "I feel the same way about you."

I don't allow myself to take in the meaning behind those words. I sling my arm around his shoulders and hang on tight. His breath catches, but I tune out that too. "All right, let's do this."

"Careful, okay?" His fingers grip my waist tighter as we start walking, pain shooting up from my ankle into my calf with each step, even though I'm barely touching the ground. Oliver is supporting all my weight without showing any sign of effort, as if I don't weigh 140 pounds.

At the bottom of the hill, he stops. "Okay, I think I'm gonna have to carry you here."

I shake my head. "Nuh-uh. I can manage."

"No, you can't. It's too steep. And if I support you like this, we'll never climb up. Not with the mud."

I groan. What a nightmare. Rubbing my eyebrows, I mumble, "How are you gonna carry me anyway?" I nod to his bag. "You have that on your back already. This will never work."

Amusement flickers in his eyes. "I've carried heavier, Charlee." Oliver slings his backpack around to his chest, then crouches down. "Come on. Get on my back and hold tight."

God, never would I have thought that I'd get a piggyback ride at twenty-six. From Oliver.

I hop up and clasp my hands around his neck as his hands settle under my thighs. "Ready?"

"No, but I don't really have a choice."

He chuckles. "Come on, sunshine."

I slap his shoulder playfully, but squeal and sink my nails into his shoulders when he gets to his feet.

He grits his teeth. "I don't usually mind nail marks, but a bit softer please."

I flush hard and unclench my grip. "Sorry, sorry."

"It's okay," he says, a flicker of a smirk in his voice. He hoists me higher up on his back, his hands cupped firmly under my thighs, as he starts the ascent. "Let's go."

My whole body is pressed against his, and I pray he doesn't notice when I wrap my thighs a little tighter around his waist. The responding sweep of his thumb against my thigh dashes all hope. The throb in my ankle is forgotten, my senses narrowed solely on the feel of him as his every muscle shifts beneath my body with the strain of the climb.

"I think I'm gonna keep you there," Oliver muses softly when we reach the top. "Easier than having you on my side," he adds a bit too quickly.

I swallow. "Yeah, okay. I like the view from up here anyway."

He clears his throat. "Good. Perfect."

We travel like this for what seems like both an eternity and a brief second, only pausing so Oliver can stretch and rest before he hoists me onto his back again. And when he does, I lean in until my face is inches away from nuzzling the damp nape of his neck, where it smells the most like him.

"How long till we're there?" I ask as we enter a rougher part of the hike. Oliver's pace is suffering from the literal weight on his shoulders. Me. I'm the weight.

"Another hour at least," he pants.

Above us, the clouds darken even more, until they're as black as a starless night.

"Doesn't bode well," I say, and Oliver immediately knows what I'm talking about.

"I'm trying to hurry, but yeah . . . let's hope whatever is brewing up there doesn't come down on us too soon."

The moment his words are out, the sky rumbles like a threat in reply.

"Fuck," Oliver mutters. "We're not going to be able to go any further."

Panic claws at my stomach. "Why?"

"Can you see the fog in the distance?" He points ahead, and I nod. "That's not fog. That's heavy rain. Heavier than this morning. We won't have any visibility."

"Then what?"

Oliver gently sets me down. "We'll have to camp."

My Charlee,

Happy New Year to you as well. What can I wish for you? A healthy year for you and your mom. A fulfilling academic semester. Endless and unconditional love.

I can't believe you talked to your sister about me. You can't see it, but I'm blushing as I write this letter. I wonder what she'd think of me, if she'd approve. I hope she would.

Your question is so silly, though. If I were living in the same city as you, would I take you on a date? Are you serious? Of course I would. A thousand times. Every chance I got.

Honestly, what you described sounds like the perfect date for me. I'd love every minute of it. How do you always find the right things to say? It's like you see right through me. I'm adding that tidbit to my Charlee folder: has magical powers of some kind.

Maybe we could go explore the forest and find all those weird animals you like to draw. You could show me how to draw one too, although, fair warning, my drawing skills are no better than a five-year-old's. I could teach you things you don't know too, like plants you can eat and the ones to stay away from. We could do some birdwatching and imitate their calls.

And maybe find something romantic to do as well. I could pack a picnic in my bag, but I'll keep the contents a surprise for now. And maybe after that, we could find a river or a lake to freshen up from the day spent running everywhere. Get sweaty all day, then jump in the lake to cool down when the night sets in. Skinny-dipping, if we dared to be bold. And we'd then run back to our tent and slide into a sleeping bag. No need for two. We'd need to raise our temperature after swimming in the cold water. Skin to skin. You tucked in my arms, your warmth all over me.

I promise you we'll go on that date one day.

I know it sounds like I make a lot of promises. But when it comes to you, I have the urge to make your every wish come true. I want you to be happy so badly I'd do whatever I could if it meant putting a smile on your face.

With love,

Your Oli

Attached article
10 things to do if you're in danger of hypothermia

CHAPTER TWENTY

All My Love

Oliver

"*C*amp?"

"Just until the rain slows down a bit," I tell a wide-eyed Charlee.

My heart is still pounding from having to climb the hill with her on my back. Or maybe it still hasn't settled from when I saw her fall into the icy water.

That image will haunt me till the day I die.

I thought I'd lost her.

For the entire trek here, I couldn't let go of her, couldn't loosen my grip on her thighs for fear that she would slip away again. I wanted her to be okay, but I *needed* to have her close to me or I would have lost my goddamn mind.

I jerk my chin toward a flat rock next to her. "Sit here while I get the tent up."

Charlee crosses her arms. "Don't boss me around."

"Fine," I sigh. "Do whatever you want to do."

I kneel and pull the folded-up tent from my bag, unroll it, and make quick work of assembling the poles. When I stand to attach the tent, Charlee is sitting on said flat rock.

I chuckle, shaking my head.

"What?" she asks.

I shrug. "Nothing." I return my focus to getting the tent ready before we're even more drenched from the upcoming storm.

Goddamn stubborn woman is what I meant to say.

"I'm sitting because I want to, not because you told me to."

I hide my smile. "Okay."

"You don't believe me? Why—*ow*!"

The poles go flying, and I'm at her side a second later. She's standing—like she shouldn't—a wince on her lips.

I press my hands to her arms. "Sit. Down. And stop being so proud all the damn time."

She listens to me this time—and without so much as opening her mouth.

Smart girl.

The tent is ready no more than five minutes later, but it's long enough that I turn to find Charlee shivering like a leaf. Shit. She needs to get out of those damp clothes ASAP, or she'll catch a cold worse than death.

I help her stand and slide my arm around her waist. "Come on, get inside the tent and change."

Charlee grabs her bag, handing it to me. "I don't think my clothes survived the fall."

I peek inside. Her spare clothes are soaked through and utterly unusable, and her sleeping bag is unsalvageable.

"Okay." I go over the available options in my head until one becomes the most obvious. *Fuck me.* "I have a spare sweatshirt in mine. Just go into the tent and change. Call me when you're done."

I make sure she's steady, then fumble in my bag until I find my sweatshirt.

"Thanks," Charlee says as she takes it.

I nod and dart away from the tent to leave her to change.

Into my shirt.

Charlee. In my shirt.

I take a slow breath, throwing my head back to the sky and closing my eyes, letting the first droplets of rain run down my face.

The universe is testing me and my restraint. Putting me in impossible situations, one after the other. Situations where her legs are tightly wrapped around my waist and all my senses are zeroed in on the warmth radiating from her body, on my fingers digging into her thighs to hold her close, her breath caressing the nape of my neck, tickling my ears, raising goose bumps with each exhale.

And now this?

I let out a bitter laugh, dragging a hand down my face to wipe the rain away. For all the times I imagined this, for all the times Charlee and I talked about it, this isn't how I expected our first camping experience would go.

"All good!" Charlee shouts from inside the tent.

I exhale sharply. No need to delay the inevitable.

I unzip the tent and slip inside, careful not to get too much water on the mat I laid down. It's not a big tent, but three people could easily fit in here, so it gives us ample room to discard our drenched clothes and boots in one corner and keep the rest of the area mostly dry.

I keep my eyes on the ground as I kneel and start untying my shoes. "Do you mind if I change quickly too?" I ask, my back to her.

I can't see her face when she replies. "Sure, go ahead." But I've gotten used to hearing her voice now, and its rough edge betrays her. I tuck that knowledge away.

I toss my vest, thermal gear, and socks into a puddle of clothes on the tent floor. In nothing but my boxers, I grab the only black shirt I packed and slide on my second pair of thermal leggings.

Behind me, Charlee clears her throat, and I can't keep my lips from stretching upward. I know I'm gonna have to look at her at some point, and we'll see if I feel like smiling then too.

"Well, this whole thing took an unexpected turn," she says, her tone heavy with derision. "Didn't think I'd be trapped in a rainstorm in the middle of the woods with you."

I laugh softly, shaking my head. "Me neither, Char. Lee. *Charlee.*" I'm glad she can't see my face burning red.

"If I recall, you did promise me a camping date once, so if this was all a ploy to get to it, bravo, Oli. I walked right into it."

Her voice is light and teasing for once, but I whip my head in her direction all the same, my eyes flashing to her face. Maybe it's the nickname she always used for me on her lips right now, or maybe it's her breaking her own rule and bringing up our past, and the *many* promises I made to her back then about that first date night. Either way, it catches me off guard.

She looks so small wearing my shirt. It reaches her knees, and she looks so cozy, so soft. So inviting. My eyes flare when they do a double take at her knees . . .

Her *bare* knees.

I ball my fingers into iron-tight fists at my sides. She's not wearing anything underneath.

It's okay. It's fine.

The thought is unbearable.

I force my mind to stay on course, to not venture into places I can't allow it to go, but one reminder works better than any cold shower ever could: *You're wearing fucking thermal tights, for god's sake.*

The last thing I need is for her to think I'm a creep. So I train my eyes on hers, not allowing—or trusting—myself to look anywhere else.

"I did promise that, didn't I? This isn't quite how I imagined it, though. If my memory serves me right, there was a lake involved."

Charlee chuckles, shaking her bangs into place. "Don't push your luck."

I sit on the opposite end of the mat, tucking my legs under me. "If you ask me, it wouldn't have mattered what we did on that date. As long as I had the chance to spend it with you."

Her breath catches, but her eyes show nothing that could betray the relaxed mask she wears. To anyone else, at least. Not to me.

"You can't say shit like that anymore," she whispers.

I bring my knees under my chin, curling my arms around my legs. "I'm sorry. It's just hard sometimes, around you."

"That's what he said."

My eyes widen, and we burst into laughter.

"I can't believe you just said that."

"What?" she asks, still laughing. "You gave it to me so easily."

My laugh dies in my throat, and so does hers. I cock an eyebrow, a silent challenge.

She chuckles, breaking the tension. "Yeah, okay, I heard it."

Outside, the rain intensifies, splattering harder on the waterproof material of the tent.

Charlee pinches her lips together. "Doesn't look like we'll be on our way soon. Should we call the lodge?"

I shake my head. "They won't send someone in this weather. We're not in a dangerous situation, so there's no need to alarm anybody."

She hums and stretches her left leg, hissing as her ankle grazes the ground.

"How are you feeling?"

It looks like the swelling has gone down, though the bruising has worsened.

"It hurts like hell. But I'll manage. I consider myself lucky to have come out of that with only a broken ankle."

"We don't know if it's broken yet," I retort.

Charlee makes a face. "Either way, it could have been much worse. Thank you, by the way."

The last words are spoken so softly, as if she meant to say so much more in those five little words.

My gaze is still on her face for my own sanity, but also because I can't seem to tear myself away from her electrifying green eyes.

"I couldn't lose you again, now, could I?"

Her throat bobs. "There you go again with shit you shouldn't say."

My eyes soften as I watch the war raging inside her, those emerald eyes catching fire while she weighs whether she likes that I'm being bold or wants to push me away. And maybe she wants to push me away because she likes it too much.

I understand. Oh, I understand how difficult it must be for her to admit to herself what I've known all along. But damn it, I can't be the only one feeling that taut thread vibrating between us.

"Maybe I should say that shit," I counter, not daring to look away. "Maybe that's exactly what I need to say. Maybe that's what you should hear."

Charlee looks at me, truly looks at me, like she's stripping me naked and holding my soul in her hands. Her stare presses down on me with a delicious weight. "Maybe."

The air thickens, barely breathable, as her admission dangles in the space between us. Her gaze slides from my eyes and burns its way to my mouth, and I can't help but do the same, watching as her lips part when my eyes linger too long on that full, luscious bottom lip.

I swallow hard, my throat drier than the hottest sand.

Charlee looks away first, tucking her hair behind her ear. The gesture would almost look shy if it weren't for the heat in her eyes. A diversion, then. To shift my attention elsewhere. To make me lose my train of thought so I won't notice how affected she is.

A valiant effort.

And what makes me tumble even farther into the spell she has me under.

Charlee is beautiful. I don't think anybody would contest that. But it's her mind, her brilliant intellect, that has me aroused like I've never been before. God, that's the sexiest part of her. That mouth, that wickedly smart mouth, irreverent and full of promises of trouble if I ever dared to go toe to toe with her, pushing her past what she's comfortable with.

I won't.

I would never.

I'd only take her hand if she'd let me, and only then would we walk out of her comfort zone. Together. I'd show her she can trust me again.

Charlee clears her throat, and I snap out of my thoughts. "I knew you'd be like that." A smile tucks her lips upward.

I return it. "Like what?"

"Lost in your thoughts. Making sure you looked at every angle and left no stone unturned. I'm not saying this in a bad way," she adds when she notices my scrunched brows. "It's just . . . I had this image of you in my mind, of how you'd be, how you'd act. It's satisfying to see I was right."

"Don't look so smug," I say, a chuckle escaping my lips. "I think I might have given you a clue or two to help you get to that conclusion."

"You mean like bearing your heart and soul to me in countless letters in the span of a year?"

Her blunt reply threatens to steal my breath. There's no malice in her words, no harshness, but the truths behind it remain too heavy to stomach.

"Something like that, yeah."

Silence settles between us. I'm moving to grab a snack bar from my bag when her hand falls on my knee and stops my movement.

As if the contact is too much for her, or maybe she realizes she's crossing a boundary she set for herself, Charlee snatches her hand back and lowers her eyes to her fingers. "I remember, you know. Everything. Every little thing you told me, I remember. Even if I don't want to."

My throat works overtime in a struggle to push my words past the knot growing there. "I haven't been able to forget a single thing about you, Charlee."

Heat colors her cheeks in a beautiful shade of dark pink. I want to trace the path of that warmth with my fingers down to her collarbone, explore every inch of her meticulously. Find out what turns that steady blush into pure fire.

"Some very annoying part of me is glad that our paths crossed," she muses, toying with a hair tie around her wrist.

I wait for her to continue, to tell me *why* she's happy that we're both here against all odds, but she doesn't.

So I gently nudge her. "On a scale of 'I walked barefoot on a Lego' to 'Trevor is a misogynistic asshole and I have to put up with him for two weeks,' where does us bumping into each other stand? In terms of annoyance."

Charlee chuckles. I'll take the win. "Somewhere in the middle, I guess."

I hum. "I can live with that. Got scared for a sec that you'd have put me all the way up there with Trevor."

She crosses her legs, settling more comfortably on the mat and blanket I laid out earlier. "Being with you again—I mean, not again, because we've never actually met in person before, but, you know, being in your life again, I guess . . . not that I'm in your life either . . ."

I look at her, amused. Is Charlee Fletcher . . . nervous?

"Let's try that again," she says. "Talking to you again brings me back to a place in my life where I was at my happiest. And where I also had my toughest moments."

I know what she means before she even has to say it. "Your mom."

Charlee nods, her eyes shiny. "She didn't make it to the end of the year. She passed away that September from cardiac arrest. Doctors told us that her aggressive treatment combined with the stage of her breast cancer had been fatal."

A wave of guilt crashes over me. I wasn't there for her. She lost her mom three months after we were supposed to meet, and I wasn't there. I should have been. I should have been and yet . . .

I wasn't.

Gosh . . . the pain she must have gone through, that awful *loneliness* she always feared. The loneliness of losing a mother. A gaping hole that's impossible to fill. And I was supposed to be the one she relied on. How many times did we talk about what would happen when the time came? That I'd fly to her, to support her and Riley in any way I could and just be there for her. Be a shoulder to cry on, a best friend. Whatever she'd have needed me to be, I would have been. Just for her. Always for her.

"I'm sorry, Charlee." My voice shakes. "I didn't think it'd happen so fast." *I didn't think you'd be out of my life by then.*

Her face is a blank mask when she says, "Neither did we. We knew it would happen eventually, but not like that. Not that brutally."

I hesitate before I place my hand on her knee, even at the risk of losing it. But Charlee doesn't move. Instead, she pushes into my touch as if seeking comfort.

"I'm not saying that for pity or to make you feel guilty," she continues, as if she can read the torment in my soul. "For years after my mom passed away, I felt like I was running away from it. Keeping myself busy, literally escaping my own life and traveling the world to get as far away as I possibly could." She lays her small hand on top of mine, and it takes all I have left in me to seem unfazed. "But I think . . . I think I wasn't truly running away. At first, maybe. But I think it turned into something else. Being with you today has made me realize that. That I might have been chasing after something this whole time."

Charlee takes a deep inhale and exhales shakily.

I wait, my heart drumming in my throat. It feels important, like she just discovered the key to a deep, buried secret she's been trying to unlock for a long time. And I crave her revelation.

"Are you gonna make me ask?" I rasp.

"Are you gonna make me say it?" she shoots back.

I flip my hand and trap her fingers between mine. "I will never *make* you do anything you don't want to."

She smiles, swiping her thumb over the back of my hand. My body reacts with the same hypersensitivity I've known all my life. The simple strokes she applies against my skin turn my nerve endings into high-voltage wires, branding me, owning me. I shudder and close my eyes, reveling in the small pleasure she's unknowingly giving me.

"I'm not ready to share that with you just yet," she says, barely above a whisper. "I think I need to sit with it a little bit."

"You'll tell me when you're ready."

She gazes at me from beneath her long lashes. "Thank you."

I peer at the roof of the tent. "Looks like the rain has calmed down a bit. How's your ankle?"

Charlee barely shifts, but inhales sharply. "Not good."

"Okay, don't try to move it again." I turn and fumble through my bag. "I might have some anti-inflammatories in here. Might help with the swelling too."

I find the bottle and pop two out, then grab some water. "Here."

She arches an eyebrow. "Are you trying to knock me out?"

"Busted," I joke.

She swallows the pills with two gulps of water and wipes her mouth with the back of her hand. "Now what?"

I unzip the front of the tent, and a gust of cold air whips across my face. "Even if we could walk now that the storm is over, the trail back to the lodge is soaked and slippery. And the sun is just setting. Might as well camp for the night and go back first thing tomorrow morning."

I look over my shoulder at Charlee, still clad in nothing but my oversized shirt, and grit my teeth.

She surveys the tent. "And how is this supposed to work?"

"The tent is big enough for the both of us. You can take the sleeping bag, and I'll sleep with these on." I nod to the jackets drying on the floor. It's gonna be a rough night. Temperatures will drop pretty low after a storm like that, but I've lived through worse. I can survive one night.

Charlee rolls her eyes. "Don't be ridiculous. We can . . . we can share."

As soon as the words are out, it looks like all she wants to do is shove them back in.

"It's okay, Charlee. I think we've had enough forced proximity for one day, don't you?"

I don't mean any of it. I could never have enough of her. I'd spend days with my face buried in her neck if I could. But I don't want to make her more uncomfortable while we're in this situation.

Something passes over her face, but I'm not fast enough to catch it. "It doesn't have to be anything more than what it is, Oliver," she says sharply. "Your sleeping bag looks big enough for two of you to sleep in. I think it'll be just fine for one night."

My eyes soften. "I didn't . . . I didn't mean it in a bad way. I just want you to be comfortable tonight, especially with your ankle."

"My ankle will be fine. I'll keep it outside," she replies with more gentleness, but still, her gaze pins me on the spot. "I wouldn't offer it if I wasn't comfortable doing so. Trust me. I can draw my own limits. Plus, I don't want you to die from the cold. Hypothermia and all, remember?"

Hey Oli,

Didn't I tell you about my magical powers? Gosh. I thought I did. I'll keep them secret until we meet, then. It'll build up the suspense so there's still a bit of mystery for when we see each other in person for the first time.

And you know what? Skin to skin doesn't sound like a bad idea, actually. Especially if I were with you. I'm very big on physical touch. Do you know what love languages are? It's how you express your love and how you like to receive it. There are five different love languages, and mine are physical touch and quality time. I'm a hugger, a kisser. Any excuse to let my hands roam freely over my person. And I need to feel it too. I need to feel loved and cherished, and nothing speaks louder to me than having a caress on my body, a touch on my face. Just the thought of your hand on my lower back is sending butterflies very low in my stomach . . . I'd rather not let my brain go down the many possible ways you could touch me, because I might combust and set the letter on fire. How funny that I'm a physical touch kind of gal, but the simple thought of your hands on me is getting me more turned on than any contact I've experienced in my life.

Is physical touch one of yours too?

Quality time is a close second. There's nothing more precious to me than spending time with the person I want to give my heart to. I want to enjoy things together and plan stuff we both love so we can connect and bond over it. Create unforgettable memories that we'll tell our children and their children about. That's what life is about, you know?

I hope I'll get to go on that date with you one day. It sounds absolutely perfect. You'll hold me, and I know that day will be one that forever changes my life.

With love,

Charlee

<u>Attached article</u>
If you don't know your partner's love language, how can you love them right?

CHAPTER TWENTY-ONE

Pancakes For Dinner

Charlee

I was so close to saying it. The truth burned my tongue, but I held on and endured the blaze.

I was chasing after the person I was when I had you. I was chasing the happiness I knew with you.

I couldn't tell Oliver. I'd barely admitted it to myself mere minutes ago. I don't know how that thought even *fits* with my own struggles to move past what he did.

For so long, I thought I was escaping my life, never stopping for a second because I didn't want to think about Mom or everything she missed out on when she died so fucking *young*. So fucking young after working her ass off all her life. She was so close to finally resting and enjoying retirement. Peace and quiet. All the plans Riley and I had made to take her on vacation and help her discover all the world has to offer. But it was all taken away from her. Just a few years, and she would have made it. Would have reaped the rewards of the hard life she led so her daughters would need for nothing.

It all went to waste.

On the day of her funeral, people had the audacity to offer Riley and me "thoughts and prayers." Prayers for what? To *whom?* What kind of divine being would take a mother's life after she gave everything she had to raise her daughters all alone? And when she'd come so close to enjoying the rest of her life? It all felt like some kind of twisted joke.

I struggled to be by myself for a long time after that. I struggled to believe in anything, to find purpose in life without my mom to show me the way. Burying myself in work helped. Kept me halfway sane.

Until it didn't. Until I realized I was still missing something else. Until I found myself in the same room as Oliver Reynolds. Until I got closer to him over the past few days than I ever thought I'd be.

I was chasing after the person I was when I had you. I was chasing the happiness I knew with you.

The words I almost uttered out loud keep resonating in my mind.

I don't know what it is about him. Why I feel so serene when he's next to me, like his mere presence is enough to soothe the incessant din of my thoughts, the restlessness in my bones. I don't feel the tug to run to the next adventure when he's next to me, or, at least, it quiets down to a faint, distant hum.

And right about now, while Oliver is getting the sleeping bag ready, I could use his logical and rational mind to calm my electrified nerves. I don't know if I'm anxious, excited, annoyed, or a freaking mix of all the above, and I need *something* to calm me down.

"Did you say something?" Oliver stops, looking over his shoulder.

"Huh?" *Shit, did I panic out loud?* I can't let him see me like this. I need to be cool, calm, and collected. I take a deep breath. "So, um, how do you want to do this?"

Oliver studies the sleeping bag, as if trying to Tetris us in without too much contact. He rubs the nape of his neck. "Um . . . I guess you'll sleep on your right side so your ankle can stay out and elevated. I'm not sure we'll both fit on our backs, though."

Color stains his cheeks, and I can bet loads of money mine are the same hue.

I look down at my bare legs. "Is this okay, or do you want me to put my pants back on?"

His gaze darts to my thighs. "No, it's, uh . . . it's fine like that," he says thickly. "Your pants are still drenched anyway. You wouldn't be comfortable, and I'd rather have you half naked instead of soaked."

I snap my widened eyes to his. "What?"

"That—that's not . . . That's not what I meant," he splutters, horrified. "I didn't mean it like that."

He mumbles "oh my god" a few times, loud enough for me to hear.

I chuckle, despite the heat coursing in my veins. What would I have done if he'd whispered that in my ear while his full weight was on me, his hands exploring my body?

Another kind of warmth rushes through me, this one heavier, lower. I can't believe I haven't had a proper orgasm in, what, a month now? God, tonight is going to be torture. The magnitude of it hits me full force, and I try not to dwell on it, even though it's not a stranger I'll be pressed up against all night but Oliver. My Oli.

"I know what you meant. Don't worry about it. But I'm sure soaked isn't a bad thing either in the right circumstances." I wink but immediately regret my poor attempt to lighten the mood when his gaze turns absolutely feral.

I yawn a bit too loudly, but he gets the hint.

"Let's get some rest," he manages to say, sounding like he could use some water. "Is that okay with you too?"

He gestures to his pantless legs. He wears only a shirt and boxers that leave very little to my imagination.

I nod. "Yep. Sounds good to me. Perfect."

I avert my gaze and start scooting to the right side of the sleeping bag, but I hiss when my foot touches the floor.

"Stop, you're gonna hurt yourself." Faster than it takes for me to protest, Oliver is at my side, sliding one arm beneath my knees and the other around my waist. Next thing I know, the side of my face is pressed against his chest, his musky scent making my head spin. A second later, he drops me gently onto the other side of the mat.

"Thanks," I whisper.

"No problem." He motions for me to slide in.

Careful not to bump my foot again, I gently fold the material on top of me, keeping my ankle out on the edge, and turn. "Front or back?"

"What?"

"Since we won't fit on our backs, do you want to have my front against you, or my back? Please don't say back to back. It's too weird."

He coughs. "Um . . . which, uh . . . which do you prefer?" He looks at my ankle. "If you sleep with your back against me, you can keep your foot outside and elevated and not put any weight on it. Might be better for you."

I smile. "Back it is." I pat the spot next to me. "Come on, I don't bite, I promise. Not when I'm fully awake anyway."

Oliver lets out a strangled laugh but slides next to me, his body heat immediately engulfing me. I try as best I can to stay still while he settles himself against me.

"Ow!" I yelp when his elbow digs into my back.

"Sorry, I don't know where to put my arms."

"Hold me," I blurt.

"What?" His question sends a puff of warm air over my shoulder.

"Just . . . put your arms around me. It'll be easier."

What am I doing? What am I saying?

"Charlee, I . . ." He lets out a ragged breath. "Okay."

He slips one arm under my neck, letting me use it as a pillow, and drapes the other over my waist as he scoots closer, bringing my back fully flush against his front. "Is that okay?"

His words tickle my skin, and I can almost feel the faint brush of his lips on my ear.

I nod, and he lets his hand fall flat against my stomach, a solid weight against me.

There's too much going on in my mind, my body, my nerve endings.

I can't figure out which part is the most overwhelming. Is it his scent that's making me lightheaded like I've drunk several bottles of the most delectable wine? Or is it the feel of his body pressed against mine, hesitant but firm? Maybe it's the wild drum of his heart pounding against my back at the same mad tempo as my own.

The sensations are overriding my central system and taking over, flipping all the switches so the only thing my mind can think about is Oliver's body behind me, his warmth. His safety.

I relax, daring to nestle a bit closer, going soft in his embrace.

"Are you comfortable?" he asks against my neck.

"Yes. Are you?"

I don't know why we're both whispering. It's not like we're going to wake the neighbors. But raising my voice seems inappropriate. Like I might burst the fragile bubble Oliver created around us. A parallel dimension, where I can give myself a respite, drop my guard, and drift into the familiar solace that is Oliver, experiencing at last what I've always felt through his letters and craved to know in person.

"I am," he replies after a while, his thumb sweeping over my belly.

I stop breathing. Does he realize what he just did? What it does to me?

"Good night, then," I rasp.

"Good night, Charlee."

I close my eyes, willing my mind to forget where I am and focus on literally anything else, but I fail miserably. And although I'm pretty sure Oliver could easily put a few inches of distance between us, I don't mind that he's glued to me. Which is . . . surprising. Because although I used to wonder what he'd feel like against me, things are different now.

But the feel of him . . . God, my body is coming alive, and all it takes is to feel him against me. It's laughable. Embarrassing, really, that his earth-and-pine smell is getting me as hot and bothered as if I've just had the most intense foreplay in a threesome.

I shift, trying to rid myself of these thoughts. But Oliver pulls himself tighter against me in response.

"Are you okay?" His breath draws a slow shiver from me. "You're all warm."

A strangled sound leaves my mouth. "You're radiating heat."

He laughs, his chest vibrating gently against my back. "Maybe I can help you cool off."

"How?"

His mouth traces the skin of my shoulder, and this time, goose bumps spread all the way to my feet. "Like this."

"I don't think shivering necessarily means cooling off," I croak.

"No?" His mouth travels up to my ear, his warm lips cooler than my skin, and I shudder again. Again and again, he plants kisses along the slope of my neck, and I lose track of why I shouldn't tilt my head to give him more room, so I do.

"You're burning up," he whispers. "Isn't this helping?"

No. Yes. Depends on what with.

His fingers caress my stomach, and I nearly lose my damn mind.

I hate this. I hate that my body is betraying me like I'm a horny teenager. I hate that I want him, of all people.

But I do. Right now, it's all I can think about.

I close my eyes. What's the worst that could happen? If I trust what his mouth and hands are telling me, he wants this too.

I push my hips into his, almost moaning when my ass meets his crotch.

Oliver inhales sharply and grips my waist firmly. "Charlee," he warns, but it's too late, because I can already feel him hardening. "Charlee . . . this isn't . . . What are you doing?"

I push farther against his length, my body melting against it.

"Nothing," I whisper coyly. "Just"—I wiggle, pleased at the sound escaping his throat—"getting comfortable."

His fingers dig into my waist. "Stop."

I halt the movement, holding my breath. Fuck. Well, now shit is definitely going to be weird.

Oliver relaxes his fingers around my skin. "Just . . . not this. Please."

"I'm sorry. I thought . . . I mean, I figured maybe you . . ." *God, Charlee, just get the fucking words out.* "Don't you want to?"

Is this what it's come to for me? Begging for sex? Ridiculous.

"I do. You know I do. But not like this."

Not like this? Okay, Mr. Sending Mixed Signals for the Last Ten Minutes. What, then? What does he mean "not like this"? Does he want me to turn around and straddle him? Or would he prefer to take me from behind? Is that the "not like this" we're talking about? Because we can absolutely negotiate.

"It doesn't have to mean anything, you know," I say, still feeling his erection poking my ass, his fingers still pressed into my skin. "We're both adults, and sex can be just that."

"That's exactly why I don't want to," Oliver replies, his voice hoarse. "I'm not a one-night or an it's-just-sex kind of guy. Sex means nothing to me if it's not with a person I love." He hesitates but adds, "You of all people should know that."

Rejection pricks at my skin like a hundred needles. Suddenly, the sleeping bag is far too small for the space my mortification takes up.

How did this sound like a good idea a few minutes ago? I *did* know him, and the Oliver I remembered would have jumped at the chance to be with me. Inside me.

Because he was in love with you then.

I shoo that damn thought away.

Not only will I be wedged against him for the rest of the night, but I've also managed to get myself super worked up.

And there's no release possible within the confines of this tent.

Oliver moves, readjusting his front. "We should sleep," he whispers, hammering the final nail in my shame coffin.

Yeah, we should.

I close my eyes with the hope that when I wake up tomorrow, all of this will have been a bad dream.

Fat chance.

I wake up the next morning to a sun-filled tent and an empty sleeping bag.

Despite all my efforts, the events of last night slam full force into my mind.

I feel awful. Not only because of the shame seeping through me or for how awkward the rest of the trip will be, thanks to yours truly, but because I've put Oliver in this position.

I rub my eyes and stretch my legs. A sharp pain erupts in my left foot and shoots up to my calf.

Ah, yes. There's that too.

Testing my balance, I press my feet to the ground very slowly. "Ow, ow, ow! Okay, no. Nope. No weight on it, gotcha."

No weight, which means I'll have to lean on Oliver all day. Great . . . just great.

As gracefully as the time I tried on my sister's high heels and face-planted in her backyard, I exit the tent, but not without losing some of my hair in the zipper in the process.

Crisp air meets my cheeks, cooling my still-burning mortification from last night. Oliver is crouched over a rudimentary fire, warming up two cups of coffee, by the smell of it.

I hop the few feet to where he is, probably waking up the whole damn forest with how loud I am.

"Good morning," he says, handing me one of the cups. "Careful, it's hot."

I nod, grabbing the handle. I blow once on the steamy liquid and bring it to my lips, humming at the rich, bittersweet notes flooding my mouth.

Yeah, this is definitely a coffee-needed day.

After I've taken a few sips, I look Oliver in the eye. "Listen, Oli, about—"

"Don't," he cuts in. His eyes are charged with something I can't quite make out. "You don't owe me an explanation or an apology. We're okay."

He smiles, his ruffled hair even messier this morning, and I wonder if it's because he got up with restless thoughts too.

"Okay," I say, my own lips stretching up, and my stomach untangles a bit.

He nods to my ankle. "How is it today? Can you walk?"

I snort. "I know you saw me coming out of that tent, and I appreciate you trying to make me feel better. I think I'll be able to manage until the lodge."

"We'll take it slow. And any time you're tired, or if it hurts at any point, I'll take it from there."

"What do you mean?"

He pushes his hands on his knees and stands. "I'll take care of you."

My dear Charlee,

This letter almost didn't make it out to you. I spotted Emile throwing my mail in the trash as I was closing the door and had to go fish it out and bring it to the post office myself before I went to class. I swear, this guy is driving me nuts. Maybe I *should* actually put something in his food. Then he'll have a true reason for hating my grandparents and me.

Of course, I know what love languages are. And I'm glad you have physical touch in yours, as it is very, very important to me. Reading that you love to touch, to hug, to kiss . . . I like that a lot. Even you thinking about my hands on you is driving me insane to the point that I can almost feel you under my fingers. I don't think it'd be a good thing for me to tell you how many times I've imagined roaming my hands over your body until they ached. Or dreamed of what your lips would feel like against mine.

I'd say words of affirmation is the other one for me. Being gifted comes with a lot of wondering moments. Most people I've talked to about this often laugh me off with "Well, how awful it must be to be good at everything you do and have a higher IQ," but they don't know what it truly means. They dismiss it as not being an issue, not being "neurodiverse enough," because if your biggest problem is that you're smart, then is it a problem at all? My neurodiversity comes with hypersensitivity, and both physical touch and words of affirmation help me understand another person's feelings and help me confirm that I have the right read on them. I tend to overanalyze everything, and without the proper signs, I get easily lost in my endless questioning. But if you show me exactly what it is you're feeling, what you feel for me, my mind quiets, and I am more at ease. As simple as that.

But on the plus side, it also comes with a heightened understanding of my senses, including touch. I feel everything more. And the pleasure it gives me . . . Let's just say that if you were here . . . I don't know, it'd probably be over in less than two embarrassing minutes.

And I don't know if I'm having the right read with you. I'm not 100% sure, even if part of me believes that I do.

I can't wait for the day I get to hold you, Charlee. It'll be the most special day of my life.

Should we exchange our numbers for when we meet? Just in case? Come up with a plan to find each other?

With love,

Oli

<u>Attached article</u>
Sparks fly: The power of touch when two people share the need for physical connection

CHAPTER TWENTY-TWO

Forever and a Day

Oliver

The day after our improvised camping trip, we land in Pine Falls, just Charlee and me. Emma texted me earlier this morning, signaling that she and the rest of the MNL crew would be on their way back shortly as well.

I haven't even started thinking about the consequences of all of this yet. Not now, not when Charlee is still in so much pain. Although I know they'll come, and I know I'll pay the price for my choices.

So be it.

I wouldn't have been able to live with myself if I had continued to drag Charlee through such dangerous terrain while she could barely put her foot on the ground. God knows how much worse it could have gotten.

Trevor was still fuming by the time we returned to the lodge after our night in the wild, but frankly, I couldn't have cared less. We packed our bags, Charlee said goodbye to Emma, and here we are now.

My leg bounces up and down while I wait in one of the hospital's worn-out chairs. The glaring lights in the waiting room are giving me a headache, and I haven't eaten since six a.m., but at least Charlee is finally being checked out by a doctor.

I sink a little deeper into the armchair, my head falling against the back of the seat with a thud. I can't stop my mind from drifting back to the last few hours I spent with Charlee in the tent. Guilt gnaws at me, despite knowing I made the right call for myself.

She wanted me. And, god, I wanted her too. I've wanted her for the last five years.

My beautiful Charlee.

She felt divine against me. I could have spent days, weeks, inhaling that distinctively sweet scent of her, peaches and vanilla, until I was high on it.

But my body's reaction to her, my need for her, that's one thing.

I simply couldn't let go and give myself to her.

It doesn't have to mean anything.

I sigh, scrubbing my hand over my face. And that's the problem, isn't it? How can it not mean everything when it's her and me?

To deny her, though. To feel how ashamed she was . . . I almost took it back and buried myself to the hilt in her warmth, but I knew that if I did, I would never forgive myself for giving in.

I want all of her, not just bits and pieces. Everything. And when she comes to that same damn realization, then, and only then, will I spend the rest of my life worshipping her body for the marvel that it is.

My pocket buzzes. I slip my phone out and unlock the screen.

Lola

> How are you back in town already?

> My texts all went through to you in one go, so I figure you have reception again.

Oliver

> Long story short, the whole trip was just awful.

Lola

> What happened?

I pause, trying to figure out how to condense the whole story into a short reply.

Oliver

Charlee got into an accident.
Slipped into a river and hurt her
ankle and her hand. We rushed
back here as fast as we could.
I'm at the hospital now, waiting
to see what's going on with her.

Lola

Oh wow. I hope it's not too
serious.

I hum to myself.

Oliver

I do too. I got a text from Donna,
though. She drove straight to Pine
Falls when she heard . . . She's at
Fir Café. We're heading there after
Charlee gets examined. I don't
know how she'll react.

The last thing I want to do is talk this through with my
boss, but I'm sure Trevor found a way to yell at her, just like
he yelled at me when I told him we were leaving, and now I
can't escape it.

Lola

Do you know what's gonna
happen? Didn't you sign a
contract?

Oliver

I don't, and yes, I did. Hoping we can find a loophole together, but I don't think Donna will be ecstatic about any of it, even if we find something. Worries for later, right?

Lola

I'm here if you need me. Are you up for a Friday dinner tonight, then?

I check the date on my phone. It's Saturday, but fuck it. I already missed two since Charlee has been here, and to be honest, I need it. I miss Matt and James too.

Oliver

Yes. See you tonight

I lock my phone, and I'm just slipping it back into my pocket when Charlee comes through the revolving doors, a crutch on either side of her and her ankle and hand wrapped in bandages.

I jump to my feet and grab my jacket, rushing to her side. "So?"

I scan her face, awaiting her answer, but I can't pick up any signs other than weariness.

"Believe it or not, I just have a sprained ankle. I tore some ligaments, which explains the swelling and bruises. But the doctor said with a couple of painkillers, I should be good as new in a few weeks."

I run my hand through my hair. "Good, good," I say as I exhale. "Does it hurt? Do you need help to get to the truck?"

Her eyes soften, and she stands on one foot, waving her crutches. "What are those for, dummy?"

"Fair enough." I chuckle. "Come on. I told Donna we would meet her at the café once we were done here."

Charlee groans. "Do we have to? Can't I just say that—I don't know? I have an emergency surgery?"

"Nice try. Let's go, little liar."

With another grunt, Charlee finally follows me. And I hope like hell that I didn't cost us both our jobs.

"Can someone tell me what the hell happened?" Donna asks from where she's seated, a steaming cup of coffee next to her. "Here I was, working on promotional material for the docuseries, and the next thing I know, I have Trevor on the phone yelling at me that you guys bailed on them and that he would unleash, and I quote, 'an army of lawyers on us.'" She looks at me from behind her glasses like she's ready to strangle the living shit out of me. "Talk. Now."

Beside me, Charlee sits oddly still. I wish I could read what's going on inside her head. I wonder if she blames me for the situation we're in.

Fuck, I hope not.

I lean my elbows on the table. "I'm sure you saw Charlee's ankle when we walked in. Before we even started our fifth day, I told everybody we needed to stay at the lodge because I could tell a storm was rolling in. Trevor didn't listen, despite my *many* warnings. He deliberately put the whole team in danger, and sure enough, Charlee hurt herself pretty badly. You think she could continue like this?"

Donna's gaze slides to the crutches lying on the floor.

"Did anyone else witness this?" Donna asks.

"Yes," Charlee rushes to say. "Everyone was there."

Donna arches one eyebrow, so I add, "Trevor threatened to sue us for not fulfilling our contracts when I said I was bringing Charlee back. I just countered with the fact that he willingly put the team in danger when he dismissed my warning. As the assigned first responder responsible for the safety of the crew, I made it glaringly clear that we should not have left the camp that day, and he stated in front of everyone that if anything happened, he'd accept full responsibility. Seems to me like a bigger case can be built against him for endangering the lives of five people despite my professional recommendations than against us for not fulfilling our end of the contract."

Donna presses her lips into a thin line. "I knew that man was bad news from the day I met him. I was hoping he wouldn't be in charge of the project when MNL approached us," she says, shaking her head. "When I saw him in my office the day you did the briefing, I wanted to throw him out." She turns her attention to Charlee, offering her a tight smile. "I'm sorry you got hurt."

Charlee shrugs. "Part of the job."

"I guess so," Donna chuckles. She places her linked hands on the table. "Look. I won't lie to you. This is a big mess. Production is stalled for now, and the crew is on their way back without enough material to make more than a few episodes. We already got a few calls from the MNL lawyers, and we might be entangled in legal drama for a while. Not ideal, but *Wild Planet* will not stand idly by while an entitled fuck endangers our reporters." Her gaze drifts to me. "Is there anybody on their team who can back your story?"

I nod. "Emma. She took our side quickly and offered to corroborate our version of the events as we were packing to leave." That shut Trevor up pretty fast, although I won't soon forget the look he shot Emma and me.

"Good, good. That'll come in handy." Donna rubs her temples like she's fighting an imminent headache. "Now for the other side of this mess. Because the project is on the rocks for now, so is your payment, and it'll be so until we settle the issue. I'm sorry, Oliver."

She really does look sorry, and so am I.

I swallow my disappointment. "It's okay, I understand."

I can already see the exasperated look Rob will give me when I tell him I need to push the deadline. Again.

I lower my head, fighting against the sting in my eyes. I let them down.

I was *so* close to making them proud, to getting my legacy back, and I failed just short of the finish line. Now Jerry's will become part of an all-inclusive resort for rich white folks, the polar opposite of what my grandparents worked for all their lives: a place of welcome and found family.

"Ben called me," Donna tells Charlee. "I told him I'd let him know as soon as we were done and I made sure you were both okay."

"Thanks," Charlee whispers.

Donna waves to the waiter and opens her laptop. "You two get going. I have another meeting in ten minutes with our lawyers to see how we can avoid dragging this whole thing out. I'll be in touch when I need you."

"Thanks, Donna." I get up and grab Charlee's crutches.

Slowly, we make our way to the car, neither of us brave enough to say a word.

After I slip behind the wheel, I turn the heat on while Charlee throws her crutches in the back seat.

"Are you okay?" I ask.

She opens her mouth, but her phone rings, cutting her off. A groan escapes her lips when she sees the name on the screen. "Hi, Ben."

I start the truck, only hearing muffled noises coming through her phone. She keeps her face stoic, and it drives me mad to be left in the dark.

"No, I know," she says. "No, it's not broken."

The leather of the wheel creaks under my grip.

"I get that. Yeah, we just talked to Donna. We will. Thank you." A pause. "I understand. Sure. You too. Bye."

She exhales a loud, trembling breath. I gaze at her, and my stomach twists at the sight of her lips wobbling.

"Charlee . . ." I reach out to lay my hand on her thigh. I move slowly to give her time to tell me to fuck off. She doesn't, so I rub my thumb over the thin material of her leggings. "Tell me what happened."

"I think I, um . . . I think I don't have a job anymore?"

Safety keeps my eyes glued to the road.

I clear my throat. "You think?"

"Well, considering this whole docuseries thing was supposed to be the Toronto office's saving grace, I guess that I didn't leave him with much of a choice." She picks at her nails as I splay my hand out on her thigh. "It's temporary, he said. Told me I was on a 'long vacation' while he figures out the legal logistics of the whole thing and tries to get me back on, but he can't afford my full salary right now. I'm not technically fired; he just won't send me out on assignments, and since ninety percent of my pay relies on the number of stories I cover . . ."

"Charlee . . . I didn't know. I . . . If I . . . Maybe I could—"

She rests her hand on top of mine. "It's done. It's okay."

I dare a glance at her, and despite her shiny eyes, I notice the hint of a smile. A sad one, sure, but it's not forced. It's almost . . . resolved. I trap her fingers with mine.

"I thought my job was the one thing in my life I couldn't live without," she says. "What was keeping me from crumbling after my mom passed away." She sweeps her thumb over my skin. "I . . . I don't think that anymore. I love what I do—*did*—do?" She laughs, and the waves framing her face ripple with the shake of her head. I can't tear my eyes away. "Doesn't matter. My job doesn't define me. I can do it elsewhere. I can still travel whenever I feel like it. I can still explore and write and draw the weirdest things I find. But I don't *need* this job anymore. Not like I used to or thought I did. And that's okay. I'm sad, but I'm okay. I think." She lets out a low whistle. "Damn, talk about a life-changing breakthrough I just made."

She chuckles, the sound light and heavy at the same time. It doesn't fool me. I can tell she's sadder than she lets on, but I don't push her on it.

"I'm sorry," I offer. "For the part I played in this." I turn onto the dirt road.

"For what?" she huffs. "Standing up for me and making sure I got home safe and sound?"

I don't know whether she means home like Toronto or home like here. I wish she meant the latter, but there is also another word for that: delusional. Either way, I'm clinging to the knowledge that she's not upset with me, that she's grateful, even.

I park the truck in front of my house and loosen a breath. It feels good to be home. "Don't move," I say as I open the door.

I walk around the truck, open her door, and unbuckle her seat belt. Gently, I slip an arm under her thighs and one around her waist.

"Hold on to my neck," I whisper.

"I have my crutches in the back, you know," she says, but she slings her arms around my neck anyway.

"I know."

I lift her effortlessly and walk toward the house, the keys dangling from one of my fingers.

Charlee buries her face in the crook of my neck. "Thank you."

My heart leaps, pulsing a little faster. "Entirely my pleasure," I say and pull her a little tighter against me.

Our moments are numbered. Now that she no longer has any obligation to be here, there's no stopping her from leaving. It's only a matter of days. Hours, perhaps. So I'll enjoy every second I'm wrapped in her vanilla-peach sweetness. I inhale deeply, willing my mind and body to commit her to memory.

For when I'll undoubtedly think of her.

I open the front door, then set Charlee down on one of the kitchen chairs. "I'm gonna grab our bags and your crutches from the truck. I'll be right back."

I jog outside, the wind a gentle caress on my burning face.

I don't want to lose her. Not again.

Fuck. I drag my fingers through my hair and push against the tears that knot in my throat, but it's too late. They roll down my cheeks, drying instantly with the wind.

I can't lose her. I need to tell her. Tell her why I never showed up five years ago. Why I'm racked with guilt and shame and grief. The project is done now, and she can't hide behind that professional pretense any longer. I gave her what she wanted. Now it's my turn to be selfish. She needs to hear the truth now. Hear *me*.

And maybe she won't forgive me, maybe she won't even understand, and maybe it will all have been for nothing, and she'll leave anyway.

But I can't leave it to fate.

She needs to know.

With a resolute stride, I head back inside the house, bags and crutches in hand. But when I walk through the doorway and see that Charlee has taken off her sweater and is wearing only a black top, grunting and stretching with one hand on her lower back, my big speech vanishes.

Instead, I say, "What's going on?"

She jumps. "Jesus. I didn't hear you come in. It's nothing I'm just . . ." She rubs her back. "I think I've been putting more weight on my right leg, and my back's a little sore because of it."

"I can help," I say a bit hoarsely.

She frowns. "How?"

"I could . . . massage you if you'd like."

She holds my gaze without flinching. "You're good with your hands?"

"I like to believe I am."

She grabs the crutches from my hands. "Then lead the way."

My Oli,

Please <u>DO NOT</u> poison Emile. He's too good for this earth. But more importantly, I intend to meet you one day, preferably not from behind plexiglass while you sport an orange jumpsuit.

I love that we both share physical touch as our love language. Things are promising to be . . . electric.

As weird as it may be, as crazy as it might sound, I have feelings for you. So, to answer your question, no. You're not reading the situation wrong. Although you not being sure of it makes me wonder if I haven't made things clear enough.

And maybe I should.

Don't you know the effect you have on me? Don't you know that I think about you every day and wonder what it would be like to lie next to you? Some nights, when I get ready for bed, I think about you. I take off my clothes and slide under my covers. I close my eyes and picture you here with me, hovering over me. Not putting your full weight on me yet, but just enough that I know you're here, your arms braced on either side of my face. And then you lean in and kiss me softly at first, your lips brushing mine with a tenderness I've never known. But as soon as you get a taste of me, you can't hold back, and your mouth turns hungry, desperate to get as close as possible. You coax my mouth open, and I willingly let you in, our tongues meeting in delicious sweeps that make me feral for more.

I imagine that my hand glides the length of your back, but in the reality of my pitch-black room, it travels down my breasts, past my navel, to where I need you most. I open my legs and slide a finger along my slit, pretending that it's you who's touching me. You take such good care of me, Oliver, that your name falls from my lips, even if you're not here. So meticulous, so detail-oriented. You stroke me, your attention focused on my pleasure, before you push one of your fingers inside me. I moan at the sensation, already feeling so full when you haven't given me what I crave the most just yet. You work your finger in and out, and my need coats it as you keep your maddening tempo. And when it's slippery enough, you add a second, and I moan your name again.

How many times have I moaned your name, Oli, while I touched myself these past few months? I can't recall. I've lost count.

I imagine that I slip one of my hands into your unbuckled jeans and wrap it around the smooth skin of your cock. I imagine you fumbling in one of my nightstand drawers for a condom just like I do to get my magic wand out. I grab it like I grip your cock and start rubbing it on my clit. My—your—fingers that were inside me trail their way up to my breast and pinch my nipple, toppling me into another galaxy. I cry out your name as my orgasm rolls over me in waves, and you're here, with me, watching me come down from the high you just gave me as if it's the most beautiful thing you've ever seen.

Did I make it clearer for you now?

I don't know how college works in BC and if our schedules are widely different, but college is ending soon over here. How about we meet in Calgary? Let's say June 21st? Then we could spend the weekend together.

Exchanging our numbers would be the reasonable thing to do, but I can't help feeling like it would ruin the mystery of this whole letter exchange we've kept up for the entire year. How about we figure out the flight logistics and then decide on a time when we can meet at the airport, at the arrival terminal? I already know what I'll be wearing, because it's literally the only dress I own: it's a steel-blue satin midi dress with quite a plunge between my breasts and thin straps on my shoulders. Can't miss it!

Oh, and let's give each other some leeway in case our flights are late or something. And if anything happens (which it won't), we can still write to each other afterward. Sound good to you?

With love,

Your Charlee

Attached article
Alberta's dying wildlife: The devastating impacts of the oil industry over the years and what we can do now to save it

CHAPTER TWENTY-THREE

Falling in Love

Charlee

Because we just got home from the hospital after a week in the wild, Oliver and I gave ourselves twenty minutes to shower and scrub the tiredness away before he goes to work on my aching muscles. Clean and feeling a bit more like myself, I join him in the living room, where he sits next to the fire, a book in his hands.

"Feeling better?" he asks when he sees me approaching. Or maybe hears me with all the noise these damn crutches make.

"Much, thank you. Sorry if I made you wait. It's harder to shower while having to hop around like a freaking bunny and not slip and crack my skull open, you know?"

Oliver laughs, the sound so rich. "Don't worry about it. I got some reading done." He sets his book down next to him and pushes to his feet. "Where do you want to go?"

I scan his house, a thought forming in my mind. *Should I?*

"I'd say the couch, but with this"—I point to my ankle—"a bed might be easier."

Oliver nods, his jaw tense. "My bed okay?" he rasps, and the sound has no business turning my insides molten like that.

"Yep, fine with me."

"Good, good." He eyes my crutches. "Can I?"

I frown until I remember. "Yes, uh . . . yes, of course."

I set my crutches off to the side and hop to him. With the same gentleness as earlier, Oliver picks me up, then climbs the stairs leading up to his bedroom, which takes up the entire second floor.

When we get to the top, I blow out an impressed whistle. "Wow. Oliver, this is beautiful."

The mezzanine looks larger than it does from downstairs. The vaulted ceiling is adorned with beams, giving the room an even more intimate quality. An inviting king-size bed sits right in the middle of the wood floor. Shelves brimming with books are built into the wall, and at the opposite end of the space, centered between the large windows overlooking the lake, sits a large bathtub. I almost salivate at the sight. I'd pay good money to have a bath in that, especially with this view.

Oliver sets me down on his bed. "Thanks. It's my favorite part of this house."

"I can see why. This is stunning."

My gaze wanders to the bookshelves again. "You have a very impressive collection between here and downstairs. What kind of books do you read?"

"A bit of everything. Fiction, nonfiction. I love true crime and fantasy. Lola's been trying to diversify my reading lately." He walks to one of the bookshelves, rummages through it, and pulls out a book.

"*Love and Other Words,*" I say, reading the title. I flip it back, scanning the synopsis. "Romance?"

Oliver chuckles. "Yep. She told me the genre is right up my alley. Apparently, I'm a 'cinnamon roll hero.'" He air-quotes the words, amusement dancing in his eyes. "Her words, not mine. I have no idea what that means, but she's usually right about things, so I'm giving this one a shot."

I laugh. "It means that you're kind and supportive. As sweet as a cinnamon roll. I'd say it fits you well."

"Oh." He blushes hard and fast. "So, um, how do you want to . . .?"

"Ah, yes. Can I lie down?"

"Of course. Here." He pushes a few pillows out of the way.

I don't know what I'm doing, but I can't back down now, the anticipation of what's to come simmering beneath my skin.

"Is it okay if I take my shirt off?"

I hear the hitch in his breath. "Y-yes, probably easier like that."

"Probably."

I strip out of it, discarding it on the floor. Oliver's gaze stays on mine for a second before it dips to my lips, my neck . . . my chest. Heat sweeps over me and pools between my legs at his intensity. Why does this feel dangerously like foreplay?

In nothing but my bra and leggings, I lie down on my stomach, my arms forming a pillow for my head.

The bed shifts next to me, and Oliver settles at my side.

"Lavender or peppermint?" His voice sounds like he hasn't used it in hours.

I smile into my arms. "Look at you, all prepared. Is this your move? You bring the ladies up here for massages?"

I keep it light and playful, but jealousy hits me like a ton of bricks, and I hate it. I hate that the possibility affects me so much when I have no right to feel this way whatsoever.

Oliver laughs, although it sounds more like a seagull choking on a piece of bread. "No, nothing like that. I like to use it in my bath sometimes. Helps me relax."

"Oh. That actually sounds nice. Which one is best for back pain?"

He studies the label. "I think the peppermint. It has anti-inflammatory properties."

He twists the bottle open and dabs a few drops on his hands before I hear the faint sound of friction. Then his hands are on me, warm and solid, pressing on my lower back with a gentleness that makes me bite back a moan.

"Is this okay?" he asks, barely above a whisper.

"Mm-hmm."

His hands knead my skin expertly, and this time, I can't help but whimper. He halts a few inches below my bra. "Can I?"

I nod, not trusting any sound coming out of my mouth at this point.

He unclasps my bra, letting the straps fall to the sides, and trails his fingers along my spine. I shiver. "So beautiful," he breathes, triggering another wave of goose bumps. His hands flatten between my shoulder blades, and he starts to loosen up my shoulders, alternating between working on a specific spot and long sweeps down my back. If he continues like this, I'm going to purr, and it's going to be embarrassing.

For a split second, words that I once wrote in a letter to him flash through my mind. Things that I wished he'd done to me, that I imagined him doing. It would be so easy to turn around and bring his lips to mine, to coax him against my bare chest and dare him to move away. I want to do that and so much more. I want him all to myself. For hours. Days. Just the two of us with nothing in between.

"You're so tense," Oliver says under his breath. He kneads a bit harder at the spot between my shoulder and my neck. "How can you function like this?"

"I think it's my default mode," I chuckle. "Never known anything else."

His fingers slide down each side of my spine until they reach the small of my back. "What are you gonna do now, then?"

He spreads his hand wide and presses from the inside out, grazing the waistband of my leggings.

"I don't know, really. I think I need to rest." I snort. The word tastes foreign on my tongue. "I've been exhausted for a long time and could use a vacation." Oliver makes small circles with his thumbs on my left side. "Oh god, that feels good."

He laughs, repeating the gesture. "You know," he starts casually, "Pine Falls can get pretty quiet during the off-season. If you want to unwind here. For your vacation, that is," he adds quickly.

I contemplate his words, the offer behind it, his desire underneath it.

It would be so easy to accept and spend weeks here, even months. Find a part-time job at the café or at the bookstore Oliver visited before we came here. It wouldn't be so bad.

And I'd be here. With him.

I wouldn't want to presume anything, but I could see him letting me stay in the guest bedroom. And it would be nice having a friend to come home to and talk to.

I mentally roll my eyes at my own words. *A friend. Listen to yourself, Charlee.* I can't even be honest with myself.

If Riley were here, she would tell me to get a grip on myself and my feelings.

But Oli isn't a friend. Truth be told, I don't know what he is. Being here with him has stirred so many things that I've been ignoring for so long, like how lonely I've been without him in my life. And while some part of me hates him for putting me through this, for making me know what it's like to miss him, to live my life without him in it, I can't deny the constant pull between us. It tugs me to him like a gravitational force I can't break away from. Through the years since we reached our tipping point, I never could bring myself to open up and trust someone again. How could I, when Oliver never gave my heart back?

It would be nice here. It really would be.

But despite my very bones wanting to move past this more than anything, despite even contemplating giving him my heart all over again, my walls are still there. Not as high, but still standing straight.

I tried to avoid the subject during this last week with him because I didn't think I needed the closure it could give me. I thought talking about it again would only bring up the ugly memories I've tried so hard to bury.

But with that comes the other side of the coin, and now here I am.

Unable to answer, because I'm too scared.

Scared that he'll hurt me, that he'll leave me again.

Scared that he didn't come five years ago because he never wanted to.

Scared to learn that he never loved me as much as I loved him.

I brought this all on myself. But I don't think I can escape the truth anymore. I need to know. I need to ask. If only so I might see what life could be here without that voice in the back of my head warning me of all the ways he could betray me again.

What happened?

I must have stayed silent for a long time, because Oliver pauses, his hands still warm on my back. Softly, he brushes some hair off my shoulder.

"I didn't mean to make you panic when I said what I just said," he says. "I like having you around. That's the truth. I'm not gonna hide that." His thumbs stroke my neck. "I forgot what it was like . . . to have something—*someone*—to look forward to. But none of it should make you stay if that's not what you want."

I swallow, going over every possibility in my mind. "I guess . . . it'd be nice to stay here a while. If you'd have me, with you . . . here."

Oliver loosens a breath. "Yes. Yes! Of course you can stay here, Charlee. I'll even have a set of keys made for you so you can go in and out and do whatever you want, even if I'm not home."

I laugh, then turn around and plop my head on my hand. "Okay, okay, before you ask me to move in and be your wife, I want to discuss something first."

He stares at me, his eyes wide as they drop from my eyes to my . . . breasts. On full display.

"Oops." A rush of heat flames my cheeks—and other parts of my body—when I see the way he's eating up every inch of me . . . "Sorry, I forgot you had taken it off."

I grab my bra, but his hand comes down on my wrist. "Don't." He swallows. "I-if you don't mind."

"I don't," I rasp.

But he doesn't let go of my wrist. Instead, he looks at me and allows me to see how much this is costing him, how much he'd like nothing more than to lay me flat underneath him.

Do it, I think, hoping it'll reach his mind.

He won't, I know that, but he's still drinking me in, and the weight of his stare hardens my peaks. That's how much power he has over me.

"Oli, look at me," I softly say. He does, and my body buckles under the emotions flaring in his gaze. "Tell me what happened five years ago."

Shadows darken his eyes. "You want to know?" he asks in a ragged breath.

I nod. "Please."

"Okay." He gathers my hands in his and looks around the room. "But first, I'm gonna need you to put your shirt on because there's no way in hell I'll be able to focus if you're half-naked."

I laugh openly, letting the sound lighten the air between us. "Okay." I grab my shirt from the floor and throw it on. "Better?"

He smiles. "No, because I miss them already. But yes, if we're about to have this conversation." He takes my hands again. "Okay. When you—"

Three knocks hit the front door.

Oliver startles and checks his phone. "Fuck."

I frown. "What? Who is it?"

He curses. "My friends. I forgot to tell you that they're coming for our usual Friday night dinner. I lost track of time. I'm sorry."

I shake my head, squeezing his hands. "It's okay." Three knocks hit again. "Go, I'll try to look decent."

"Are you sure?"

"No, but I'll try, I swear."

He laughs again, and it fills a hole in my heart. "You always look gorgeous, especially when you don't even try." He leans in and kisses my forehead, and for a second, nothing exists but us. He rests his head on mine and whispers, "Later?"

I nod. "Later."

Charlee . . .

I'd like to know what went through your mind when you wrote me your last letter. Did you sit down and think, "Let's see if I can make Oli combust without even laying a single finger on him"?

Do you have ANY idea what your words did to me? What you made me do? I couldn't hold it in, Char . . . Reading you, picturing you like that . . . I needed the release.

And I did. God, I've never come so hard. Do you know why? Because of you. I pictured all that you wrote and more. It's like you've awoken something in me that I didn't know existed. Wild and filthy. I want to be filthy with you. I want to explore you until you beg me to stop, commit every inch of you to memory so I can replay everything in my dreams. I'd learn what makes you go off and devote my days to making you come again and again and again until you cry out from madness.

But you know what would drive me over the edge? Your taste. If I ever get my mouth on you, Charlee . . . I can't promise I'll behave. That's what I thought about after reading your last letter. After you imagined me fucking you with my fingers.

You know what I'd do next?

I'd bring those very same fingers to my lips and lick them clean. And because your taste would drive me wild, I'd pull your thighs up, my thumbs digging into your skin, and I'd lower my head until my mouth came flush against your center. I'd play with your clit, sucking, swirling, nibbling. I'd give it all the attention it deserved until it swelled on my tongue, so plump and ready to explode. Then I'd go for the final blow. I'd slide my fingers inside you again, curving them slightly so I'd rub that spot that'd make you come on my hand and tongue.

Do you know that I'm stroking myself as I write this? I can't help it, Charlee. You have me slowly pumping myself while I write all the dirty things I'd do to you. Hard and hot in my hand, wishing like hell it was yours instead. Would you take me in your mouth if I asked nicely? Would you kneel before me in nothing but a thong and swallow me between your pretty, wet lips? Would you let me fist your hair and guide you over me until you can't fit a single inch more? What a sight you'd be, Charlee . . .

In case this wasn't clear, I have feelings for you too.

And I can't wait to see you in June, just so I can tell you how much. It's a date for June 21st. I went ahead and booked your flight. You'll find the airplane tickets in the envelope, so I hope you don't open your mail like a crazy person and rip it in half. If you happen not to use your return ticket, that's fine too.

No numbers, then. A gamble, but I'm sure it'll pay off when we finally meet. I'll be the one at the arrival terminal in dark pants and a warm yellow sweater, desperately looking everywhere for the beautiful woman wearing a gorgeous blue dress.

Just three more weeks, and I'll be with you. I'll see you soon, sweetheart.

With love,

Your Oli

PS: Last article of the year! I feel like my writing has improved so much since we started the program, and a lot of that is thanks to you and the great feedback you've given me. Thank you for being an amazing critique partner throughout this whole thing. And for becoming so much more to me now.

Attached article

Lake Louise, once the jewel of Alberta is now the most Instagrammable place in the world. Behind the scenes of a digital phenomenon.

CHAPTER TWENTY-FOUR

Missing You

Oliver

I run my fingers through my hair and smooth out my shirt while I take the stairs two at a time.

"Coming, coming!" I shout when the knocking starts again.

I jog to the door and swing it open. "Hey, guys."

"There he is!" Matt booms from behind Lola. He holds up the two six-packs he holds. "I brought the supplies."

Lola rolls her eyes as she pushes past me and hangs her coat. "Remind me to never skip a Friday dinner ever again. He's been insufferable the whole way here."

"Which is like a three-minute drive, Lola," Matt shoots back.

James approaches and opens his arms, bringing me into one of his classic bear hugs. "It's been too long, brother."

I clap his back. "I know. I'm sorry. Work has been keeping me busy."

He eases away, arching a brow over his thick glasses. "Work, huh? Lola filled me in on *work*."

"Did she?" My eyes narrow to Lola, who smiles very sweetly in my direction. "I'm sure she had a lot to say."

"Not really," Matt chimes in. "Just that we might meet your *work* tonight." He shakes out his long hair before gathering it back up into a bun. "Is she here?"

My mind wanders to Charlee, half-naked in my bed.

Yes, she's here. She's here and willing to talk to me. She's absolutely stunning and breathtaking, and all I want to do is kick these idiots out of my house and savor her. Talk things out and learn everything there is to know about her.

"*Oh*, Oliver is hiding something," Lola croons. "Look at that blush."

I roll my eyes. "Yes, she's here, but I forgot to tell her you guys were coming, so take it easy on her." I stare at Lola. Then Matt. "Please."

"They'll be on their best behavior," James says, clasping his hand on my shoulder. "Right, guys?"

Matt puts his hands up. "You know I'm here for you, man. I'm Team Oli forever, no matter what. I'm just curious to meet the woman you gave up the last five years of your life for. Never thought we'd be here, to be honest with you."

"We're excited to meet her." Lola takes my hand. "But we got you. Always."

"Thank you." I smile at them, taking in the unwavering loyalty in their eyes. My family. Not by blood, but by choice.

Bound by unconditional love rather than lineage, making it the most beautiful bond of all.

"So," James says, looking around. "Where is she?"

"She's, um . . ." Realization hits. *Fuck.* I left her upstairs, *in my bedroom*, with her crutches in the kitchen. She's gonna kill me when she tries to come downstairs and gets stuck.

I sigh, knowing none of them will let me off the hook with this one. "One last thing. Charlee hurt herself during the trip. She has a hard time walking without her crutches. And right now, she might be stuck upstairs."

They all stare at me.

Matt breaks the silence first. "Upstairs?"

"When you say 'upstairs,' you mean *your room*, right?" Lola adds. "Charlee is in your bedroom. Right now."

I nod. "She is."

"Wait," Matt blurts, a laugh bubbling in his throat. "Are you telling me that we just cockblocked you?"

"You didn't *cockblock* me. We were just talking and her back hurt, so I . . ." *Why am I telling them this? Jesus.* ". . . offered to massage her."

Matt howls a laugh that fills the entire house. It's so loud I can't even hear the sound of Lola and James cackling.

Yeah, I brought this on myself.

"Man, you've been out of the game for too long," Matt says after a while, wiping the corners of his eyes. "I'm sorry we arrived at a bad time, though." He nods toward the stairs. "Go on, go get your girl so we can finally meet the mysterious Charlee."

I throw a worried glance at Lola, who smiles at me reassuringly.

"Best. Behavior," I say through my teeth. I walk back upstairs, finding Charlee sitting on the bed, her bra and shirt back on, her hair as wild as it's ever been.

"I forgot you couldn't walk down by yourself."

"I forgot I've been acting like a princess and made you carry me upstairs without my crutches."

We both chuckle.

"It's gonna be awkward," I warn her. I nod toward the stairs. "They like to tease me sometimes. Don't read too much into it."

She shrugs. "It's okay, I can handle it. Guys are very predictable and not so subtle when it comes to sexual jokes. Don't worry about me."

If anybody can keep up with Matt, it's her. They might rival each other when it comes to their temperament.

"Come on, they'll give me more shit the longer we stay up here."

As if it had already become a habit and my new favorite thing to do, I lift her up and take her downstairs.

Three pairs of eyes zoom in on us as soon as we reach the ground floor. "Everybody, meet Charlee. Charlee, this is James, Matt, and Lola."

I set her down on a chair and bring the crutches to her.

"Hi, everybody." Charlee waves briefly and smiles. "Sorry about that dramatic entrance."

"Oh, no, you're fine," Lola says. "It's not every day we see Oliver carrying a woman like that."

Matt snickers, and I shoot him a warning glance.

"How about a drink and some fresh air?" I ask in an absurd attempt to change the topic.

Charlee looks around until her gaze lands on the back of the couch. "Do you mind if I borrow your sweater? I haven't unpacked yet."

I swallow the desire rising in me at the thought of her wrapped in my clothes again, or the fact that her scent will be clinging to the fabric afterward, too aware of my friends watching us like hawks. "Not at all. Go ahead."

Charlee takes the sweater and pulls it on, and then everybody grabs a beer and their jacket and makes their way to the deck, where the Muskoka Chairs are waiting for us.

It's chilly out, but with a jacket on, it's comfortable, and the perfect way to end this interminable day.

"So, Charlee, tell us. What is it that you do exactly?" James asks, crossing one leg over the other.

Charlee tips the bottle to her lips. "Well, that's something currently up in the air since I just got benched."

Matt spits out his beer. "I'm sorry," he says between coughs. "I wasn't expecting that."

"It's okay." Charlee waves him off. "I'm still in the denial phase. I think."

I'd say. I'm nervous about how calm she's being about this, and I wonder when reality will set in.

"What do you guys do?" she asks as she settles further into the chair.

"Matt has a flower shop, Lola owns a bookstore, and I'm the most boring one of the group," James says with a hint of a smile as he pushes his glasses up his nose. "I have a regular nine-to-five job working as an accountant. I used to handle Jerry's finances before—"

"Now he does all our taxes," I cut in, earning me a curious look from Charlee. "Which between the bookstore and the flower shop keeps him pretty busy, right?"

Lola's narrowed eyes are scrutinizing me, so I just shrug and zip my jacket the whole way up.

"I'd never have guessed that you own a flower shop," Charlee says to Matt, her gaze doing a double take on his bushy beard.

Matt smirks, showing his huge hands. "These fingers? Some of the most delicate in all of Pine Falls. According to the flowers, of course."

We all roll our eyes, except for Charlee, who lets out a laugh.

"What's it been like to finally come here? Do you like Pine Falls?" Matt asks Charlee, and I feel her going rigid next to me. His question, as banal as it sounds, holds a million implications. None of which either Charlee or I have been able to talk about so far. And Matt, with his usual finesse, just walked right into it.

Charlee takes a swig of her beer. "It's been . . ." She glances at me quickly before dropping her gaze to the bottle. "It's been unexpected, but familiar too, in a way. I . . . I really like it here."

Lola hums. "It's easy for a place to feel like home when you're with the right people."

I whip my head to her. She's already watching me, the love of a sister in her eyes. She's right, though. Home is wherever these three are.

And to my surprise, Charlee nods too. "Perhaps you're right about that."

James clears his throat, the wind pushing through the dirty-blond strands of his hair. "Oli, what do you say we get dinner started?"

"Sure." I turn to Charlee. "Wanna come?"

"I think I'm gonna stay here a bit, if you don't mind."

"Not at all. You staying too?" I ask Lola.

Lola smiles, settling deeper into her chair. "I think I just might. Go on, boys. Charlee and I are hungry."

The girls chuckle while James gets up and nudges Matt's foot. "Come on, big guy. You're coming too."

"I want to stay," Matt says.

"I think not. Up." James widens his eyes, and Matt finally gets the message. So do Charlee, Lola, and the whole town.

I turn to Charlee as I walk away. "Text me if you need anything, okay?"

"Okay!"

Matt blows out a breath as we walk toward the house. "You are so fucked, Oli. It's way worse than I thought."

"You don't know what you're talking about." I open the front door and head for the kitchen. "What are we gonna eat anyway? I didn't have time to go grocery shopping. Maybe we should order something."

James sits at the kitchen table, Matt in tow. "Lola stopped by and left some stuff in your fridge this morning. You know how she is when you come back from trips."

I open my fridge, and sure enough, I find everything I need to cook our traditional Friday night dinner.

"What did I do to deserve you guys?" I grab the potatoes, cooking cream, and grated cheese and set them on the counter.

"Is this a real question for which you want the answer?" Matt deadpans. "Because I can make you a list in two seconds."

I chuckle, fumbling in one of the drawers for the peeler. "It was rhetorical. My way of saying I'm lucky to have you in my life. Who would go grocery shopping for their friends just so they can have food after a week away?"

"Hey," James says, "you're cooking *us* dinner, so to me, it sounds like a good deal."

Matt gets up, rounding the counter. "Can we help? Or are you gonna shoo us away again because we didn't cut the potatoes the 'proper' way?" he says, taunting me. If you ask someone to *slice* the potatoes, you don't expect to find them in cubes.

"Just sit your asses down, okay?" I get the steaks out of the fridge, add salt and pepper, and slide them onto a pan in the oven on low heat.

"Charlee's nice," James says, not bothering with subtlety. "How was it, seeing her?"

I keep my focus on peeling the potatoes and say, "Like someone knocked me unconscious over and over again. I still can't believe she's actually here. How many times have we talked about this?"

"Honestly? More times than I think is healthy," Matt says. When I give him a look, he adds, "Oh. Rhetorical again, sorry."

"Remember two weeks ago when I was helping you set up your stand for the Autumn Festival?" I ask Matt, and he nods. "I was trying to write a letter to her, and I couldn't come up with anything to say. You told me at that moment that I should let go, and I remember thinking that you were right."

"But then?"

"But then, a week later, I'm meeting her in the flesh for the first time in my life, and it's like everything clicked into place. Everything in me went so calm, so still, for that brief second before I freaked out, that I just knew. What were the odds, right? What were the odds that I'd finally come face-to-face with the woman I'd thought about for years? If this wasn't a sign that I should not give up on her, then I don't know what is."

Matt lets out a long whistle. "I don't know if I believe in signs, but I'll agree that it's a pretty wild coincidence. And for what it's worth, I'm happy you hung on to her, even if I thought you were crazy at times and hated watching you be so miserable." He and James exchange a look. "Seeing you pining over a woman for years when we didn't know anything about her, except for how disastrously it ended between you guys? It wasn't always easy to accept. But now we understand why. We've never seen you like this, Oli."

"Your whole face lights up when you look at her," James adds as he nods. "Hers too, for that matter."

I try not to let his read of Charlee settle too deep within me. He doesn't know her, not really. Not like I do. If only things were that easy.

I shake my head. "I'm not sure where to go from here. You should have seen how angry she was when she first saw me. I thought she was gonna rip my head off."

Matt snorts. "She sure does look feisty." He elbows James. "Don't you always say he needs someone to shake him up?"

"Sure do," James agrees. "Well, she might have been angry at first, but I'm sure she's okay now, right?"

I concentrate on slicing the potatoes just right before dumping them into a pot of boiling water.

"Oli?" James insists. "Tell me you guys had a talk about it. She knows what happened, right?"

He doesn't need to say it for me to understand. They were all there when it happened. They all waited with me for days, taking turns on Oliver watch.

I brace my hands on the counter and let out a defeated sigh. "We haven't talked yet, no."

"*What?*" The chair creaks under Matt's weight. Next to him, James frowns but stays silent. "How has it never come up? Weren't you together twenty-four seven?"

"We were, but she deliberately said at the beginning that she didn't want to talk about it, and I respected her choice. And we were *just* about to broach the subject when Lola banged on the door earlier."

James and Matt exchange a look before he says, "Oli. You have to tell her."

Charlee

"How did that happen?" Lola asks, nodding toward my ankle.

It's just the two of us sitting in the red Muskoka Chairs on Oliver's deck, sipping our beers while watching the sun set on the lake. I could get used to this view. I could get used to a lot of things here, I realize.

"Fell into the river." I grimace. "Oliver pulled me out."

She hums as if to say "Doesn't surprise me."

"*What?*"

I whirl toward the booming male voice coming from inside the house.

Lola snorts and shakes her head as she brings the bottle to her lips. "Ignore Matt. He can be a bit over-the-top sometimes."

"I noticed. Quite the opposite of Oliver."

"True. But they love each other the most. Oli helped Matt through his first heartbreak a few years ago. They, uh . . ." She glances at me furtively. "They both dealt with it at the same time and got through it together."

Unease claws at me. I don't want to know that. I don't want to know that Oliver fell in love with someone else and had his heart broken.

"That's good that they had each other, then," I say, a bit more harshly than I intended.

"Yeah, it was. Matt decided after that disaster that he'd throw himself into what he loves. He quit his job and opened a flower shop. Took us all by surprise, but damn if it's not the best thing that happened to him. And Oli was there almost every day. He made all the stands for the flowers in the store."

My brow rises. "I didn't know Oliver made furniture." As far as I knew, he dabbled a bit in woodworking with his grandfather, but furniture? That's a whole other level.

"Oh, he does," Lola says. "He made the bookshelves for the bookstore too. He loves carpentry. I think he loves it even more so now that Jerry isn't here anymore."

I finish my beer, then start pulling off the damp label. "He told me about his grandpa and how much time they spent in the shed." I touch the base of my neck, feeling the necklace beneath my fingers.

She nods, her eyes lost in the distance. "Hours and hours. It's different now. But when he needs to take his mind off things, that's where he goes. Do you want to see it?"

I cast a hesitant glance toward the cabin. It sounds like the woodshop is a special place for Oliver, and I'm not sure he'd like me there, especially without him. I get the feeling I'd be crossing an invisible boundary that I shouldn't be crossing.

Lola seems to read my thoughts. "He won't mind. Don't worry."

"Are you sure? I don't want to make him uncomfortable."

"I'm sure." She gets up. "Come on."

I pick up my crutches and walk with Lola to the workshop. She pushes the burgundy door with a grunt. "I keep telling Oliver to change this freaking door because it's so . . . damn . . . heavy."

Finally, the door slides all the way open and reveals a large room covered in wood dust and littered with machinery I can't name. Dozens of chairs and tables and furniture of all kinds are crammed into the space. I move closer, running my finger along the dusty surfaces. The furniture looks like it's been stored there for years, but the lack of wear suggests otherwise.

On one of the machines lies a long wooden plank with *Oli's* engraved in thick cursive letters.

"What's that?" I ask, not sure if Lola is close enough to hear me.

She comes to stand next to me. "Oliver's unfinished project."

I frown. "Is he changing the name of Jerry's?"

It's Lola's turn to look confused. "What do you mean?"

"Isn't it a new sign for the restaurant?"

Lola presses her lips together.

"What?" I ask when she doesn't say anything.

"Not my place to say." She shakes her head, mumbling something I don't catch. "I really think you should talk to Oliver, Charlee. Seems like there's a lot you don't know."

"I don't understand." I don't speak riddles, and I don't see how a piece of wood with his name on it requires a conversation. It's been a long day, I'm tired, and my patience is running thin. So it's no surprise that my answer came out a tad curt. And from the way Lola's mouth twists downward, it seems like we're both veering toward irritation.

"I have known Oliver for a long time, Charlee, and believe me when I tell you that he's only ever loved a handful of people in his life. But there's one person in particular he's never been able to move on from. And it's been eating at me every day to see him hang on to someone who didn't love him enough to reach out to him and try to understand what happened in his life." Her eyes soften, even though she delivered a solid blow right to my gut. "I'm sure you're a good person if Oliver couldn't let you go, but I'll be Team Oli forever, no matter how amazing you seem to be. And the man over there"—she nods toward his house—"is worth fighting for a hell of a lot more than you have so far."

I'm too stunned to speak. So Lola goes in for the kill.

"Do you know why Oliver wasn't in Calgary to meet you five years ago?" She takes a step forward and places her hand on my upper arm, squeezing once. "We all have our demons and reasons for not wanting to dredge up the past, but this might just be one of those times when it's worth experiencing the pain and reliving the unhappy memories, if only for the chance to rewrite parts of them."

She pats my arm and walks away. And I stay there, on a precipice, contemplating for the first time in five years if I should make the jump.

Toronto, July 30, 2018

I've been asking myself for weeks now what happened on June 21st. I've been trying to solve the equation by myself, thinking I didn't need to write to you to understand.

At first, I thought that you had booked the flight on the wrong date and I had misunderstood somehow. But I brought all your letters with me to Calgary because I was so excited to show them to you, and sure enough, the date was right. Maybe you hit a snag on the road that delayed you. That was my second thought. And then, after I tracked down each flight coming in from Vancouver and spent all my waking hours at that terminal before coming back alone to the hotel, my hope that you'd show up started to fade. On the fourth day, I packed my bags and left.

What the fuck, Oliver? What. The. Fuck?

I've spent the last month banging my head against the wall and trying to figure out why you never showed up. Did something happen to you? Why haven't you written to me since?

Of course, there's a simple explanation that I've refused to admit to myself, but as I write this last letter to you, I have no choice but to face the harsh truth: I was just a pastime, a class to pass. And why not have a little fun in the process, right?

I hate myself for writing you this letter, Oliver. I've tried so hard to solve this on my own, to move on and be strong, but to no avail. Riley gently encouraged me to start putting my words down. She says it will help me turn the page. She's the one who picked me up at the airport when I got back. She was rooting for us so badly. I don't think I've ever cried this much in front of my sister. Poor thing didn't know how to console me.

Did I dream our story? Did I make it more than it really was? For the first time in my life, I thought I'd found a best friend and a love that transcended all reason and space. Not only someone who understood me but who truly saw the person I longed to be.

I gave you my trust. I gave you my heart. I gave you <u>my soul</u>.

I should have known better. I won't make that mistake twice.

Since you've never written back to me, I don't hold out much hope that you'll take the time to reply, nor do I necessarily want you to. Maybe you won't even open the envelope when you see my handwriting, or maybe Emile won't deliver it. Was that a lie too? Does the French mailman really exist, or did you make him up?

What does it matter anyway?

All that's left is to wish you a good life. In my dreams, we lived it together. In my dreams, we met, and everything finally made sense. Everything clicked into place. In my dreams, you didn't break my heart. No, you held it in the palm of your hand like the most precious prize on this miserable earth.

I wish I could say I wish you the best, Oliver, but I'm not there yet.

But I can say without a shadow of a doubt that I loved you. And I wish you had loved me too.

Goodbye.

Charlee

CHAPTER TWENTY-FIVE

Moon

Charlee

For the rest of the evening, Lola's words echoed in my head like a song I couldn't get rid of.

After managing to unscrew my feet from the floor of Oliver's workshop, I joined the group in the kitchen as if nothing had happened. Lola was all smiles, and when I came in, she threw a gentle, understanding look my way without anyone else noticing. Only Oliver paused as I walked past Lola and James to sit in one of the living room chairs. There were no hard feelings between Lola and me. I held none, and I knew she didn't either. And yet her words kept running over and over in my mind.

Dinner was a relaxed and cozy affair. Everyone sat around the table and shared the wonderful meal Oliver prepared. Something stirred in me when I saw him look so comfortable, so laid-back, with one leg crossed over the other, his arm draped over my seat as he tilted his head back and laughed openly at something James said. So at ease that he didn't shy away from my gaze when I caught him quietly looking at me as Matt was telling us all about the flock of fifty-something women who kept strolling past his stall at the weekly Pine Falls Farmers' market, batting their eyelashes at him, not minding that their husbands were a few feet behind them.

I have no intention of letting that feeling go.

Yet I couldn't shake the incessant need to talk to him. I needed to talk to him now.

So when, around ten p.m., Lola not so subtly hinted that she and the guys needed to leave us alone, I almost breathed a sigh of relief that was heard across town.

"It was nice meeting you, Charlee," Matt says, bringing me into a hug. "Take good care of him, okay?"

I nod, swallowing down the emotions I feel at Matt's approval, and say goodbye to Lola and James.

"I'll walk you guys out," Oliver says before turning to me. "I'll be right back."

And I understand what he's not saying. That even if we're tired, even if it would probably be better to wait until tomorrow, we're having this conversation tonight.

I pick up the glass of wine Oliver poured for me during dinner and walk around the living room using one crutch. I've never seen a house with so many bookshelves. Even here, the walls are literally lined with dozens and dozens of books on wooden shelves that are reminiscent of the stunning beams that decorate the ceiling. Has he read them all? How many hours has he spent stretched out on his couch by the fire, dreaming of imaginary worlds?

I could get used to being here, I think. Reading, enjoying the peace and quiet of his house, watching the rain fall outside through the big windows of his bedroom while I take a nice, hot bath. And why not have him find me like this one evening when he comes home from work? I wouldn't mind.

My thoughts are interrupted by my phone buzzing in my pocket. I put my glass down on one of the shelves and fish my phone out. I roll my eyes when I see the name.

"I thought I told you I wasn't reachable for two weeks."

"And yet here you are, on the phone with me," my sister says. "I just wanted to check in, see how you were."

I frown. "What do you mean?"

"PR is a big world—a gossipy one, at that—and we get mixed in with lawyers a lot. I've heard rumblings and rumors about something happening with MNL and *WP*. I got worried."

"Yeah, well, do not freak out."

"Of course not," Riley says with a hint of panic in her voice. "Especially when you ask me not to like that."

"I hurt myself. Nothing bad, I promise. Just a bruised ankle. But we had to come back earlier than planned, and the filming stopped. We're waiting to see where it'll go, but from what I've heard, nowhere good."

"Did you get your ankle checked?"

I roll my eyes again. "*That's* what you focus on? Yes."

"Good. Yeah, it doesn't bode well for a peaceful resolution. MNL has solid lawyers too. If Ben needs any help, let me know. I can put him in contact with some good friends."

"I will, thank you. Listen, I gotta go. Oliver's friends are here."

"Who?"

Oh, yeah. I forgot she doesn't know.

"Erm . . . long story. Remember Oliver from college? So, he's a journalist for *WP* too and was assigned the project I'm on. Lots to talk about, huh? Okay, bye!"

"Charl—"

I hang up, text her two kiss emojis, and slip my phone back into my pocket. I would have been on the phone for hours if I hadn't cut the conversation short, and I don't feel like having a full dissection of the situation I'm in without having had a chance to talk it through with Oliver first.

Seeing as how he's still out front saying goodbye to his friends, I continue my tour around the room, noting the alphabetical order in which the books are arranged. Bookshelves become drawers and cabinets, the fronts of which are tastefully decorated with swirls of wood carvings. No doubt Oliver's work, which surely means he made everything here.

I survey the space in utter disbelief. I never knew his little hobby had developed so much. He has real talent.

I'm about to turn around when one of the half-open drawers catches my eye. Or rather, what's inside.

Frowning, I reach out to open it—no. I shouldn't. Even though it looks an awful lot like—

No, Charlee.

I'm not going to snoop through someone else's things in their own house.

I glance at the drawer, then at Oliver, who's still chatting with Matt, James, and Lola at the front door.

Fuck it.

I pull on the drawer, opening it wider.

"What . . .?" My fingers shake as I take the first envelope from the stack. Addressed to me. Dated a bit more than three weeks ago.

Slowly, I open the unsealed envelope, then unfold the letter.

Charlee, this will be the last letter, and after five years, I think it's time to call it quits, don't you think?

I scan the rest of the words. "What the fuck is this?"

Dropping the letter, I rummage through the pile of envelopes in the drawer. How many are there? Thirty? Fifty? A hundred? My heart races in my chest.

April 20, 2023.

February 3, 2023.

October 14, 2022.

May 6, 2021.

All these letters were never sent. All addressed to me.

And it goes on and on back to . . .

My stomach plummets to my feet. Back to July 10th, 2018.

What kind of sick joke is this? Tears blur my vision as I try my best to pull the letter out with my shaking hands.

Dear Charlee,

I don't know where to start, what to say, or how to begin to apologize. Right now, you're probably back home, and I realize now that I don't know where "home" is when you're not staying at your dorm address. And it's driving me crazy to think about you waiting for me when I . . .

God, Charlee, where do I even start?

I cry openly, my tears falling onto the paper. To hell with it. Let them ruin it for all I care. My eyes continue to scan the words as I furiously wipe my cheeks.

I wanted to meet you so badly. I was packed and ready to go. Lola was set to give me a lift to the airport. I knew I was hours away from meeting the love of my life. And then everything was ruined. My entire life has crumbled, and what's left now lies in ashes.

Tears that aren't mine already stain the paper. My thumb grazes the letter as if it can feel the sadness through the years.

*And even though you're probably furious, I hope you'll find it in
yourself to forgive me once I—*

"What are you doing?"

I whirl around to find Oliver staring at the letter in my
hand. "What is this?" I breathe, raising the letter in my fist.
"*What is this, Oliver?*"

He moves forward, palms up as if he knows the wrong
step, the wrong word, could make me bolt. "It's a letter,
Charlee. That I've been holding on to for years." He's close
enough now that I notice his damp eyes. "Please," he rasps, and
moves another step closer. I take one back.

I don't have a damn clue what he's pleading for. All I want
is for him to start talking. Start explaining why he left me at
a fucking airport terminal alone and dared to continue to
write to me.

Who does that?

I slam the letter against the edge of the bookshelf. "Where
did you go on June twenty-first? Why did you never show up,
Oli? Never try to contact me? Do you have any idea what it
was like for me to wait for you for *days*, only to realize you'd
never come? To have thought I meant something to you
when, in truth, I was nothing but someone to pass the time
with and discard at the first chance you got?"

I'm shouting now, but I don't care. I'm being unfair, but I
don't care.

The dam has finally burst, and my anger needs out.

Guess I'm regressing to the second stage of grief, or maybe
I never truly accepted the loss. Because I *did* lose him—and a

piece of myself with him. Being with him for the past week has made me realize that, and I hate it. He had no right to take that from me. No right at all.

He drags a hand down his face, and when he speaks, I shudder from the coldness of his voice. "Get in the truck."

"*What?*"

The next step he takes has him almost flush against me, towering over me in a way that makes my knees buckle. He grips my waist, holding me firmly upright. "You want to know why I never came? You want to know why I let slip the only chance to meet the woman I love more than anything?" His eyes search mine frenetically. "Get. In. The. Truck."

I gulp my pride down at being ordered what to do and don't say anything back.

He lets go of me and strides to the front door, grabbing his jacket and wrenching the door open. "Are you coming? Yes or no?"

His display of anger takes me by surprise, but I guess everyone has buttons that can be pushed. Maybe I hurt him. Maybe he didn't like what I said. Fine. If we're keeping score, he still has a long way to go to match what he dealt me.

"Yes." I lean on my crutch as I walk to him and take the jacket he hands me.

Let's get this over with, once and for all.

CHAPTER TWENTY-SIX

Would That I

Oliver

The drive to the restaurant is dead silent except for my fingers drumming on the wheel the whole time.

Nothing but someone to pass the time with.

That she could think that after all we shared.

Beside me, Charlee keeps her attention on the road too, dodging every glance I occasionally throw her way. I shouldn't have snapped at her at the house, but that comment? Was she trying to hurt me, or does she really think that? Whatever the case, her daring to reduce our relationship to that gets my blood boiling. She has no right to do that. She can be angry, disappointed, or sad all she wants, and she can take it out on me, but not on what we had. I won't let her do that.

I park my truck across from the restaurant and turn off the engine.

"What are we doing here?"

"This," I point to the newly renovated building with the For Sale sign, "used to be Jerry's."

Her eyes narrow. "What do you mean 'used to be'?"

You can do this, Oli. What's one more time reliving it when you've already done it a hundred times?

I look up at the brand-new building. "A few years ago, Pine Falls endured one of the worst fires in its history. A tourist camped nearby and started a fire, despite warnings of extreme heat and a ban on campfires given the drought. It caught in a blaze and spread all the way to town. It took the fire fighters several weeks to extinguish it completely. There was a lot of damage, and many people lost their homes and businesses. Including my grandparents." The lump in my throat grows tighter, so I pause for a moment before continuing, "Because Jerry's was a staple of Pine Falls tourism, the building was rebuilt exactly as it was."

It's just not mine anymore. My greatest shame. So close. I'd been so close.

"When did Jerry's burn down, Oliver?" She looks at me, horror in her eyes. She knows when. She understands. So why does she need me to say it out loud? What difference does it make?

Charlee grabs my arm and squeezes hard. "*When?*"

"June twentieth," I say as I look at her, soft and full of regret, and rest my hand on top of hers.

"Twenty eighteen," she whispers, like she didn't want to believe it, tears rolling freely down her cheeks.

I nod, not a sound breaching the knot in my throat, and bring my thumb to her face to brush away her tears, until my finger becomes as damp as her face. "Jerry and Carol were sleeping when the building caught on fire." I fight to get the words out, still stroking her cheek. "I wasn't home that night. I'd been with James, Lola, and Matt. I was seeing you the next day and needed to be with my friends because I was *so* nervous. I'd never been that nervous in my whole life."

"Oh, Oli . . ."

"I wasn't there, Charlee. I wasn't there. If I'd been home, maybe I would have been able to smell the fire and wake them up. But I wasn't there."

Years of therapy taught me that "what if" and "if I had done this or that" were futile and only served to torture me further. They don't change the outcome and only add weight to the excruciating guilt I still carry.

Twin tears spill from my own eyes, so I rest my head against hers, my hand still cupping her face, as she drags her hand across the back of my neck and clings to me.

"It's okay, Oli, I'm here."

I nod, breathing her soothing scent into the deepest parts of my soul. "They woke up to thick, dense smoke," I say, unable to control the tremors in my voice. "They made it to the hospital, where they called me. Matt drove me there and stayed with me the whole night while my grandparents got tests done. The tests showed that their lungs were destroyed because of how much smoke there had been in the house.

They . . ." Five fucking years later, and I still struggle to say it. "They passed away the same night from smoke inhalation."

I bite down a sob at the memories of that night. Everything I had, everything I loved, went up in literal flames.

I drop my hands to my lap, but before I can fall apart, Charlee slips her hand from my neck to my jaw and tilts my head up to meet her green eyes, shining with tears. "None of it is your fault. You hear me? *None* of it."

The gentleness in her voice could bring me to my knees if I wasn't already sitting down. I've never heard her use that tone, yet I feel like I've always known it.

"It's hard for me to remember that sometimes," I whisper.

My grandparents, the restaurant, Charlee.

Loss after loss after loss.

All in the span of twenty-four hours.

And every time, a common denominator: should have been there, should have bought it back, should have made it to her.

Could've, would've, should've.

Enough to press on my chest and knock the air out of my lungs on bad days.

"Look at me, Oli," Charlee says, keeping her index finger under my chin. Her eyes soften, like a featherlight brush on my cheek. "I'm sorry. I'm *so* sorry."

Tears well up again in her eyes and trigger mine. "I'm so sorry," she repeats until her sobs and the words blend into one. She drops my chin to clutch the jacket at my shoulders, her tiny, fragile body shaking with her heaving breaths.

"You couldn't have known, sweetheart." I hold her tight against me as my hand sweeps down and up her back. Her tears mixed with mine soak my jacket and break my heart a thousand times over.

When she pulls away after a moment, her eyes search mine, questioning, full of hesitation and doubt. My gaze drifts to her lips long enough to provide the answer to her question.

Slowly, her lips brush mine in invitation. I kiss her, this time more fervently, my hands cupping her face and drawing her even closer, as if this might be the only kiss I'll have the chance to steal. Something in me breaks. The last rampart collapses and lets everything through. No corner of my body is spared by the surge of raw emotions wreaking havoc from within. Sadness, grief, shame. These I'm used to. But not the almost painful relief of kissing Charlee. Finally. As if my body has been deprived of it for so long, knowing it needs her lips, her taste, her warmth to be whole.

Her answer is swift and feverish. She drops all pretense and presses her mouth to mine as though our tomorrow isn't promised. Our lips part, and I taste the salt of our tears mingling with the delicious sweetness of her tongue against mine, inhaling her sugared scent until the world around us blurs.

I didn't know how much I needed her lips until she laid them on mine. How much the soft ways in which she kisses me would patch the holes left by my guilt. How much her mouth would ease the pressure that's existed in my chest since that dreadful night.

I blamed myself for not making it to her, for leaving her in the dark for so long, for making her believe she didn't mean anything to me. And I feel her pain in every flick of her tongue. Pain for me, for herself, for what we could have been. For what I've lost. I feel the whisper of her forgiveness. Of her understanding. I feel and hear everything she doesn't say but puts into our kiss.

And that's all I need to lose myself in her.

I suck on her bottom lip, and she rewards me with a whimpering sound that alters a fundamental part of me. It rewrites my brain chemistry to make the need to hear it again my core desire. Finding other ways to get it out of her.

"Take me home," she whispers against my mouth as her fingers scrape the hair at the base of my neck. "Please."

I nod, my lips still on hers, still tasting her. "I'll take you home, Charlee," I say, pulling back. "I'll take you home and we'll talk, and if you want more, I'll give you more." I make sure she looks at me and sees how much I mean my next words. "But I need you to promise me that you won't ever say again that you were someone I passed the time with. Or I'll never forgive you for thinking yourself as meaningless to me."

Her chin wobbles, but she swallows her rising emotion and nods, stroking my cheek once. "Promise."

CHAPTER TWENTY-SEVEN

Comfortable

Charlee

A nother kind of tension fills the truck on the drive back. My body is hyperaware of every move Oliver makes, like Earth can't shake the sun's orbital pull.

The restaurant.

Guilt and shame will come, and Lola's words are already coming back to me with the strength of a slap in the face. *Oliver is worth fighting for a hell of a lot more than you have so far.*

But if I allow those feelings to pass through now, I'm not sure I'll be able to stop crying for the next five days. I'm not sure I'll be able to forgive myself for thinking the worst of him. So for the moment, all I can do is rearrange the memories, sort through the dozens of scenarios I created for myself and forget them one by one as the truth dawns on me.

Oliver didn't leave me. He didn't abandon me.

Much remains unknown, and more questions arose with his confession than I have answers to, but I can no longer question this truth.

And oddly, that's enough for me.

I don't need all the details. I don't need all the answers. Not right now. Not when the only thing I allow myself to feel is my need for him and how right it felt to kiss him. Not when all I can think about is how to get his lips on mine again. Fast.

"Almost there," Oliver says, eyes on the road, and I don't know whether he said that to me or to himself. I can't tell if he's sensing my restlessness or if he's just as on the edge as I am.

He nearly trips out of his truck when we arrive at the house but grabs the door before he hits the ground face-first.

I stifle a laugh. "Take your time. I'm not going anywhere."

Still, he's next to me in a flash, opening my door. He unfastens my seat belt as if I can't do it myself, then hoists me out of my seat. "Aren't you?"

I wrap my hands around his neck, holding his gaze. "No."

I'm not entirely sure how many layers there are to this no, or how many I want there to be. All I care about is the heat of his body against mine, that feeling I've been dying to know for years. Everything else can wait.

Oliver's lips slowly stretch into a smile. "I like the sound of that."

I laugh, pushing his shoulder gently, but it only makes him tighten his hold on me. "It's unfair. I'm not thinking clearly right now. You can literally make me say or do whatever the hell you want."

His eyes travel to my lips in a dare. "Yeah? That kinda makes me want to try it. See for myself."

"Do your worst," I breathe, my thighs clenching.

"If you insist."

He crashes his lips against mine as he kicks open the front door and bolts to the kitchen, where he sets me down on the counter and wraps my legs around his waist. I gasp as every inch of his solid body molds against mine. I feel his hardness everywhere, *especially* there. And all I can think about is that I'm kissing Oliver.

I'm kissing Oliver.

"I don't know where to start." He trails a flurry of kisses down my neck while his hands grip my waist, keeping me close to him. I'm just a rag doll in his arms, waiting for him to play with me for hours. "So many possibilities." He nibbles my earlobe, and I whimper. "So much power you've just given me, Charlee." His hands slip under his sweater I'm still wearing, toying with the shirt underneath. "Could drive a weaker man to madness." His hot breath skitters along my jaw until he reaches my lips again, hovering over them. "Not me, though. No. I can handle it. I'll show you how worthy of you I am."

"Please," I whisper, tugging on his shirt collar and bringing him down to me.

My lips meet his teeth as he laughs against my mouth. I open for him, and the feel of my tongue colliding with his puts an abrupt end to his teasing.

"Can I touch you?" he asks. Pleads.

"I thought I told you I was yours to command."

His eyes turn a dangerous shade of dark. "Just making sure."

He presses his hands on my ass and slides me to the edge of the countertop. I yelp and tighten my legs around his waist.

"I can't see you with this thing on." He grabs the hem of the sweatshirt and pulls it over me, throwing it somewhere in the room.

My shirt is next, then his, and suddenly, he pauses, his throat bobbing. And I understand. I'm in the same state of wonder. Of shock. How many times have I pictured his chest beneath my hands? And now that he's right in front of me . . .

"My dreams do not come close to doing you justice," he tells me, echoing my own thoughts.

Gently, the very opposite of his urgency a few minutes ago, he lets his hands run down my arms in an impossibly tender touch. A thousand shivers riddle my skin, and I wouldn't have thought of it twice if it weren't for the fact that a simple caress has never aroused me so quickly or so much.

It's him, my body seems to say. *It's always been him*.

His fingers wander back up my arm, running over my shoulders and down on my collarbone. Oliver watches my immediate reaction with deadly focus, as if transfixed by how easily my body responds to him.

"Do you like that?" he asks in a breathless whisper.

"Yes."

He lets his index finger trace the curves of my breasts, dipping into the narrow path in between before stroking his thumb over my bra, applying enough pressure for the fabric to rub deliciously against my hardening nipple.

"And that?"

I moan. "Yes."

Oliver drags the fabric down, and my breasts spill out. I feel him twitch between my legs as he sucks in a breath, then releases it, the cool air a nice relief against my burning skin.

"You're exquisite," he murmurs as he dips his head and hovers above them, my body already begging for release. Cupping my breast, he places a chaste kiss on the tip of my nipple. "Simply exquisite."

"Oliver . . ." I groan impatiently.

He lifts his head enough for me to read the undiluted lust in his eyes. "I've had five years to fantasize a thousand times over what it would be like to touch you, to kiss you, to taste you. To just *see* you. So I'm gonna need a minute. Let me savor it."

He lowers his head again and closes his mouth around my breast, sucking on my hardened peak while his right hand gets busy with my other nipple. The growl that bubbles in his throat sends a pang straight to my core, and my legs clench around his waist in a desperate attempt to get some relief.

I find my grip in his hair and revel in the softness of it between my fingers.

Nothing will ever feel as good as this. Nothing ever did. I don't need to tell him anything; he knows what makes me squirm, and that's why he lays his tongue flat on my nipple, giving it a few flicks before licking it so thoroughly I cry out.

"Please!" I'm so close to my release. "Please, Oliver."

"I'm right here, sweetheart," he says into my skin. "I'll always be right here next to you."

His lips leave my chest, and he slides his hands up to cup my face. He finds my mouth once more, pouring all of his devotion into this one kiss.

"Lie down," he says.

I obey, a thousand goose bumps pebbling my skin at his order.

Oliver smooths a hand down my stomach until it reaches the waistband of my leggings. It's unfair, really, to see him still dressed when I know he'll have me naked in a minute.

He bends down and presses a kiss to my hip bone. "Can I take these off?" His voice is low and ragged, as if the mere thought has him struggling to breathe.

"Yes."

My head thumps on the counter as Oliver drags my leggings and underwear down my legs so slowly that my heart flutters in my chest like it's about to flatline. I need him. Now.

"You're torturing me," I whine.

"But isn't it the best kind?" His mouth moves south, but still not where I want it to go. Where I *need* him to go. "The anticipation." Another kiss lower. "The guessing." Lower. "The thrill."

He grasps my thighs and pushes them up against my stomach, baring me fully to him. I'm vaguely aware of a curse falling from his lips, but the open-mouthed kiss he presses against my inner thigh drowns out everything else around me.

"Relinquish control," he hums, and merely grazes my center with the tip of his nose, inhaling. A ghost touch, that's what it is, and I need more. So much more. "Goddamn, Charlee. Vanilla and peaches are quickly becoming my new favorite flavors. I want it all over me."

"Oliver, *please*." My pulse is racing through every inch of my body, my blood drumming through my veins and swirling to that bundle of nerves desperately waiting to be stroked.

"I love when you beg, sweetheart. I could hear you do it for hours. Tease you until that's all you do. Beg me. You don't understand the kind of power I feel having the woman that you are begging for me."

He exhales, kissing me softly *right* there. I choke out a moan of frustration and try to wiggle myself closer, but his fingers burrow deeper into my skin and stop me from getting the relief I need.

"Unfortunately, this sort of torture goes both ways, Charlee. And if I don't taste you on my tongue in the next few seconds, I'll go fucking insane."

He lowers his mouth and takes my clit between his lips, sucking greedily. The sensation runs through me so thoroughly that I let out a loud gasp, my eyes rolling to the back of my head. All the teasing he's lavished on me peaks at that exact moment, my clit like a simmering volcano on the verge of an eruption.

God, he knew what he was doing a minute before, but this? No more thoughts cross my mind as he worships my body and flicks his tongue over me with the devotion of a man eating his last meal.

"Fuck, Charlee, I can't get enough," he growls against me, and I buckle under the vibrations rumbling through me. He looks up at me and presses my thighs wide. The pure, unfiltered arousal in his gaze could have been my undoing if it weren't for his next words.

"Will you come on my tongue? Can you do that for me, sweetheart?"

I nod, swallowing a whimper at the absurdity of his request, because those words alone, the way he looks at me with a hunger I've never seen on any other man or woman's face, could make me climax on the spot.

Oliver grins. "That's my girl."

Oh god.

He dips his head again, licking me thoroughly, and when I think I can't handle anything more, he adds the pressure of his thumb to his tongue and pushes one finger inside me.

My body gives out.

I grab a fistful of his hair as I burst on his tongue and use his face to ride the wave of the orgasm shattering through me. My back arches, but he holds me in place, sucking every drop I give him, guiding me until my vision no longer blurs and my surroundings start to appear again.

Oliver softly kisses my navel before he straightens and bends over my spent body.

"Hey," he whispers, brushing my sweaty bangs out of my face. "You okay?"

The adoration on his face melts something deeply unyielding in my chest. "Of course I am." I bring his wrist to my lips and place a small kiss there. "I'm more than okay. You, on the other hand . . ." I rise up on my elbows, eyeing the erection tenting his pants.

He drops his gaze there too, palming himself. "I don't mind. Don't worry."

"I want to."

He lets go of his crotch and pulls me to him, my breasts pressing against his naked chest, and I moan at the burning feeling rising inside me again as I wrap my arms around his neck. He feels so thick between my thighs.

"Believe me, me too." His hands glide along my sides, the rough pads of his fingers scraping my bare skin. "Especially when you make those little sounds. But we've had a very, very long day, and we're both exhausted. We need to get some rest."

He nibbles the soft place below my ear before he whispers, "Besides, I plan on taking the entire day tomorrow to learn everything about you—and have your mouth on every single inch of me."

I tighten my hold on him, refusing to give him the satisfaction of seeing my face aflame. God, this sounds like something I can definitely get on board with. "Excellent plan."

Oliver chuckles. "Come on, let's get you to bed."

I let him lift me up, my legs around his waist, and carry me to my bedroom entirely naked in his arms, as if there's nothing more natural than allowing him to see every bit of me without filter, without makeup, without disguise. I bury my head in the hollow of his neck, breathing in the pine-and-musk scent that has become so familiar, and let my hands explore the sturdiness of his shoulders and his back.

"Tomorrow, Charlee," Oliver grunts, his bulge still heavy between my legs.

"Sorry," I say, hiding my smile in his neck.

I'm not sorry at all.

He opens the door to the bedroom I stay in and sets me down on the bed before he unfolds the covers and motions for me to get under them. "Come on."

I don't know why, but I'm suddenly gripped by the overwhelming urge not to let him go. I'm afraid that I'll wake up alone tomorrow and none of this will have happened, and I'd still be a woman without answers. A woman who wouldn't know what to make of the man in front of her.

I can't go back to that.

"Sleep with me tonight. In here."

His brows crease. "What?"

"Don't make me ask twice. Please, Oli. Just sleep, nothing more. I promise."

"Are you sure?"

I see the surprise in his eyes. It's as if spending the night next to each other crosses an even more intimate line than sex. And deep down, it does, especially to him. I'm not stupid. What we just did wasn't just about releasing any sort of tension between us, and one of the reasons he didn't want me to touch him is probably because he's still assessing which way things will turn out, whether I'm actually going to stick around. If he can give me all of himself. Sex holds a lot of meaning for him, and I get that. He wants to protect himself, and that's perfectly fine.

I know it, and he knows it, but neither of us says it.

"I'm sure," I say and try to convey my certainty in my voice. "Please stay."

He bends toward me and cups my face. "Of course I'll stay if you want me to, sweetheart. Anything you want. Always."

"You mean that?" I murmur, another kind of emotion rising in my chest, one I haven't felt in so long I can't even find a name for it.

"Every word." He spies the goose bumps on my skin. "Come on, you're gonna catch a cold. Under the covers. Now."

I laugh and do as I'm told and take the left side of the bed, careful not to put too much weight on my ankle, although the pills they prescribed me at the hospital have been doing wonders for the pain.

Silently, I watch as Oliver strips off his pants, and I get an unobstructed view of his perfect, biteable ass. His fingers hesitate at the waistband of his boxers. He turns to me, chuckling when I avert my eyes.

"It's okay. I don't mind you looking. I, um . . . I usually sleep with nothing on. Is that okay with you?"

"Of course," I say. In reality, I'm screaming inside. I know I said we were only going to sleep, but Oliver seems hellbent on testing me tonight.

I turn off the light before I can get a glimpse of any parts of him I haven't yet discovered.

The covers rustle beside me, and a second later, I feel the warmth of his body inches from mine.

"Can I hold you?" he asks softly.

"Please."

The weight of his arm settles on my waist as he wraps it around my belly and tugs me close.

"Sorry about that," he says as his cock grows hard against my ass. "I can't control or hide the effect you have on me."

I caress his arm with my fingertips. "Don't worry about that. I like it."

He hums and places a kiss in my hair. "I like it too."

It occurs to me then, before sleep sweeps me away, that we're lying in the same position as we were a few nights before in the tent. And yet everything is so different.

CHAPTER TWENTY-EIGHT

Evermore

Oliver

I wake at eight o'clock to the sound of birds chirping in the trees and to Charlee at my side, her chest rising and falling in soft, sleepy sighs.

I blink, chasing sleep away from my drowsy eyelids, or possibly because I can't believe what happened last night. What's happening right now. It's like living in a daydream, as if the last five years never happened, as if I didn't spend them writing hundreds of letters that I never sent.

I wasn't sure how she was going to react to the reason I never showed up, why I let her down. It could have gone either way, really. Sure, she'd have understood, who wouldn't have? But my absence left scars, whether I like it or not, some too deep for even the most reasonable of explanations to heal. How many exist or whether they can be erased, I don't know.

Time might do the trick, if she gives it to us. Yet when I look at her, so peaceful, so in need of me, a glimmer of hope that all isn't lost kindles in the depths of my soul.

She hasn't moved all night. She's still in my arms, her back against my chest, stark naked.

My gaze roams down her coppery hair, her ribs, her hips, uncovered by the sheets. The rest is cloaked in covers, but my mouth and tongue remember perfectly what lies beneath. Have already mapped out every detail of what she liked so I can do it all over again tonight. And the day after that. For as long as she'll let me.

Charlee stirs, stretching like a cat before pushing her ass into my now unmistakable hard-on. "Well, good morning to you too," she mumbles.

"Good morning, sweetheart," I whisper into the nape of her neck.

I didn't think she could smell even sweeter, but the warmth that radiates from this particular spot in the morning is a concentrated shot of serotonin that will run through my nervous system for the rest of the day. I could get used to this. And I don't know if I should entertain that thought without putting my heart on the line.

"I don't mind getting woken up like this every day." She turns until her face is nuzzled in my chest.

I don't think she realizes what she's saying. What those words do to me. To my heart.

Say the word and I'm yours, Charlee.

"I'm a simple man, you know." I stroke her hair. "Just holding you like this, I'm content."

Her hand travels down my chest, my waist. She stops a few inches above my cock, as if asking for permission. "I wouldn't mind spending a few more hours in bed . . ."

A chuckle bubbles in my throat. "Trust me, I'd like nothing more than to stay right here with you, but I need to take care of a few things that unfortunately can't wait much longer." I splay my hand on her backside, gripping the soft flesh there, and draw her snugly against me.

She fits so perfectly.

"We'll pick this up when I come back, okay?"

She lifts her head and kisses my jaw. "Sounds like a plan to me. I'll go brew some coffee for you."

She moves to get up, but I tug her back to me, and she yelps.

I claim her mouth before she can say anything else. "Five more minutes."

I knew I shouldn't have gotten out of bed this morning, but my regret only grows stronger now that I'm at town hall.

"He'll be with you shortly," the receptionist says. She looks to be in her late forties, sporting thick round glasses.

"Thanks," I mutter as I drag a hand down my face.

So much has happened since we got back, and so quickly, that I haven't had time to sit down and actually process what my decision to bring Charlee back here means. In the moment, it felt like the easiest choice I'd ever made, but now that I'm about to tell Rob the news, the finality of it is sinking in.

The door swings open, and a big man with graying hair pokes his nose through. "Oliver, come in."

I exhale sharply and follow him, closing the door behind me.

Rob sits behind his desk, his fingers linked on top of his protruding stomach. "What can I do for you, Oliver? Are you finally here to make me an offer?"

I sit in the other chair. "No. I'm here to ask you to reconsider selling to Oscar."

The chair creaks when he leans in. "We've already gone over this. This deal is good for the town. It's good for business and for the people here. You know how it gets during fall and summer. We need the space for tourists, and Oscar will give us that."

"Part of the reason why we have so many tourists, Rob, is because of places like Jerry's." I rest my elbows on my legs to stop them from jiggling. "Give me a year. I know it's a lot to ask, but I can bring you the money in a year. You have my word."

Rob shakes his head. "What happened to the cash you were supposed to get really soon?"

I got my girl back, that's what happened.

I've always known she was the love of my life, even if we never uttered the words that would have spoken it into existence. But I felt it all the same. Even more so now that I know the feel of her on my body, now that her scent is imprinted all over me. She's mine and I'm hers, and there's no need for words when I feel it so deeply in my bones.

"It's a long story," I say, forcing my focus back on the mayor. "It might take longer than planned, but I'll get the money. I just need more time. Please, Rob, you know how important this is to me. You agreed. I gave you everything I could each time I had a bit of money to pay the taxes. I've been pitching in for building maintenance. You told me you'd wait. If not for me, then do it for Carol and Jerry's memory."

Shadows flash through Rob's eyes. "Look, Oliver." He holds his palm up on his desk. "Your grandparents were friends, and I've known you since before you could even walk. When I told you I'd look after it until you got your stuff together, I meant it. But I also have to look out for this town, and I'm sorry, I really am. There's nothing I can do. I have people breathing down my neck about this, and I need to make a decision soon and sell the damn place. I'm not thrilled either about Jerry's going to someone like Oscar, despite what you or the people in this town may think, but it's the only viable option I have right now. It's been on Pine Falls's finances for too long, and it needs to go. I've given you five whole years. I gave you time, kid. If you can't buy it back now, then it'll go to Oscar. My hands are tied."

I take the punch to the gut without letting it show. I failed them. Again and again. It was a long shot, but still, I held on to a glimmer of hope that I'd be able to sway him. Unfortunately, the fondness he used to harbor for my grandparents wasn't enough, and this was the last card I had to play.

"Thank you for your time, Rob," I say and get up.

He rises, meeting me at the door. "Don't beat yourself up, Oliver." He claps a big hand on my shoulder. "Eyes on the future now. Stop looking behind. You did everything you could."

"Thanks."

The door closes behind me, and with it, my family's history.

CHAPTER TWENTY-NINE

Sweet

Oliver

"Charlee?" I throw my boots in the entryway. I've only been gone a few hours, but I remember her mentioning wanting to get some fresh air, as much as she could with her ankle anyway.

"On the couch."

The mere sound of her voice loosens a few knots in my muscles. I walk over to her, finding her curled up in a blanket, a book in her hand. The sight knocks the wind out of me, and the absolute truth hits me with full force. This is her home. Nowhere else. I need her to realize that.

I swallow the rising tide of my emotions, not ready to dump them on her yet. My gaze drifts to the fireplace. I lift an eyebrow. "You lit a fire?"

She shrugs absently. "Cozier with a book."

I come closer, bracing a hand on the back of the couch, and lean over her, placing a kiss on her forehead. "How was your morning?"

"It was nice," she says, a rosy hue tinting her cheeks. She straightens from her lounging position and puts the book on the coffee table. "I walked along the lake for a bit. Oh, and I took a bath in your bedroom when I came back. I hope you don't mind. I've been dying to try it out since you showed it to me yesterday."

I've seen her naked. I've seen her come on my tongue. And yet the images of her alone in my bedroom with nothing covering her but warm water and soap set off a chain of chemical reactions in my system that flows straight down to my crotch.

"Not at all."

Charlee looks at me more intently and frowns. "What's wrong?"

"What? Nothing."

She pulls on my elbow and forces me to sit down across from her. I drape my arm over her middle. "I can see it on your face, Oli." She pokes the spot between my eyebrows. "Just here, and . . ." Her fingers skim my cheeks and caress the corner of my mouth. "Right here. I can tell, you know. You're my favorite book, and reading you is ridiculously easy. Especially when your mouth droops like that."

I twist my head and nibble her finger. She shrieks and pulls it away, giggling.

"I stopped to see Lola for a while at the bookstore, then I went to Rob's office. The mayor," I add in case she forgot.

"*Oh*, sounds very official."

"Not really. Rob has known my family for a while and, well . . ." God, where do I start? What can I say that won't riddle her with guilt or make her run away? "Remember the guy you punched at the bar when you arrived? Remember what I told you about him?"

She nods, her brows scrunching. "That he was a real estate mogul, and you hated his guts because he wanted to turn Pine Falls into Lake Tahoe 2.0?"

I smile. "Precisely. One of the buildings he's been eyeing for a while now is what used to be Jerry's."

Her frown deepens. "You're selling it?"

"No." I shake my head. "Quite the opposite. I wanted to buy it back."

"I think you've lost me here. Didn't the building go to you once . . . you know . . .?"

"Once my grandparents passed away?" I finish for her. "Yes, it did. But it was also severely damaged in the fire. The insurance money covered the repairs, but I didn't have a job at the time, didn't have anybody to provide for me either. Suddenly, I was on my own, with no family, no income, and a whole building that wasn't in great shape to take care of. So I struck a deal with Rob. Unofficially."

I should have been cleverer. Should have made him sign a contract or something. Not hope that the man who went fishing with my grandpa more times than I can count would have my best interest at heart. What's the point of having a higher-than-average intellect if I let my grief and despair make my choices?

"We agreed that the town would buy the building from me so I could use the money to provide for myself. I left a sum to Rob to cover the taxes, any needed repairs, and building maintenance. The restaurant was classified as some sort of landmark, and when I was able, I'd buy it back. I had this whole plan of renovating the building and filling it with pieces I've made myself, hiring a chef to whom I could teach the family recipes . . ."

My throat tightens, but I fight the sharp burn in my eyes. Charlee must sense it, because she runs her hand up my arm that cages her against me. "You can do it," she pushes softly.

My fingers close around hers, willing her strength to spread through me. "I've had some money set aside since, but not enough to close the deal. Especially because each year, I've used some of it to pay whatever I could in costs that the city was forking out. A few months ago, Oscar made Rob an indecent offer. Because Jerry's borders a lake with a lot of nature around, there's a lot of potential to expand for tourism. Rob saw an opportunity and has been pressing me to meet my end of the bargain we made."

"And you have nothing to back up what he told you five years ago . . ." she whispers. "What an asshole."

I shake my head. "No, Rob's not an asshole, but I see how you'd think that. He's been trying to help me out for years. *I* was the one who failed to get it back in time. I can't blame the guy for wanting to move on."

My heart starts to gallop in my chest at the thought of what comes next. The *why* behind my visit to his office today. I was so close. I turn the words over in my head, rearranging them, flipping and twisting until I can find the perfect order that won't make her bolt.

"I might have told him recently that I'd come through with enough money soon, and I asked him to give me a month. Which he accepted." I scan her face, but I see nothing but patience and her full attention. I exhale a sharp breath. *Out with it.* "That was before this whole MNL debacle. The money from the docuseries would have given me enough for a down payment, but since it's up in the air now, and I'm not sure when or if I'll ever see the money . . . With no guarantees, Rob refused to give me more time. He's selling to Oscar."

Her jaw goes slack. "Did you lose your last chance to buy your grandparents' restaurant because of *me?*" Her voice goes up two octaves on the last word.

Well, she went there fast.

I scoot closer, needing her reassuring presence against me. "You didn't make me do anything. It wasn't because of you. You have no power over the choices I make, Charlee, nor how I react to things. This is on me, and me only."

"But Oli—"

"There is no 'but.'" I lean a few inches from her lips. I search her eyes, forcing her to see what's in mine. "You're not in a better place than me in all of this. Shit happens that we can't always predict, and not everything goes according to plan. I'll live. It's a hard one to swallow, I'll give you that, but I'll live. And besides . . ." My thumb strokes her cheek as I graze my lips over hers. "I choose you every time, sweetheart. You over everything else. Forever and always."

"Come here." She hooks her fingers behind my neck and pulls me down the last inch left between us until our lips meet and her warmth fills my mouth. I crush my weight on her as I angle my head so I can take her deeper, relishing the way our tongues dance, just as our souls have been intertwined since our pen-pal years.

It's life-changing and world-bending, and everything in me snaps into existence at the touch of her lips on mine. There's nothing remotely ordinary about this kiss, not when I feel the last walls of her fortress crumble as her fingers claw at me and pull me even closer, as if she's trying to make up for the last five years we lost.

"Why did you never send me those letters?" Charlee asks, panting against my mouth. "Why did you never try to explain everything to me?" She kisses me again, unable to stay away too long. "I wondered for so many years what I'd done wrong. Why you never came."

I rest my forehead against hers, not letting her get an inch away from me. "And how would you have liked me to do that? You weren't staying at uni anymore, and you weren't going back. Believe me, I tried to look for you, for a long time. But you were off the grid too, and I couldn't find you anywhere on social media. I had no way to contact you, Charlee. None." I let out a bitter laugh. "Which sounds absolutely ludicrous in the times we live in, but we truly committed to the whole letter-only thing, huh?"

She chuckles too, playing with my hair between her fingers. "We did, and that's what made this so special. But in hindsight, it definitely had its downsides. What about the one I sent after we were supposed to meet? Did you get that one?"

I draw back, frowning. "You sent me another letter?"

"I did."

I pause, running through the sequence of events in my mind. The months went by, each one slower than the last, but I never received a single letter from Charlee. Actually, come to think of it . . .

"The fucker," I grunt between my teeth. "That fucking stubborn old French bastard."

"Who are—*oh*. No, he wouldn't have . . . Would he?"

I scoff. "Oh, he would have. I was staying at Matt's for a while, got my mail redirected there and gave his address directly whenever I could. But now that I think about it, I don't recall receiving one single piece of mail from my old place. Emile must have kept everything. He's retired now. Fucking finally."

Charlee bursts out laughing.

"It's not funny!"

"A little bit, though," she heaves between cackles. "Emile really didn't give two shits. I can't believe he's part of the reason why we never heard from each other again. Part of our story, in a sense. Think about it. Had he given you my letter, you would have gotten my address. We could have figured out what had happened, and we probably could have arranged to meet again once our lives calmed down." She shakes her head, incredulous. "I should be so fucking pissed at the guy, but the whole thing is so ridiculous that I can't find it in me. Aw, man, I wish I could meet him."

"Well, that can be arranged," I mumble. "He still lives in his burrow like a hermit."

Charlee's lips stretch upward, and she lays a hand on my arm. "I think we'll let a few months go by before we do. I wouldn't want you to lose your shit in his face."

My heart stumbles on her words, hope blooming in my chest faster than peonies on a hot summer day.

A few *months.*

"Wise decision. I'll send him a strongly worded letter instead."

The sound of her laugh tingles my heart. "You do that." Her eyes soften. "So that explains quite a bit . . ."

"It does." I brush her bangs to the side just so I can see all of her beautiful face. "You know, your eyes are the color of where I love to be the most."

"Where is that?"

"The forest. When I look at you, it feels like I'm there. Everything goes quiet; I breathe easier. I lose myself in those green eyes until I forget where I am. And then you smile, or you say something sassy, and I snap back into the present. Every time I look at you, you whisk me away to my favorite place. It's you. You're where I love to be the most."

I lean down and kiss her gently, her lips like feathers against mine.

When she looks at me, I catch a spark of nervousness before it disappears. "There's something I've been meaning to tell you for a long time and never had the guts or the chance to."

"And what's that?" I ask.

The air is growing thicker around us, but her body underneath me keeps me grounded and focused. I could stay like this for days. Weeks. I'll never get used to it.

"That I love you. So thoroughly and unmistakably. I've known I loved you, the person you were, your soul, before I knew what you looked like, but I didn't want to simply write it down on a piece of paper. It seemed too important to be read. I wanted you to hear it from me. I never got to say it, and I hated you for a very, very long time for it. For making me love you, for showing me what it truly meant to be loved for who I was deep inside, then disappearing—or so I thought—before I had the chance to come clean about my feelings. But now I can. I can, and I'll say it again and again, because fuck if it's not a weight off my chest to finally be able to. I love you. I love you so much, Oliver. I've never been so sure of anything else in my life."

I'm stunned into silence. My mind can't catch up with my heart, which has taken off in a sprint and is about to jump out of my chest. Words blur and tumble, tripping over each other in my mouth, and I'm left with no coherent thoughts with which to form a sentence.

I'm overwhelmed and overpowered by my emotions. It's been a long time since I've felt like this.

"Please say something," she whispers.

The worry in her voice snaps me out of it, and I blurt, "I love you. God, I love you, sweetheart. It's never been up for debate. Not even for one second. I'm sorry. I'm just processing all you've said. If someone had asked me a few months ago whether I thought you'd say that to me, I'd have told them that the most likely thing I'd get out of you would be a slap in the face. But you can read the letters I've written to you over the years. There's not a single one where I don't mention that I love you from the depths of my being. Not a single one. It's as if you were etched into my soul, into my bones. I've known for years that you were mine and I yours. Soulmates. That's what we are."

And as if the words were taking shape in the air around us, becoming tangible as they left my mouth, the bond between Charlee and me grows stronger.

"We are." She smiles and tugs me to her mouth, claiming me as completely as the words she just uttered did, only with another kind of intent. "Take me upstairs."

I smile against her mouth. "You don't have to tell me twice."

I scoop her up and almost run to my bedroom, where I lay her down on my bed. I can't get enough of this, of her in my bed.

"Come here," she moans.

"Where do you want me?"

She spreads her legs. An invitation. My knee sinks into the mattress, but my attention is drawn to something lying in the opposite corner of the bed. I freeze.

"Charlee?" Her name comes out strangled.

"Hmm?"

"What is that?"

She looks in the direction of where I nodded, and crimson splotches creep up her neck. "I cleaned it, I promise. I must have forgotten it after I took a bath."

I pick up the long, curved object with the rounded tip. "Did you use this while you took a bath? In my bedroom?" I ask, exhaling sharply as I hold the silicon magic wand in my hand.

"I did." She scrambles onto her knees, reaching to grab it, but I hold it out of range.

"Fuck. You packed a vibrator? To come here?"

"I didn't know I'd be staying at your place. I'm sorry. I shouldn't have used it here."

I inhale deeply. "Correction: you shouldn't have used it *alone*."

"*Oh*," she says coyly, and raises her eyes to me. "Do you . . . do you want to use it on me? Now?"

I stare at her incredulously. "Do I want to use it on you? Yes. Yes, I do."

A Cheshire cat smile spreads across Charlee's face, and my cock springs to attention.

"On one condition, then." She crawls on the bed until her hands reach for the waistband on my pants and start to unbutton them.

"Anything," I pant as she brings the zipper down.

"I want to take care of you while you take care of me."

"Charlee," I grunt, "I don't think I'll be able to hold it in if you—"

She palms my length through my boxers, and a growl rumbles through my chest. I lose my train of thought. "I want to. Please, Oli."

I imagine parting those plump, inviting lips with my cock, the very same ones she's currently pushing into a pout, begging me *again* to let her have her way. I can't deny her anything. But if I'm about to lose my damn mind, I might as well do it my way.

"Do you trust me?"

"Yes," she says, and the speed with which she replied makes my heart swell.

"Take me out, sweetheart."

Her breathing picks up as her fingers hook into my boxers and push them down, letting my erection pop free. She's felt me against her, but her eyes still linger in surprise on what is entirely hers, and I can't help but grin.

My gaze drops to her leggings. "My turn now, okay?"

"Okay," she says in one breath.

I help her lie back, then pull her leggings down her thighs, her knees, her calves, until they're completely off, and fling them to the floor. My eyes trip on where her underwear should have been and where, instead, I stare at her bare pussy.

"You're not wearing underwear?" The words come out strangled, tight.

Charlee looks at me, amused. "Going commando with leggings isn't unheard of. It's more comfortable like that, especially when I'm just lounging around the house."

"Are you telling me this will be a regular thing?"

Her skin turns a shade of pink darker. "Yes."

I hum, pressing my fingers deeper into the flesh of her thighs. "I hope you don't mind being bothered, then. I won't get much done if I see you in those."

Her breath hitches. "Bother me as many times as you want."

"I'll start now, if you don't mind?" I drop a kiss on her collarbone, taking a long whiff of her scent. Grabbing the edges of her sweater, I peel it off, and it soon joins her leggings on the floor.

"Absolutely stunning," I say as my lips trace the edge of the fabric of her bra. I unclasp it to reveal her perky breasts. "I want you to lie down on your back, face over there." I point to the edge of the bed.

While she moves into position, I quickly remove the rest of my clothes and pick up her magic wand. Just the idea of using it on her makes me impossibly hard and gratifies something inside me far more than my own pleasure ever could. Something different, a kind of pride in knowing that I'll be the one who gives her the release she needs. Of drawing it out of her.

"Like this?" she asks me, her head dangling slightly off the mattress.

I curl my fist around my throbbing length at the sight awaiting me: her back is arched up from the bed, her pointy breasts ready to be consumed, her beautiful, toned legs bent at the knees, and between them, her center already glistening with her arousal.

"You're perfect," I murmur as I come to stand above her.

Her gaze brimming with mischief, she flicks her tongue out and licks my balls, and the world explodes around me. It's all too much. One lick, and I'm fighting the urge to come on her beautiful face.

Fuck, this is going to be tough.

"I'll give you one minute, Charlee. One minute to do anything you want to me, and then I'll bury myself deep inside you and never come out. Are we on the same page?"

"One minute," she nods, grinning. "Start the timer."

I turn on the vibrator, the sound thrumming softly between us. The faith she puts in me is enough to make a man blind with lust. "Open up for me, sweetheart."

I don't know what it is, but she unleashes my filthiest, most primal instincts, and all I want to do is make a proper mess of her.

She wets her lips before parting them, and slowly, I slide into her warmth, groaning when she seals her lips around me and her tongue swirls around my tip. She hums, and the sound drives me out of my skin. All the muscles in my body strain from the effort not to spill into her mouth as she takes her time and draws me in deeper, inch by inch.

My head drops between my shoulders. "*Fuck*. Fuck, fuck, fuck."

In a split second of lucidity, I remember the magic wand in my hand, and with what little willpower I have left, I place the vibrator on her already engorged clit while my free hand cups her breast and pinches her nipple tight enough to pull a whimper from her lips. The sound reverberates through my cock. Without thinking, I sink deeper. Her hands find purchase on my ass as she digs her nails into my skin and holds me in place, showing me just how much she likes it when I fuck her mouth hard and fast.

"Thirty seconds," I pant, the tension already coiling down my spine as I circle the toy along her slit. Her legs start to clench together, but my hand comes flat against her inner thigh, keeping them wide open. "I want to watch when you come, sweetheart. Let me see."

Her thighs go obediently slack against my palms, and my heart threatens to give out.

"I love you so much," I breathe as I pump faster into her mouth while her legs start shaking. "Jesus, Charlee."

There are no words powerful enough to describe the hundreds of emotions that surge through my body at the speed of light, illuminating every inch of me until they burst into a beam of white light in my chest.

I have just a few more seconds before I fill her mouth, and there's no fucking way I'll allow that to happen. Not when I don't know her boundaries. Not when I want to feel her around me.

"Can you take me deeper?" I pull back enough for her to give me a pleading "yes," and I smile, rolling a rosy peak between my fingers. "You're such a good girl, Charlee. Such a good girl."

I need her to come, and fast. And judging by the way her clit pulses under the toy, she can't be far off, so I angle myself lower and nudge my cock into her mouth until it hits the back of her throat.

One.

Two.

Three thrusts.

Charlee takes everything I give her and sucks me until I lose my mind, but I don't ease the pressure I apply on her, and her legs tense around the vibrator.

"Give it to me," I grunt, teeth clenched, pushing my orgasm down, down, down.

In a flash, her muscles contract, and her body convulses beneath the brunt of her release that soaks the sheets.

"Oliver!" she cries out when I withdraw from the wet heat of her mouth and her lungs fill with the air I've deprived her of in the last few seconds.

"I'm here, I'm right here." I toss the vibrator somewhere, then lie down next to her and stroke her body until she stops shaking. "God, Charlee, that was the hottest thing I've ever done in my life." I kiss her hair, her cheeks, her mouth. "That was incredible. *You* were incredible."

She clasps her hands firmly around my face and guides me away so she can look at me. "I love you so fucking much."

I laugh and bury my face in the crook of her neck, hiding the happy moisture that dampens the corners of my eyes.

"You're not walking away this time," she says low in my ear. "This time, you come inside me."

I let out a ragged breath against her neck and shake my head as I heave myself above her. "I'm so glad you were able to come before," I say, chuckling. "Because I'm afraid this won't be my best performance."

"I don't care if you last thirty seconds or thirty minutes. I just want to feel you inside me."

"Let me get the condom. I'll be right back."

I hoist myself up, but she tugs me down, and I have to brace my hands on either side of her so I don't come crashing down on her.

I chuckle. "Not that the idea of getting you pregnant isn't tempting, but I'd rather we wait a while so I can enjoy having you all to myself for a bit."

"Not that I don't like the thought of carrying your babies one day, but I have an IUD, and I'm clear about everything else. If you are too, then I don't want anything between you and me. Not anymore."

I shut down the images of Charlee's swollen belly. *One thing at a time, Oliver.*

I actually don't remember the last time I was with a woman. It's been so long. Maybe two, three years? It takes time, effort, and willpower to pursue something with a woman who stirs my intellect, and after Charlee . . . Well, it was hard to fill the empty space left by a woman like Charlee. Hard as fuck.

"I'm clear too." I push her knees apart and settle between her open legs, bringing my tip to her entrance. My hands are shaking, but from lust or trepidation, I'm not sure.

Inch by inch, I push my cock inside her, withdrawing and pushing in again to let her adjust to the thickness of it. I blow out a breath when I sink another inch deeper. Who am I kidding? I need to adjust to *her*, because she's gripping me so tightly and I'm already fighting the urgent pressure building in my balls.

Because she feels so good.

Because I've imagined this more times than I would ever admit.

Because it's her.

The thought breaks something in me and snaps the little restraint I had as I rock the last inches in one hard thrust that draws a choked sound from her mouth.

"Fuck, Charlee," I groan when I feel just how soaked she is. How perfectly she hugs me. "You're killing me."

She tilts her hips in response, and my vision goes black.

I start to move lazily over her. If I take her rough, I'm not giving myself more than two pumps before I spill my release inside her. Especially not when her lips open wider and wider with each of my thrusts like it's just a matter of time before she cries out my name, and, god, when she does, I'll topple right behind her.

So I keep my unhurried pace, my hands on each side of her waist, and marvel at the sight of her beneath me, at her body colored with warmth and passion, at her breasts bouncing in harmony with the tempo of my hips.

Because I have apparently no sense of self-preservation and am greedy as fuck when it comes to her, I bend down and suck her nipple into my mouth, giving her just enough pressure that she arches her back and lets out a sound that makes me feral for more.

The latch on my control pops.

I'm so close.

My pace increases, and the muscles in my lower abdomen strain as I force myself to hold back the rising tide threatening to spill over.

Not yet.

"*Yes*, oh my god. Just like that," Charlee hiccups as her hands fly to my arms, her nails digging into my flesh.

My head falls forward, and my gaze is drawn to where I slide so perfectly in and out of her.

"*Fuck.*"

"Do it, Oli. Fill me up, *please.*"

God, she's going to make me come from those words alone.

I grunt. I can't finish without her. I *need* to get her there.

In one desperate movement, I circle her waist with one arm and lift her upright against my chest, her legs straddling me as I drive my hips up in long, hard pumps. She yelps and grips my shoulders, leaving crescent moons there too.

Jesus, this goddamn woman.

She can mark me anywhere she wants, however hard she wants. I've been hers for years already, way before her body, her scent, her touch were all over me.

I palm her breast and lower my mouth, sucking hard, while I push into her until my cock hits that spot deep inside her.

I keep up the pace and hold her upright as best as I can as her legs clamp around my thighs and her pussy tightens its hold on my cock.

"Right . . . there," she gasps, tilting her head back. "Yes, *yes.*"

Her hips buck and her whole body tenses, and I hold her firmly seated on my cock as she flies over the edge and drags me down with her. There's no holding back the surge coiling at the base of my spine. It rises through me, hot and thick, and spills into her, wave after wave, her name on my lips like a desperate plea as we ride out our orgasms together.

"Oh god." I release a breathy laugh, and she hums as if there's nothing else to say that can explain the life-altering experience we just shared.

I don't know how long we stay like this, how long I stay buried in her warmth, her legs folded around my waist while her fingers thread through my hair. But at some point, she pulls back gently, and I see the tenderness sweeping her features as she whispers, "You're the place I love to be the most too," then kisses the unspoken promise onto my lips.

CHAPTER THIRTY

Big Time

A MONTH LATER

Charlee

I t's been a month. A month of not being able to get
enough of each other. A month spent discovering and
rediscovering each other in the most intimate and profound
ways, talking plans for the future and having dinner with his
friends, who are now my friends too. Especially Lola, now
that she has warmed up to me. Or maybe she was just testing
me at first to see if I was worthy of her best friend. To be
honest, I'm still not convinced I am. How can I live up to the
sacrifice he made for me? How can I make it up to him? I've
spent the last month going over every option, *any option*, to

get his family legacy back, and I might have found a solution. But it's a long shot.

A month that flew by in a whirlwind.

And no words have been uttered about a potential date for my departure.

I've been on the West Coast for almost two months now, and Oliver still hasn't asked me to stay for good. Why hasn't he asked? I need him to tell me he wants me to stay. I don't want to overstay my welcome or take for granted that I can just stay however long I want. Why can't he just . . . ask me? I don't want to go home now.

Home.

I snort as I pull a pair of warm socks over my black leggings and tie my hiking shoes in the entryway. What a weird concept now. Can I really call Toronto my home when I'm not even sure when I'll have a job to come back to? Or when ninety percent of my time has been spent outside the country over the last five years?

And now that I've been here, now that I've had a taste of life with Oli, Pine Falls is home. And for the first time in I don't know how long, I don't want to run anymore. I don't want to leave. The urge in me that used to thrum with impatience every time I stood still for too long has quieted down. I no longer feel the constant need to search for risk and adrenaline. All I'm looking for now is that safe and grounding feeling to never leave me. My time with Oli has made me feel like I belong somewhere when I've never felt that way in my life, except with my sister. That I belong to someone.

"How's the ankle?" Oliver asks when he joins me with our bag.

I rotate it for show, barely feeling any discomfort. "Good as new."

He bends down and drops a quick kiss on my lips as he smiles. "I'd hate to have to carry you again."

"As if you'd object," I say and gently poke his chest.

He snatches my wrist and pulls me up to him, laying my hand flat on his heart. "Any excuse to keep you close to me."

His index finger comes under my chin, tilting my gaze to his. His lips part, but a knock on the door stops whatever was going to come out of his mouth.

"Ignore it," I whisper.

Oliver chuckles. "They're just behind that door, sweetheart. They can probably hear us."

"Charlee! Oliver! Open the door!"

Bang, bang, bang!

I whip my head toward the door at the voice. "Emma?" I fling open the door.

"Do you know how many houses I had to knock at before someone told me where you lived? Why isn't there a street name on the path that leads here?" she asks Oliver as she pushes past me and falls onto the shoe bench. She waves at me. "Hey, you. I wasn't sure you'd still be here, but I guess I was right about whatever was going on between you two while we were filming. Glad to see it was enough to make you stay a bit longer. Damn good guess, though. Otherwise, I would've come all the way here for nothing."

Oliver and I exchange a puzzled look. *What is she talking about?* He shrugs, as if he can read the question in my mind.

"Are you okay?" I ask. "What's happening? Why aren't you in Toronto?"

Emma straightens in her seat. "Yes, I'm okay. A lot is happening. Because I needed to see you. More questions?" She looks at our backpacks, then at us. "Were you on your way out? Am I interrupting something?"

"We were," Oliver says. "I'm taking Charlee somewhere, yes. Can't say where." He flashes me a grin. "It's a surprise. But we can spare a moment to chat. We're not in a rush and it looks important. Come on, let's settle somewhere more comfortable."

Emma rises and follows us to the living room, where she sits down on the couch with Oliver while I take the armchair.

"You're the last person I expected to see today," I say.

Emma laughs. "Well, this won't be the least surprised you'll be, let me tell you. Have you heard about what's going on with MNL? Shit is going down."

"Yeah, we heard bits and pieces." Oliver nods. "Donna has been filling us in. Ugly stuff."

"'Ugly' wouldn't be the term I'd use, but that's definitely one way to put it," I say between clenched teeth.

The aftermath has been dire for Trevor, especially since Emma, and, surprisingly, Nick and Axel, corroborated our side of the story, prompting other scorned employees to come forward with their lengthy list of Trevor's abuses of power.

"*Wild Planet* and Movie Night Live lawyers are still going through the fine print of our contracts and ironing out the last details," I say, "but as far as we've heard, Trevor is out. Right?"

"Oh, he is. Absolutely," Emma says, a smug smile pulling her lips upward. "Listen, I'm gonna give it to you straight, Charlee, and this stays between us for now, because you're technically not supposed to know until the big boss at MNL calls you next week, but I wanted to tell you in person."

I frown. "What are you talking about?"

"I'm taking over. The docuseries. Every single project Trevor was on. I'm in charge now." Emma leans her elbows on her knees. "I have every intention in the world of finishing what we started, and I got the green light to bring you back on board. Both of you."

My jaw goes slack. "The filming is back on?" I glance at Oliver, who mirrors my expression, his brows high under the thick mass of hair falling on his forehead.

"It is," she says. "We're set to get back there next fall, enough time for our lawyers and *WP* to agree on a few final details."

Oliver blows a sharp breath out. "I didn't expect this."

"Oh, I have more." Emma pats his knee, her stare fixed on me. "You have a gift, Charlee. I watched the few tapes we managed to get from the trip and, god, I wanted to follow you everywhere you went. You're not meant to hide behind a pen. You're cut out to be in front of the camera. Ditch the written press. Come work for me at MNL. We have an open position, and I want you on my team. It'll be nothing like what you've been doing at *Wild Planet*. No rushing all over the place. Two documentaries a year, and the rest of the time, you can enjoy your life quietly."

Oliver's hum of approval punctuates her incredulous offer.

I don't know what to say, don't know what to think. I always thought that the only way I'd leave Ben and *Wild Planet* would be if the offices went under, and with the documentary back on track, Toronto should survive. So to just leave Ben and be in the spotlight full time? Is that really what I want?

Remember the rush in your blood when the red light of the camera was on, the giddiness of bringing such priceless moments to life for thousands of people?

I can't lie to myself. It was *fun*, and Emma and I made a hell of a team. A new challenge. New adventures. I glance at Oliver. There's something new here too that I can't ignore—or leave behind.

I can feel Emma watching me, so I tear my eyes away from Oliver and say, "Can you give me a few days to think about it?"

She smiles and stands. "Absolutely. Call me before the end of the week, okay?"

"Will do." I walk her back to the front door as Oli waves goodbye.

"Thank you," I say and bring her into a hug. "I need to go see someone in town," I whisper in her ear, "and Oliver can't know. Ask me to drive you back."

"What are you up to?" she asks in my hair.

I grin when I pull back and zip my lips. "Righting a wrong."

"Hey, would you mind driving me back to town?" she says loud enough for Oli to hear. "Someone very nicely dropped me off earlier."

"Uh, sure. Oli?"

He pokes his head out from the kitchen. "Yeah?"

"I'm driving Emma to . . ." I look at Emma for any clue as to where she's staying.

"The Butterfly Inn," she chimes in.

"I'll be back in thirty, okay?"

Oliver smiles. "Sounds good; drive safe. Emma, nice to see you."

Two seconds after I drop off Emma, I push through the doors of town hall.

"Is he in?" I ask the person at the front desk, who looks ready to aim pepper spray in my face.

"Yes, but he's in a meeting." She stands, but it's unclear whether she wants to bolt or block my path.

I smile sweetly. "Well, not anymore."

I walk to the door with Rob's name on it and push it open. "Well. My timing couldn't have been more perfect," I say wryly as my gaze falls on Oscar, who sits in front of the mayor.

Rob bunches his eyebrows. "I'm sorry, who are you? We're in the middle of something."

I shake my head vehemently. "Oh no, don't worry. I won't take too much of your time." I move forward and lay a hand on Oscar's shoulder. "This gentleman and I are already acquainted, aren't we?" I squeeze hard, and Oscar hisses, wrenching his shoulder out of my grip. Satisfied, I hold my hand out to Rob. "Charlee Fletcher. Nice to meet you."

Rob shakes my hand, a frown still on his forehead as his eyes dart between me and Oscar.

"What is going on?" Oscar rages next to me.

"Oh, yes." I open my bag and pull out a thick book, letting it fall with a thump on the mayor's desk. "According to Pine Falls's bylaws, not only do classified historic buildings have to be voted on unanimously by the council before they can be sold, but the purchaser is required to maintain the integrity of the building even after taking ownership of it, since the historic classification remains." I open the book to the right page and point to the section in question. "It took me a while to find it, but it seems to me that with this, Oscar can kiss his expansion plan goodbye. Right, Rob?"

Rob studies the paragraph as if he doesn't know his own regulations by heart. "Hmm . . ."

"Robert, who cares about a bylaw when I can boost Pine Falls's economy tenfold?"

An exasperated sound leaves my mouth. "As if the town needs that." I turn my attention to Rob. "I know your back's against the wall. But do you really want to sell to someone who disrespects your town's history like that?" I tsk in Oscar's direction before I turn back to Rob and plant my hands on his desk. "I have a better idea. Just hear me out."

CHAPTER THIRTY-ONE

Bloom

Charlee

"S he dropped quite the bomb," Oliver says as we climb into his truck after I come back from "driving Emma back."

I nod. "I sure as hell didn't see any of that coming. I'm glad that Trevor got booted, though."

"Me too." Oliver starts the engine and places one hand on the back of my seat as he backs the truck up. "I called Rob while you were with Emma."

I whirl my head to him. "You did?"

"Yeah." He puts the car in neutral, then turns to me. "It was weird. I wanted to let him know as fast as I could that I would be able to get him the money next fall, just in case there was a slim chance he hadn't sold to Oscar in the past month. Guess what?"

My heart hammers. "What?"

"He told me the deal with Oscar is under review. Didn't tell me much more, but when I asked for a delay until next fall, he said he'd think about it. He might have another potential buyer, so he couldn't really give me his word."

"Already?"

He sighs. "Yeah. I hope it's not anything serious."

I place my hand on his thigh, squeezing lightly. "I'm sure it won't be. You'll get it back, Oli. I'm sure of it."

"Thank you, sweetheart." He lays his hand on top of mine. "The faith you have in me is what keeps me fighting for it."

I smile, rubbing my thumb on the coarse fabric of his pants, and nod to the road. "Now. Are you gonna tell me where we're going?"

This man woke me up at five a.m. today, and although he did so in a way that had me curling my toes and crumpling the sheets in my fists, it was still five in the morning. On a Friday. Not that it means anything now that I'm officially on the unemployed train.

He brings my wrist to his lips. "Do you remember when we wrote to each other, the time you told me about that awful date?"

His breath skitters along my skin, making me shudder. I want him. All the time. It's a problem.

"I do," I say, a bit strangled.

Oliver hums, his nose brushing the thin skin just below my palm, and inhales softly. "Remember what we talked about after that?"

I paw through the thick fog that has settled over my memories through the years. I haven't forgotten anything, but it's all been under lock and key for so long that my first instinct has always been to refuse to delve into it. "If I do recall, I said that I thought about you the whole date."

Pride, and something else, heat his gaze. "And? Come on, I'm sure that beautiful brain of yours has the answer somewhere."

I frown, narrowing my eyes. "We talked about what our ideal da—" I snap my eyes to his.

"I made you a promise five years ago, and I'm a man of my word. Welcome to our first date, sweetheart."

"It's not technically Caliper Lake Park, but it's beautiful too," Oliver says as we trek through the woods a couple of miles outside Pine Falls. "And teeming with weird things crawling everywhere." He throws me a conniving look.

"I haven't sketched in years." I jump over a small hole in the ground.

"Good thing I packed some supplies, then."

I slip on a root covered with moss, but Oliver grabs my arm and steadies me. "I can't always be here to catch you, Char. At some point, you're gonna have to learn how to walk."

"Well, maybe stop being so damn surprising and throwing me off guard all the time," I retort with the strength of a kitten, because all I want to do is rub myself against him and purr.

He lets go of my arm and slips his hand in mine, resuming our hike. He's been weirdly quiet today, and I don't know if it's because he usually gets like this when he's in nature or if it's because of something else. Something that's apparently been bothering him since we left home, given the tension steadily radiating from his body.

I push the thought aside and tilt my head upward, admiring the conifer-lined sky. It's probably nothing serious.

"Do you know this species?"

"Cypress pine," he says. "You recognize them because of their scalelike needles." At my impressed scowl, he smiles. "I've spent way too many hours running around here. This forest holds no secrets from me."

His gaze slides to me, the weight of it like a gentle caress. "See those purple flowers over there?" He points to my right, where little bells cluster around dense green vegetation. "Do you know what they're called?"

"How would I know that?"

He chuckles. "Fair enough. They're called bleeding hearts. They're believed to have medicinal properties and are often applied for pain relief."

I take in the delicate flower. "Could have come in handy when I tore my ankle. What about this one?" I take a small red berry between my fingers. "It looks delicious."

Oliver looks at the fruit closer. "Don't eat those. They're toxic. Though their name is very sweet."

"What is it?"

He smiles, tossing the berry away. "Orange honeysuckle."

I turn and wrap my arms around his neck. How can a simple gesture heal so many little wounds wrought over time? "Were you always the one raising your hand first in class?"

His palms rake along my sides possessively. "I was. Proudly."

"Nothing about this statement surprises me." I bring him down to me and place a kiss on his soft lips. He groans against my mouth, and I open for him, letting him take what's his.

"We have a hike to finish, Charlee," he says against my mouth. "And lots of other things to do, according to your perfect date itinerary." His hand drags down my back and cups my ass. "We'll get to that tonight. I promise. I want to fuck you under the stars."

I swallow a whimper and struggle against the molten lava tumbling down to my core. I wouldn't mind pausing the hike if it meant having him take me against that tree over there.

Oliver grinds me against his crotch. "Hike first. Come on."

We spend the day trudging through the forest and climbing the steep mountainside under the blazing sun. At some point in the afternoon, we encounter a family of flying squirrels, and Oliver insists that I draw them. It takes me much longer than it would have a few years ago, and although I balked a little when he handed me the notebook he'd carefully packed, once I held the pencil in my hand, it was like riding a bike. And witnessing the awestruck expression on his face made me feel a kind of pride I'd never experienced before.

Despite the weariness slowly creeping into my bones, every second spent exploring this place he knows so well is magic. I'll never forget it, no matter what happens after tonight.

"We're almost there," Oliver says. He takes my hand and leads me down a smaller path that twists between the trees and disappears into the thick vegetation. The tension in his shoulders loosened as the afternoon wore on, but he now looks jittery as we make our way down the narrow trail. I want to ask him what's on his mind, but I'm not sure he wants me to know. So I push it away. Again.

After what seems like an eternity of being whipped by branches of all shapes and sizes, the path clears and yields to a lake with water of such emerald hues, I wonder if the bottom isn't covered with the exact gemstones.

I sling my backpack off my shoulders and drop it to the ground. "I can't believe my eyes." With the last rays of the sun filtering through the tall pines surrounding the lake, the water glitters, reflecting the countless colors of the rainbow. "I didn't know water could be so pure."

Oliver slips his arm around my waist and tucks me against him. "When I was a kid, my grandpa and I came here to camp all the time. We would build a fire over there," he nods toward a strip of sand running along the lake, "and then camp next to it. Sometimes, we stayed here for days and never saw a soul. It was perfect."

I lean my head against his shoulder. "Thank you for bringing me here."

His fingers slip under my chin and tilt my face until he peers into my eyes. "I want to show you everything."

I lift myself on my tiptoes and kiss the corner of his mouth, losing myself in his comforting scent.

"What was that for?" he murmurs against my lips.

I cup his face, bringing him down to me for another one. "For holding out hope. For not giving up."

"On you? Never, sweetheart."

My heart squeezes. "I did. I gave up. I was so mad."

"It's okay. I forgive you," he says. "I had enough in me for the both of us."

I would have melted to the ground if not for the solid grasp he has around me. "How about we get the tent and fire ready and go swimming in the lake, huh?"

He must pick up on my unspoken invitation because his fingers flex on my waist. "Already on the schedule, ma'am. If memory serves me right, your perfect date included a swim. Without any clothes."

His words warm my blood until my skin feels tight and overheated. "It did," I whisper. I wouldn't mind running to the lake right about now, but Oliver releases me and takes my hand, leading me to the patch of sand.

When we get there, I take care of gathering twigs and larger branches to build a fire in the middle of a set of stones that have already been placed in a circle, and Oliver busies himself with the tent.

"So, um, do you have anything planned when you go back to Toronto?" he asks after a while, his focus zeroed in on pitching the tent.

I bring some branches and twigs and strategically place a few fire starters. "Not really, no. Probably see my sister," I reply, my tone as detached as I can force it. I strike a match, and the wood catches fire.

Oliver kneels in front of one of the tent's pegs and pulls the material taut before placing the pole in the loop. "Riley will be happy to see you. It's been a while." There's an edge to his voice, and I don't know what to do with it.

"Yep. She's always hounding me for sister time, so it'll be nice."

He hums—*just hums*—like there's not a billion other things he could say. Like "stay."

Ask me to stay! I want to scream at him, but the words get stuck in my throat.

So we both stay silent. I wish he wouldn't let the quiet settle. I wish he would take the leap I desperately want to take for once in my life. But instead, he finishes putting the tent up, and when I'm sure the fire will keep burning, I walk to my bag and rifle through it until I find the blanket and lay it out on the sand.

I take off my hiking boots, then remove my sweater, tossing it onto the blanket. "I'm going for a swim," I say to Oliver. I don't wait for his answer. I need to sink underwater and forget the disappointment rising in me. I slip my clothes off piece by piece until I'm wearing nothing but my skin and the bear pendant around my neck.

"Charlee, wait!"

But I'm already halfway into the water. The cold chills me to my bones, but I don't care. I wet my shoulders and the back of my neck, and without a second thought, dive into the limpid water and lose myself to the roaring in my ears. When I rise to the surface, I spot Oliver removing his underwear and diving into the freezing lake.

Before I know it, he's caught up with me, staying just a few feet from where I am.

"There's something I've been meaning to talk to you about." He's out of breath, panic contorting his face.

"Go ahead," I reply calmly, even though my heart is pounding in my ears.

"I had this whole speech planned. I wanted it to be perfect. To deliver it when we were snuggled in front of the fire, but I can't wait any longer, and, honestly, fuck the speech. So, here's the blunt truth, Charlee."

He's next to me in three long strokes. "Stay with me. Charlee, I—" He rakes a hand over his anguished features and looks at me, his arms keeping him afloat. "I can't bear to see you go. I don't know when you plan to leave for Toronto, if you've booked your tickets already . . ." He huffs shakily, and I try to do the same, but the air doesn't go through. "This"— he widens his arms desperately—"is your home." He places his hand over his heart. "*This* is your home. Don't go. Please. I need you here."

My mind goes quiet, and the bad thoughts that were spreading through me like weeds are ripped out in one fell swoop.

This was what he was mulling over all day?

I feel almost foolish for scaring myself like that. I know what he's like. I should have known it was eating him up inside, that he'd study it from every conceivable angle before bringing it up to me.

I mentally face-palm myself.

It's almost funny that he thinks I need any convincing, though.

But before I can tell him exactly that, he grasps my waist and pulls me to him, erasing the last few inches that were separating us. "I know my offer terrifies the wildcat in you, that you love your freedom more than anything and you never stay in one place for too long. I don't want you to think I'm not on board with Emma's offer. I hope you go for it. It'll be an amazing opportunity for you, and she's right—you're a natural in front of the camera. You shine, and I'm mesmerized every time. I'll never stop you from going places. I just want to be the home you come back to once you're done wandering the world. I'll wait for you to come home to me."

I chuckle, bracing my hands on his shoulders while my feet keep kicking the water below me. "Don't you know by now? Haven't you asked yourself why I'm still here?"

He huffs out a strangled laugh. "I figured I was coming dangerously close to your stay limit."

"Silly man." I shake my head. "I don't want to leave. I never want to. I've been waiting for weeks now for you to ask me to stay."

His eyes warm to a rich shade of brown, almost gold. "You have?"

I nod, all of a sudden, I feel so light. So at peace with that reality. "I don't need to run anymore. I've found you. I'm exactly where I want to be."

Oliver sucks in a breath, then dives straight for my mouth, claiming me as if the world were about to end. "Say that again," he growls against my mouth. "Tell me you're mine."

"I'm not leaving, Oli," I pant, grasping him harder. "I'm yours. *I'm yours.*"

I tie my legs around his waist and feel him already hard between my thighs. His hands clamp on my ass, tugging me flush against his length, and I yelp when his tip teases my clit beneath the water.

"My perfect girl," he whispers again and again into the crook of my neck, like a prayer to a higher power, and with one arm holding me to him, he swims us back to shore.

When his feet touch the ground again, he effortlessly rises out of the water with me still in his arms and sprawls us out on the blanket, soaking wet.

In the glow of the fire still burning on the beach, Oliver maneuvers me onto my side and leans over me, folding my upper leg to my chest. I want him so bad I can hardly think, and I could scream in relief when he finally pushes inside me in one long thrust, holding on to my hip like he might shatter into dust without an anchor point.

"Charlee, Christ, look at you. *Look at you,*" he groans as he pounds into me, hard and unyielding. "You're fucking glowing for me."

I understand exactly what he means, because the sight of him dripping with water that trickles down the muscles of his torso as if he's been fucking me for hours, his wet hair in a wild mess, makes me lose my sanity. The last rays of sun dance behind him, and with the gleam of the fire and the reflection of the light on his glistening skin, he almost looks godly.

"You're mine," I gasp as he sinks deeper inside me. His hand grips the flesh of my thigh like a saddle handle, and I know that tomorrow morning, I'll wake up to the mark of his fingers there.

"Again. Say that again."

My inner walls grip him tighter. "You're mine," I moan, pressure building low in my belly. "You belong to me."

"I'm yours. Mind, body, and soul." Oliver thrusts into me a few more times before his orgasm tears through him and echoes in the young night, my name on his lips as he spills inside me. It's enough to push me into my own abyss and make me see stars.

Oliver slumps against me and buries his head between my breasts, his chest heaving. "Welcome home, sweetheart."

I burst into laughter, half-delirious from my lingering climax, and hold his face to my limp body, stroking his damp hair. "I love you."

Neither of us moves. We lie naked under the stars, his head on my chest, my fingers in his hair, gazing up at the constellations. After a while, Oliver's gentle breathing lulls me into my own slumber, so I close my eyes.

The perfect first date to start the perfect rest of our lives. Just like he promised.

EPILOGUE

Everywhere, Everything

SIX MONTHS LATER

Charlee

"I'm gonna bring this to the car, and I'll be right back," Riley says, with a box full of glasses in her hands.

"Wait for me. I'll bring my equipment too." Avery grabs her camera and lens bags and meets Riley by the door.

I stack the rest of the cups, food, and bottles of champagne into the boxes on the kitchen counter. "I think we might need to take two cars to get there."

"Josh and Miles drove with Lola's car, so we can use your rental, Riley," Avery says when they come back.

"Sounds good!" my sister yells as she walks out with another box in hand.

Avery types something on her phone, and a second later, it rings. She puts it on speaker. "Everything okay with you guys?"

Josh's voice fills the kitchen. "We're doing great. Don't worry, baby," Avery's husband says. "Miles is fighting with some of the decorations, but otherwise, everything's under control. I told him to let me handle it, but your brother is a little stubborn. Did you know that?"

"You're the stubborn one who keeps asking me if I want help when there's so much to do," Miles argues. "I would be more helpful in the kitchen."

"Honey, be nice," Riley chimes in as she walks by and rolls her eyes, whispering, "Worse than children" to us.

"All right," Avery chuckles. "We'll be there soon. Love you."

"Be safe. Love you," Josh says and hangs up.

"On a scale of one to ten," Avery says as she closes another box, "how much should we be worried that we left them in charge of setting everything up?"

"Probably ten if Lola wasn't there to supervise them," I say, laughing nervously. I pick up my phone to text Matt.

Charlee

ETA ?

Matt

We're packing things up.
Will bring him back to you
on schedule, boss.

Charlee

Thank you.

I set it down. "We should get going in thirty minutes so we have plenty of time before James and Matt come back from their camping weekend with Oli."

Avery smiles. "We'll be ready. It's gonna be perfect, Charlee. Go on, go change. We'll finish loading the boxes in the car."

I blow out a sharp breath. "Okay. Thanks, Ave."

"No worries."

I climb the stairs two at a time, trepidation seeping through my every pore. I haven't been able to stand still for the past week, but the last two days have really done a number on me. Luckily, Oliver wasn't here to see me lose my mind.

I make my way upstairs to the walk-in closet, where I arranged all my clothes after moving in, and fumble through the few dresses I own. It's rather warm for April, and I can't help but think that this is a sign that Carol and Jerry are looking down on us, warming us with the pride I know they've always carried for their grandson.

I pick out an outfit I haven't had the heart to look at in a long time: a steel-blue midi dress that hugs my narrow waist in soft satin and highlights the curve of my breasts, thanks to the plunging neckline. Emotion claws at my throat at the memories of the last time I wore it and how different things are now from that doomed day.

"Everything is going to go perfectly," I tell my reflection as I dab some mascara on my lashes and shake my hair into place.

"Char, we're good to go!" Riley calls from the kitchen downstairs.

"I'll be right down!"

I draw three deep, slow breaths and let the air fill my lungs and cool the heat drumming in my veins.

I've spent the last six months planning, scheming, and organizing. It all comes down to today.

I still can't believe I've managed to pull this off.

So far, at least.

Riley didn't hesitate when I called her right after I stormed out of Rob's office and asked her for something I'd never asked for in my entire life: money. I'm sure she had a ministroke over the phone when that happened. Her sister, asking for help. When she shared my plan with her husband, Miles texted his sister, Avery, right away to see if she'd be available to immortalize today's event.

And then came James, Matt, and Lola, who all heaved a sigh of relief when I told them my idea and asked them to embark on this project for Oliver—and to pitch in however they were comfortable.

And with the help of everybody Oliver and I hold dear, I bought his family's restaurant back.

The trickiest part was getting Rob to agree to give up his multimillion-dollar deal with Oscar. It took more than just me barging into his office that day. Dozens of people showed up at the mayor's office after I dropped old-school flyers in their mailboxes, all of them with a story of how Oliver helped them renovate their roof, brought food for them after a hospital visit, or took care of their kids for a few hours.

"It's the least we can do," they said when I asked if they'd be willing to help me close the sale. "We miss the place as much as we miss Jerry."

Truth is, Rob wasn't indifferent to this turn of events either. All he wanted was for Pine Falls to stop footing the bill for the building. And when Riley hooked him up with one of her land development contacts to assess expansion options for the existing hotel, it sealed the deal. He even agreed to play along when Oliver kept on calling him to get updates on the sale and almost blew up our plan. Fortunately, Rob stayed tight-lipped, and Oliver's expectations remained low but not crushed.

It really did take a village.

I wailed the whole drive back after I left Rob's office with his signature on the sales contract, and when Oliver jogged to my car to greet me, I jumped his bones right there in the back seat, no explanation needed.

I fasten the last buttons on my dress, my skin heating at the memory.

Every day spent by his side has been like that: always wanting him closer, craving him, never having enough. Sometimes, I wake up in the middle of the night and find him asleep next to me, softly breathing, and wonder what I did right in a past life to deserve a second chance at loving this man—and to have my love returned tenfold.

In all my years of scouring the world in search of the rarest beauty, never would I have imagined that I'd find something far more precious here in Pine Falls, in the arms of the man who wrote to me for five years, never giving up on us. Never would I have thought that this town would become my sanctuary.

And today, Oliver gets his back.

Oliver

"I still don't understand why I need to wear a tie for tonight," I say as I tighten the knot at the collar of my cream-colored shirt.

"Because," Matt says from his bathroom, "we're finishing this boys' weekend with a true gentlemen's night out. And we're doing it the proper way."

James adjusts his cufflinks, casting a furtive glance in Matt's direction before focusing back on his shaking fingers.

Weird.

Why does he look nervous? "You okay, man?"

He huffs a laugh. "Yeah, just struggling with these." James holds out his wrists. "Two days in the wild, and I've forgotten how to wear formal clothing." He straightens the lapel of his suit jacket. "It's so *tight*."

I reach for James's wrist and lock the cufflinks properly. "There you go."

"Thanks, Oli." James checks his watch. "Oh, we gotta go or we'll be late for t—"

"Our reservation," Matt cuts in, throwing James a warning glare.

I frown. "What is up with you two? Where are we going?"

"Just a nice restaurant, but we don't want to arrive late, so if we're all ready, let's get this show on the road."

I run my fingers through the waves atop my head, trying to put my hair into some semblance of order. "I hope you're not dragging us to another 'adult' club. I still have awful nightmares."

James shudders. "Me too."

"It's not my fault. I was told it would be a tasteful experience," Matt retorts, tying his hair in a neater-than-usual bun. "How could I have known it was a BDSM swingers' club?"

"The *name*, maybe?" I suggest.

Mistress Munch, in neon-pink letters. Five minutes in, James and I had sprinted out of there.

"I don't want to get back home too late," I add. I check to see if Charlee texted again, but I've only received one message from her since I got my signal back.

Charlee

> I can't wait to see you tonight.

God, I miss her. As much as I loved being with the guys, I miss touching her, feeling her against me, waking up next to her supple body, breathing in her vanilla-and-peach scent.

I'm ready to go home to her. Listen to her tell me about her weekend, share mine. And like every night since she unpacked her suitcases and made Pine Falls her home, I want to love her until she forgets her own name and I can't feel anything but her all over me.

"Oli."

I snap out of my thoughts and find Matt looking at me, amused. "We need to go."

"Put this on." James holds out a black blindfold to me.

"What? Why?" I look at Matt. "This really does sound like a Mistress Munch situation all over again."

"Put. It. On," Matt says. "Trust me."

We're parked a few blocks away from the edge of Pine Falls's main street, an eerie quiet hovering over the town. I don't understand what's going on, but whatever the guys have planned, I want no part of it. I just want to go home. So the quicker I play along, the quicker I can get away.

"Give it." I grab the blindfold and slide it over my eyes, and just like that, Matt resumes the drive, only to kill the engine two minutes later. "Can I take it off now?"

"*No*," Matt and James say at the same time.

"Okay, okay, calm down."

They get out of the car. I hear my door open, and a hand grabs my forearm. "Careful with the step," James warns.

Fresh air whips my face, and is that water I hear rippling in the background?

"Stay here. We'll be right back," Matt calls as his footsteps echo away.

"*What the fuck, guys?*"

But no answer.

I shake my head, resting my hands on my hips. I'll never get home at a decent hour. I hear a door open, and a waft of air carries a sweet smell I'd recognize in a heartbeat.

"Charlee?" She lays her fingers on my chest, and my arms circle her waist, bringing her closer to me. "What are you doing here? What's going on?"

"If I take this off," she says, ignoring my questions, "will you keep your eyes closed until I say?"

"Yes," I breathe, my heart picking up speed.

Gently, Charlee pulls the band off my face, and light filters behind my eyelids. She slips her hand in mine and laces our fingers together. "Open your eyes in three . . . two . . . one."

She squeezes my hand. I flutter my eyes open, and stare at . . . my grandparents' restaurant. The newly renovated facade . . . and the closed curtains . . .

What is this?

I look up at the wooden sign over the entrance. The one I spent months perfecting in my woodshop.

Oli's.

I whirl to face Charlee, who stands next to me in a beautiful summer dress I somehow feel like I've seen before, tears streaming down my face. "What is this? What is going on, Charlee?"

She smiles warmly, stroking my hand with her thumb. "This is yours. Oli's is yours."

I huff a sharp breath. "What d-do you m-mean it's *mine?*" My sobs drown my words, and I choke on the emotions that flood me. "What about the potential buyer Rob told me about?"

She wraps her arms around my waist, holding me tightly against her as she guides me to the door. "It's me. I'm the potential buyer. I'll explain everything when we get home and it's just the two of us. But right now . . ." She pushes the door open, and a room full of people yells, "*Surprise!*"

"Right now, you get your restaurant back."

I look around, recognizing familiar faces through my thick tears. Lola, James, and Matt are all sobbing messes like me. Rob is smiling, tears sparkling at the corner of his eyes. And is that . . . *Emile* nodding in my direction? There are others I've seen a couple of times before, like Riley, Charlee's sister, and her husband, Miles. And from the camera clutched between her fingers and pointed at me, I assume that's Avery, Miles's sister and wife to the tall, elegant man standing close behind her, Josh.

They're all gathered in my grandparents' restaurant . . .

My hand shoots up to my mouth, and another sob breaks free from my lips when I take in the room filled with chairs and tables straight from my shed.

I turn to Charlee, her eyes red and damp, and cup her face between my palms. "I can't believe you did this for me," I murmur just for her. "I don't know what to say, what to do." She laughs, a melody I will never get enough of. "Is this real?"

She wraps her fingers around my wrists, the touch grounding me. "It's real. And it's yours. Ours."

I groan and bend down, pressing a kiss to her soft lips. I taste the salt of her happy tears on my tongue. I want to do so much more, but a room full of people doesn't allow for my hands to wander below her dress, so I keep it to a gentle flick of my tongue against her lips, a promise of exactly what's awaiting her when we get home.

Someone claps. Matt, probably.

I laugh, pulling myself out of her embrace. "First round's on me!" I shout, and the room explodes in cheers.

For the next three hours, I drown in the throngs of people packed into the restaurant. Champagne flows freely, as do the delicious appetizers Miles concocted. I catch up with people who used to be regulars here and others I don't know, all stopping and thanking me, while the woman I love is tucked against me. Jerry's was always a magical place for me, but I never imagined how important it was to so many other people. Seeing the restaurant so alive, so full, all these years later . . . I understand it now.

And when, around midnight, I close the door behind the last person to leave, when the room falls silent for the first time and I can truly grasp my surroundings, the place of my childhood, reality sets in. This isn't a dream. It's happening.

I let out a shuddering exhale and turn to find Charlee, Riley, and Josh sitting around a table in the middle of the room while Avery stacks glasses behind the bar.

"I don't even know where to start," I say as I join them and sit next to my . . . girlfriend? No. The word feels wrong and profoundly weak. Wife, maybe, one day. Soulmates is what we are, but she's more than that.

Love of my life.

She's the love of my life.

I pull the chair she's seated on closer to mine and wrap an arm around her shoulders.

She nestles against me. "We'll start from the beginning. Tomorrow. Everything you want to know. But tonight, we celebrate."

"It was a great night, man." Josh nods. "Congratulations."

I laugh. "Congratulations? You guys are the ones who pulled it off. I didn't do a single thing."

Josh flashes me a grin. "True."

"You haven't seen the best part yet. Oops, there it is," Riley says, just as Miles comes out of the kitchen with a tray in his hands.

"Fresh macarons to end the night. By yours truly," he announces and sets the tray in the middle of the table. "Don't worry, Oliver. Charlee already begged me to give your chef my recipe."

"You mean, you offered it before I even had time to think about asking," Charlee counters, and Riley laughs, snuggling close to Miles.

"While we're offering things," Avery says as she comes around the bar and sits on Josh's lap, "I took some photos of the restaurant's facade with the new name earlier today. With the ones from tonight's event, you should have plenty to work with if you ever need to do a little promotion."

I swallow hard. "Thank you." I look at these people, these wonderful families, who came through for me. "I-I don't know what to say, how to repay each of you."

"I'm sure you'll learn quickly, if you haven't already," Riley starts, "that there's little I wouldn't do for Charlee. And because you're holding a piece of her heart, that now includes you too."

Charlee lays her hand on my thigh as she looks at me with a world of tenderness in her gaze. I grasp her fingers in mine, and my universe redraws itself the second I meet those green eyes. The place where I love to be the most.

And as we stretch out the night until the first light of morning, etching the first indelible memories of Oli's into our minds and the very soul of this place, my gaze is drawn to the wall where photos of Christmases spent with customers at Jerry's over the years hang. All the Christmases I can remember are displayed.

I swallow roughly, my eyes stinging again when I notice one I have never seen before, and it takes me a second to realize what I'm looking at. Standing in front of a Christmas tree in what looks like a living room are Charlee and Riley in their red and white pjs. They look a bit younger than they do today, and between them, with her arms wrapped around their shoulders, is a woman with a Santa hat covering her head who beams at the camera. The same smile I've seen on her daughter's face time and time again.

Charlee's mom.

The hollowness of her cheeks and the paleness of her skin leave no doubt as to her health, but for that one picture, all three of them look infinitely happy.

My eyes move to the next frame, a photo of my grandparents in the kitchen as they're getting ready before the holiday lunch hour, looking straight into the camera I was holding when I took that shot.

I smile, a twinge of sorrow shadowing my heart at the fact that they couldn't be here to see us make them proud. But as I stare at the two pictures hanging side by side, I could almost swear that they all smile right back.

ACKNOWLEDGMENTS

I apologize in advance if things get sappy (they definitely will), but what else do you expect from me?

I don't think I've ever experienced the kind of unconditional love that my best friend, Katie, gives me every day, and that's why I want to thank her first. You are the most precious thing in my life and I am so lucky to share this world with you, my favorite Harry-loving Swiftie. I love you to the moon and to Saturn.

To my beta readers, Payton, Grace, Gen, Jessica and L.H.: your help, endless support as I made adjustments, long conversations by text, voice memo and phone, all of it is worth more than you'll ever know. Thank you, thank you, thank you. Without you, this book would not be the story you hold now in your hands.

To Gen (yes, you get thanked twice) and Emma. Finding your friendship has been the highlight of my year. Thank you for being my number one cheerleaders throughout this process, and welcoming me in your lives.

Letizia, thank you for coming up with Emile, my favorite angry mailman. There's a little bit of you in this book, and that makes me very happy.

To my editors, Caroline and Beth: it's been a wonderful experience working with you guys, and I can't wait to do it all again. Writing and publishing a book is stressful enough, but with the right team, it almost feels easy.

To Leni, the illustrator of my dreams, and one of my dearest friends. Your professionalism and talent are second to none, but it's having you in my life that makes me the happiest. Thank you for making my books what people are drawn to, but most of all, thank you for brightening my days with our daily conversations. And fuck AI.

To Anna, you absolutely talented sorceress. Thank you for drawing all the pre-order merch for Unbearably Yours and for literally creating the perfect hair for Oliver. I don't think anyone should be allowed to look this hot, but here we are. I adore you and am so grateful to have had you on the team. To many more collabs in our future. And fuck AI too.

To David. Well, you already have the book dedicated to you, but I guess I can thank you here too. You're the best golden retriever/cinnamon roll boyfriend a girl could ask for, and I love you so much.

To my cats, Berlioz and Troopie, and every time you decided to sit on me, on my computer, or to bite my feet until I got up and fed you. Thank you for reminding me to take breaks.

To Emily (@emilysbookshelf_), Kelley (@kells.books), Emily @librarybyemily), Jess (@readwithme.jess): your unwavering support since day one has meant a lot to me. Thank you.

Finally, last but not least (in French, we say that we save the best for last), to you, my readers. This indie publishing business isn't always easy, but you make it *so* worth it. It's not lost on me that I'm privileged to write stories that are read by hundreds of people, that you buy my books and take photos, that you post, talk about them, create amazing aesthetics: I am truly lucky to be surrounded by this incredible community. So to you, my book girlies (and boys?), who spend an unhealthy amount of time daydreaming about book boyfriends (just like me). I hope Oliver makes the list.

ABOUT THE AUTHOR

Originally from France, Elodie moved to Montreal, Canada in 2014 to pursue her studies in politics. An avid reader since childhood, it wasn't until 2021 that she rediscovered her love for books, especially romance novels.

Never one to do anything half-hearted, Elodie has shared her love of reading with other book lovers on her Bookstagram (@elosreadingcorner) where she has found an incredibly supportive and inspiring community.

When she's not immersed in reading or analyzing public policy, you can find Elodie baking sweets for the whole neighborhood, cuddling with her cats, or hunched over her keyboard creating love stories everyone can dream of.

FOLLOW HER ON

Instagram/Threads @elosreadingcorner
Tiktok @authorelodiecolliard
Twitter/X @elocolliard

Made in the USA
Middletown, DE
04 September 2024

59764564R00241